One of the few Israeli crime thrillers to become a bestseller in its native land, *The Missing File* is now commanding international attention.

'A wonderfully satisfying detective story with a real knockout finale. A tense, gripping page-turner that I devoured in two days – it's hard to believe it's a debut'
S. J. Watson, author of *Before I Go To Sleep*

'Impressive! That is what first comes into my mind after having read the Israeli author D. A. Mishani's novel, *The Missing File*. D. A. Mishani writes with profound originality. His main character, Inspector Avi Avraham, is a quite remarkable man on the stage where detectives dance. A truly interesting story, well written. It will find readers, I am quite sure. Once again: impressive!'   Henning Mankell, author of the Wallander series

'Its vivid characters and setting linger in the memory'
*Sunday Times*

'Marks the start of what could become a fine detective series, centred around a striking character . . . Mishani's bittersweet story hums with humanity'   *Daily Mail*

'Mishani, the crime fiction editor of an Israeli publishing house, clearly knows his field, and in Steven Cohen's smooth translation he delivers a solid brainteaser . . . A thoughtful character study of a good man deeply troubled by issues of innocence and guilt'
*New York Times*

'Outstanding . . . Mishani, the editor of international fiction and crime literature at Keter Books in Israel, puts his expertise in the genre to good use in combining the procedural and the puzzle with artful misdirection'   *Publishers Weekly*

'A compelling debut in a complex case aimed straight at the reader's heart'   *Kirkus*

D. A. Mishani was born in Holon, in Tel Aviv, Israel in 1975. He has worked as the News Editor for Tel Aviv's leading daily newspaper, *Haaretz*, as the Editor-in-Chief of the *Haaretz Book Review* and as Editor of Israeli fiction and international crime fiction at Keter Books publishing house. He wrote *The Missing File* while studying in Cambridge. Now a full time writer, he lives in Tel Aviv with his family.

*The Missing File* was the first crime novel written in Hebrew to be nominated for the Sapir Prize, the Israeli equivalent of the Booker Prize. It gained unprecedented international attention and was published in more than fifteen countries. The second novel in the Detective Avraham series, *The Possibility of Violence*, was published in 2013 in Israel and will be published in 2014 in the UK.

# THE MISSING FILE

## D. A. MISHANI

Quercus

First published in Hebrew in Israel in 2011 by Keter Books as תיק נעדר
Published in the UK in 2013 by Quercus
This paperback edition published in 2014 by

Quercus
55 Baker Street
7th Floor, South Block
London
W1U 8EW

Published by arrangement with Harper, an imprint of
HarperCollins Publishers, New York, New York, USA

A CIP catalogue record for this book is available
from the British Library

PB ISBN 978 1 78087 651 1
EBOOK ISBN 978 1 78087 650 4

10 9 8 7 6 5 4 3 2 1

Printed and bound in Great Britain by Clays Ltd, St Ives plc

Typeset by Ellipsis Digital Limited, Glasgow

To Marta

*Comment s'étaient-ils rencontrés? Par hasard, comme tout le monde.*

DENIS DIDEROT, *Jacques le fataliste et son maître*

# PART ONE

# I

Across the desk from him sat a mother. Another mother.

She was the third he had seen this shift. The first had been too young, and pretty too, with a tight-fitting white T-shirt and wonderful collarbones. She had complained that her son had been beaten up outside the school yard, and he had listened to her patiently, promising that her complaint would be dealt with seriously. The second had demanded that the police send out a detective to follow her daughter and find out why she speaks in whispers on the telephone and locks her bedroom door at night.

All his recent shifts were made up of similar complaints. A week earlier, a woman had complained that her mother-in-law had put a curse on her. He was sure that the duty officers at his station were out there stopping people in the street and asking them to come in and file ludicrous reports to make fun of him. He wasn't aware of such complaints being filed on the shifts of the other investigators.

It was 6:10 p.m., and if there had been a window in Inspector Avraham Avraham's office he would have seen that it was starting to get dark outside.

He had already decided what to pick up for dinner on the way home, and what to watch on the television while he ate. But first he had to ease the concerns of the third mother. He stared at his computer screen, waiting for the right moment.

3

'Do you know why there are no detective novels in Hebrew?' he then asked.

'What?'

'Why aren't there any detective novels? Why doesn't Israel produce books like those of Agatha Christie, or *The Girl with the Dragon Tattoo*?'

'I don't read much,' she replied.

'Then I'll tell you. Because we don't have crimes like that. We don't have serial killers; we don't have kidnappings; and there aren't many rapists out there attacking women on the streets. Here, when a crime is committed, it's usually the neighbor, the uncle, the grandfather, and there's no need for a complex investigation to find the criminal and clear up the mystery. There's simply no mystery here. The explanation is always the simplest. What I am trying to say is that I think there is very little chance that something has happened to your son. And I am not just saying so to ease your mind. The statistics say so, and there don't seem to be any worrying signs that things are any different in your son's case. He'll be home in an hour, maybe three hours, tomorrow morning at the latest. I can assure you. The problem is that if I decide now that your son is missing and that the case requires immediate attention, I am obliged to send out officers to begin looking for him right away. Those are the procedures. And I can tell you from experience that there is a chance we will find him in a situation in which you wouldn't like us to find him. What do I do if he is found with a joint in his hand? I won't have much choice, and will have to open a criminal report. So you see, I don't think there is any point in starting to search for him now, unless of course your gut feeling tells you that something has happened to him, and you can give me some kind of sign or explanation why you think so. If that's the case, we will open a missing-persons file now and begin looking. If not, we should wait until tomorrow morning.'

He fixed his gaze on her, trying to assess the impression his little speech had made. She appeared lost. She wasn't used to making decisions – or insisting. 'I don't know if something happened to him,' she said. 'It's not like him to disappear like this.'

Another fifteen minutes or so went by with them sitting there like that, in his small room, face-to-face. He hadn't had a cigarette break since 5:00 p.m. His pack of Time was on the table in front of him, a small black Bic lighter on top of it. He had lighters in both pants pockets, and in the pocket of his shirt too.

'Let's go over the main things again and agree on what you can do when you get home if he isn't back yet, okay? You said he left for school as usual. What time did you say it was – ten to eight?'

'I told you, I didn't check. But it was the same as every morning, perhaps a quarter to eight.'

He pushed his keyboard aside and used a simple pen he had found in his drawer to jot down short sentences on a blank sheet of paper. He had an odd way of holding the pen, close to the tip, with all his fingers, the ends of which were already dotted with blue ink.

'The precise time isn't important,' he continued. 'Did he take his backpack as usual? Did you notice if he took anything out of the ordinary, if his backpack was particularly full, if there were clothes missing from his closet?'

'I didn't check.'

'And when did you notice he hadn't taken his cell phone?'

'During the day, when I cleaned his room.'

'Do you clean his room every day?'

'What? No, not every day. Every now and then, when it's dirty.'

She seemed to him to be the kind of person who did in fact clean every day. Small, with small hands, sitting there on the edge of the chair, leaning forward, a faded black leather handbag on her lap. She had one hand on the bag and the other was clutching a small cell phone, an old Samsung model, in blue. And this bent-over mother, with a son of sixteen, was his age, perhaps a year or two older. No more than forty. He jotted down none of this because it meant nothing.

'The phone was turned off, right? Isn't that what you said?'

'Yes, it was off. It was on the desk in his room.'

'Did you turn it on?'

'No. You think I should have?'

It was the first question she had asked him. Her grip on her handbag tightened, and he thought he heard her voice perk up – as if he had said that the moment she turns the phone on, it will ring and her son will be on the line to assure her that he is well and on his way home.

'I don't know, ma'am. In any event, I suggest you turn it on the moment you get home.'

'I had a bad feeling as soon as I found the phone,' she said. 'I can't remember him ever forgetting his phone.'

'Yes, you said so,' Avraham continued. 'And you called his school friend only in the afternoon, right?'

'I waited until four because he's a little late sometimes. They have a long school day on Wednesdays and he gets home at three, three thirty. I called at four.'

'And you believe his friend, right?'

Her reply in the affirmative began decisively but faded into a sense of hesitancy. 'Why? Do you think he lied? He could hear I was worried.'

'I don't know if he lied or not, ma'am. I don't know him. I only know that friends sometimes cover for one another and that if your son decided to cut school for the day and go into Tel Aviv to get a tattoo, for example, he may have told his best friend and asked him not to tell anyone.'

Would I have done the same? Avraham wondered to himself. And did kids still use the phrase 'to cut school'? Maybe it was because she sat there so motionless, so frightened to be in a police station, or maybe merely because it was late, but he chose not to tell her he had studied at the same school, that he remembered the mornings on which he had walked down to the bus stop at the top of Shenkar Street to wait for Line 1 or 3 to take him into Tel Aviv rather than go to school. He never used to tell anyone, not even the few friends he had. And he had a good cover story ready in case he bumped into one of the teachers.

'Why would he do that?' she asked. 'He's never done that before.'

'Perhaps, and perhaps not; it's worth checking. If he isn't home when you get there, I suggest you call his friend again, some of his other friends too, perhaps, and try to find out if there are any particular places he sometimes goes to. Maybe he has a girlfriend you don't know about. And try to remember if he said anything about having plans for Wednesday. Perhaps he said something and you have forgotten?'

'What plans would he have? He didn't say anything to me about plans.'

'And what about his siblings? Perhaps he told them something that would ease our minds? Or another family member – a cousin, grandfather?'

His question again seemed to awaken something in her, the semblance of a thought, but just for a brief moment. Or perhaps he was mistaken. She had come to the police station in the hope of finding someone who would take responsibility for her son and would start looking for him, and the conversation had confused her. She shouldn't have been sitting there at all. If her husband had been in the country, he would have been sitting there in the office in her place, making calls from his cell phone, threatening, trying to pull strings. Instead, she was being sent home alone, with instructions on how to look for her son on her own, while the policeman sitting opposite her spoke about him as if he were someone else. The fact that he had started speaking to her in the plural to make her feel she was not alone in her concerns wasn't helping. He got the sense that she wanted the conversation to end, yet didn't want to go home. He, on the other hand, wanted very much to go home. And just then, without her noticing, he wrote the name Ofer Sharabi at the top of the sheet of paper, crudely underlining it twice.

'He hardly speaks to his brother and sister,' she said. 'His brother is five, and he isn't very close to his sister.'

'It wouldn't hurt to talk to them. Anyway, do you have a computer at home?'

'Yes, there's a computer. In his and his brother's room.'

'So here's something else you can do; check his e-mails, his Facebook page, if he has one. Maybe he left a message there that would explain things. Do you know how to check?'

He knew she wouldn't do it. So why suggest it even? She'll

8

go home to wait and jump up every time the phone rings or at the slightest noise in the stairwell. And even if her son doesn't get back tonight, she'll still do nothing. She'll wait until morning and then come back to the station – dressed in the same clothes she won't take off all night. She'll come back to him.

The room was silent. She hadn't answered his question about the computer. Perhaps she was offended. Or maybe she was too embarrassed to admit she didn't know how to check it.

'Look, ma'am, I'm really trying to help. Your son doesn't have a criminal record and you tell me he isn't caught up in anything out of the norm. Regular kids don't just disappear. They may decide to cut school, to get away from home for a few hours, or be too ashamed to come home because they think they've done something unforgivable. But they don't simply disappear. Let me paint you a possible scenario: your son decided not to go to school today because he had an important exam and wasn't ready for it. Do you know if he had an exam? Ask his friend perhaps. He wasn't prepared and he's used to getting good grades and didn't want to disappoint his parents. So he didn't go to school and wandered the streets instead, or went to a shopping mall somewhere and was spotted by a teacher or someone else who knows him. And he got scared and was sure the whole world would know he cut school. So that's why he didn't come home. That's what happens with regular kids. So if you aren't hiding anything from me, you have nothing to worry about.'

Her voice shook. 'What do I have to hide? I want you to find him. He can't call without his phone . . .'

The conversation was going nowhere. It was time to end it. Avraham sighed. 'Your husband will be back in only a few days, right?'

'Two weeks. He's working on a cargo ship headed for Trieste. He can get off only when it anchors for the first time, in four days.'

'He won't have to get off anywhere. Where are Ofer's brother and sister now?'

'With the neighbor.'

He suddenly realized he had said the boy's name out loud for the first time during their conversation. Ofer. And it was such a beautiful name. He immediately changed his first name to that of the boy – like he always did when he heard nice names. His head played around with another name he would never have: Ofer Avraham. Inspector Ofer Avraham. Superintendent Ofer Avraham. Chief of Police Ofer Avraham announced his resignation today owing to personal reasons . . .

'I suggest you go home to your children, and I assure you we won't see each other tomorrow. I'll get someone to call you in the morning to check up on things.'

He placed the pen on the sheet of paper and leaned back in his chair. She didn't get up. If he doesn't tell her in plain words that the conversation is over, she won't leave. Perhaps he could ask her a few more questions. She clearly didn't want to be left on her own.

And only then did Avraham notice that while they were talking, he had inadvertently doodled a blue stick figure at the bottom of the sheet of paper. A long line for the pelvis, stomach, and neck together. Two diagonal lines at the one end for the legs, and two lines at the other end for the arms – with a circle above for the head. Tied around the circle was something that looked like a rope. And dripping from the circle were blue drops of blood. Or maybe tears? He had no reason for doing so, but placed his hand over the drawing. His fingers were stained with blue ink.

The skies above the police station and the Holon Institute of Technology were almost pitch-black when Avraham left the building. It was past seven. He turned right at Fichman Street and left onto Golda Meir, getting swallowed up among the walkers along the exercise path that stretched between the Neve Remez and Kiryat Sharet neighborhoods. He tried not to get caught up in their walking pace. Slower, slowly. It was a pleasant early-May evening. There wouldn't be many like it in the coming months.

His slow pace caused small traffic jams among the walkers behind him. Most were twenty or thirty years older than him, in tracksuit pants and T-shirts. They'd slow down and hesitate for a moment before stepping off the path onto the sand and quickly striding by the uniformed policeman and onto the asphalt again. A woman old enough to be his mother bumped into his arm and turned to mutter, 'Excuse me,' and he suddenly became aware of the noise of the traffic on the road, as if someone had just removed a set of earplugs from his ears.

He hadn't heard anything for a few minutes. He had been listening only to himself, an internal dialogue. He couldn't forget that woman. He recalled the murder of Inbal Amram in 2006. The court ruling was mailed out to every policeman in the country. It found that the police had been negligent in their search and were responsible for her death. But the circumstances were very different. The son of the woman who had sat in his office earlier hadn't disappeared at night. And there was nothing at this stage to indicate the need for any urgent missing-persons procedures or for mounting a comprehensive and expensive search operation. He had even taken the time, in the presence of the mother, to make some calls to hospitals in the area. None had reported admitting a boy by the name of Ofer Sharabi or anyone matching his description.

Before leaving the station, he had asked to be notified about any relevant report on the matter, to be called in the middle of the night if necessary. He had told the mother how to keep searching on her own, and had left the duty officer with a description of the black backpack with its white stripes – an Adidas knockoff – in case it came up in reports about a suspicious object in the area. Any other course of action would have been a waste of resources – and could land him in hot water. But if something were to happen to the boy that night, something he could have prevented, they'd really let him have it. He regretted his little speech about detective novels and crime statistics in Israel. Inbal Amram was murdered by a car thief who didn't know her – a carjacking that went wrong.

The dunes between Neve Remez and Kiryat Sharet, the two gray neighborhoods he had lived in all his life, were almost gone – replaced by apartment towers, a public library, a design museum, and a shopping mall, glowing in the darkness like a space station on the moon. At the halfway mark to Kiryat Sharet, the bright neon signs of Zara, Office Depot, and Cup o' Joe beckoned to his left, and he thought about crossing the street and going into the mall. He could get a coffee and a cheese sandwich and sit at one of the empty tables outside to quietly watch the soothing motion of the car headlights and think for a while. As he did most nights, he chose not to.

He wanted to think about other cases he was working on. One, in which he didn't have a single lead, involved three burglaries within a week on two adjacent streets in the Kiryat Ben-Gurion neighborhood. All had happened during the day, when the occupants were out. Clean break-ins. No broken locks or sawed bars. The burglars seemed to have had precise information on the comings and goings of the occupants. And they were obviously good at opening doors and locks without much noise. These weren't random break-ins by dopeheads. They stole jewelry, checkbooks, cash. And broke into a safe in one of the apartments.

It was a frustrating case. His only real line of investigation was to wait for the next burglary and hope that the thieves would leave something behind for forensics to pick up. They hadn't done so yet. Or perhaps some of the stolen property would turn up in a raid on a warehouse somewhere and there'd be someone to question. And he had a hunch that he dared not confess to in team meetings. That only one of the three burglaries was a real one. That only one had any significance to the burglars. And the thing they were looking for, and perhaps found, had nothing to do with money or property. The other two burglaries were staged, to throw the police off the scent.

He had had some success with his other case – but things had gone wrong over the last two days. Igor Kintiev, a twenty-year-old who had been discharged early from the army, was arrested in connection with a series of sexual assaults on women south of Tel Aviv, along the Bat Yam promenade. They had taken place on and off over a two-month period. Kintiev was picked up by detectives who were on a stakeout operation. They noticed him walking back and forth along the promenade, following women – mostly older than him, in their forties at least. He'd follow them and then turn and walk in the opposite direction, or cross the street, until he found another one to follow. He was picked out in a lineup by four of the seven victims. When first questioned, he denied everything, but then, two days ago, he opened up and confessed to the sex crimes and to dozens of crimes that had nothing to do with the original investigation, like setting fire to a retirement home up north two years ago, or an unreported case of attempted arson at a restaurant in 2005.

He was a strange kid, and his Hebrew was odd too – distant. His mother had stayed back in Russia; his father died in Israel. He had no fixed address. He had lived for a few months in a rented basement in the North, and then moved six months ago to the apartment of relatives in Bat Yam, for work purposes. Avraham didn't believe a word he had said. During one of the assaults, Kintiev had gripped the arm of a fifty-year-old cosmetics marketing manager and forced it into his pants – in the middle of the promenade, on a Friday evening. He was picked up without any ID papers on him and no money at all. In his backpack they had found a brand-new sophisticated compass and a copy of Shai Agnon's *A Simple Story*, a special edition for schools – its worn, blue, soft cover peeling apart. The first page displayed a handwritten dedication dated August 10, 1993: *To Yoela, a simple love story lost.* The name of the inscriber had been erased with Wite-Out.

Avraham didn't know why he thought the things he did. For no apparent reason, he had formed a picture in his mind of the computer screen in the room of Ofer Sharabi and his brother. An old, heavy monitor, in a shade of cream – or so he saw it. He was primarily concerned, however, with the age difference

14

between the children. A sixteen-year-old boy, a fourteen-year-old girl, and a five-year-old. Why were there nine years between the girl and the young son? Why would a couple that starts having children suddenly stop and wait such a long time for the next one? Perhaps it had something to do with the family's financial situation, health issues, a marriage crisis. Or maybe the mother had been pregnant before then and had lost the baby? Why the hell does everything need an explanation?

His mind wandered to eight in the morning. The three children leave for school and kindergarten, and the mother remains alone. The apartment's quiet. The rooms are empty. There's a soft sound coming from the white living-room curtains. What does she begin doing first? Wander through the empty rooms? The boys' room – a large space, with a bed that folds into a sofa and a desk on which the old computer monitor sits. On the other side, a child's bed, and a sideboard. And the girl's room – small, whitewashed, with a long mirror hanging on the wall opposite the door, in which the mother comes face-to-face with herself. In his imagination she is carrying a washing basket.

Five young boys and girls were standing at the number 97 bus stop on the main road at the entrance to Kiryat Sharet. The line's final stop was in Tel Aviv. One of the young girls was showing one of the boys something on her iPod. She was short and stocky, but noisily cheerful nevertheless. Dressed in unflattering black tights and a gray Gap sweatshirt, she tried to coax the boy into putting the earbuds into his ears. He refused, acting as if he were disgusted by the idea. Without meaning to, Avraham fixed them with a stern gaze. They were silent as he passed by, smiling in his wake. The girl with the iPod might have made some funny gesture. Was Ofer there among them? He must be. And if not there, then at a different stop.

Toward the end of his talk with the mother, just before she agreed to leave, she told him that Ofer had run away from home twice before. He wasn't yet twelve the first time. He walked – 'in flip-flops,' she said – more than six miles, to his grandparents' house. It was on one of the holidays, after a fight with his father. A year or so ago, he fought with her too, and left the house that afternoon saying he wasn't coming back. He returned after nine, in the end, let himself in with his key, and went straight to his room, without a word about what he had done that evening. They never spoke about it again. Avraham had asked her why she hadn't gone to the police then too, but she didn't answer. Probably because the father was home at the time.

An image froze in his mind. He didn't know exactly what the boy looked like, but he could see Ofer Sharabi placing his black bag on a bench in a dimly lit, deserted public park and lying down on his back. He's covering his body with a gray sweatshirt – like the one on the girl at the bus stop. He's getting ready to go to sleep. There's not a soul there aside from Ofer. And that's good. He's not in any danger.

Avraham passed by the building in which he had grown up – 26 Alufei Tzahal Street. His parents' home. He inadvertently lifted his head to look up to the third-floor window. Everything was shut tight. Not a sign of life. How long had it been since he was last here? The shutters of the second-floor window were open, and a shirtless man sat there on the windowsill with his back to the street, his face turned toward the glow of the living room and the sounds of the television set coming from it. The news would be on soon. The man spoke to someone in the apartment, maybe his wife in the kitchen. He was one of the neighbors who a few years earlier had found Avraham's father lying in the stairwell after the stroke.

He continued up the road and went into the supermarket. He thought for a moment about changing his plans, about cooking himself a nice dinner that would clear his mind of all his thoughts and make him happy. Maybe a simple bottle of Côtes du Rhône with some packaged ravioli that he could boil and then top with some olive oil and grated cheese. But his bubble popped again. He went over to the refrigerated section and took out a small single-portion tub of spicy tahini. It took him a while, but he eventually found a semi-fresh bread roll among the few items that still remained on the bread shelf, feeling them with his bare hands. He added a small box of tomatoes to his basket as he approached the cashier. Had he not forgotten to take the sheet of paper on which he had written the address, he would have gone home, got in his car, and driven to the building where the mother now waited. He would have staked out the place until he saw Ofer Sharabi walking into the stairwell and heard the mother's shouting or weeping. He would have slept easier. But he forgot to take the paper – even though he had folded it into a small square with the intention of putting it in his shirt pocket. Perhaps he didn't want to take the drawing that had startled him for no reason. He had an idea: he could call Ilana for advice. If Ilana told him to return to the station and put out an urgent missing-persons report, that's what he would do despite the late hour. But if he called her, he would again be exposing his insecurity, and he didn't want to do that. He paid with a credit card so as not to spend the small amount of cash in his wallet.

He returned to Alufei Tzahal Street, passed by his parents' home again, and decided against going up. His father was probably sitting in the dark in front of the TV, staring at the news. It was the worst time to disturb him. If his mother wasn't out walking, she would be sitting at the kitchen table and speaking on the phone. He wasn't in the mood for listening to her. Besides, he could already hear her voice playing in his head as she spoke to some friend: 'Oh my, it's Avi. I must go heat up something for him to eat.' He preferred to eat on his own and watch an old episode from the third season of *Law & Order* that he had seen countless times before. It was on Channel 3. He discovered something new each time he watched – another mistake in the investigation, a new way to acquit a defendant. He walked down the road and turned left, continuing for another three or so minutes past dark, silent buildings before reaching his own on Yom Kippur Street.

He'd leave his cell phone by the bed that night in case someone from the station called.

## 2

Ze'ev knew why the police cars were there the moment he saw them parked outside the building. It was a gut feeling, a sharp searing of his conscience, from deep within. He knew, too, that he was ready, but didn't know for what just yet.

It was strange – as if his life had secretly steered him toward this moment over the last few years, without any awareness at all on his part. He felt something explode inside him, like an unexpected birth: the moment he saw the patrol cars, a different person emerged from him, someone who had been inside him for years, waiting. With Elie's birth, it had been the opposite. They had prepared for nine months, but his arrival had hit them like a bombshell, out of nowhere. The parents within them that were supposed to emerge didn't. They both became children again, so very helpless.

He saw the patrol cars from the intersection, while waiting for the light to change. There were two of them parked at the entrance to the building, both with their front passenger doors open. A uniformed policewoman leaned against one, speaking on a cell phone. He parked his motorbike alongside the entrance to the building and walked into the stairwell. The door was open and voices were coming from the floors above. He passed by the door to his apartment and went up to the third floor. The door to the Sharabis' apartment was open too and a policewoman was standing at the entrance. Doors are open when a disaster has occurred, he thought. Perhaps that's what he had felt. Something opening.

The policewoman noticed him and asked who he was. 'My name's Ze'ev. I'm a neighbor from the second floor,' he replied, and asked her if something had happened. Standing firm at the entrance to the apartment, as if to indicate to him that he wasn't allowed in, she said nothing had happened. He hadn't thought of going in.

Michal was sitting on the sofa in their living room. Elie slept beside her. She was still in her pajamas and was watching *Dr Phil* on the TV. The shutters were closed and the apartment was dark. He asked if she knew what had happened at the neighbors', but she hadn't even noticed that there were police cars outside the building and that something was going on. He was home early, and she was surprised to see him. She quietly asked if he wanted something to eat. Then she took Elie to his room, carefully so as not to wake him, and opened a small crack in the shutters on the balcony to look outside. She went over to the door and peeked out into the hallway. Two policemen were bounding down the stairs, and she quickly shut the door again, asking, 'Perhaps they were burgled?'

Ze'ev said they wouldn't send out so many police to deal with a burglary.

'It's frightening. What could have happened?'

'Nothing terrible, I'm sure,' he answered, hugging her close.

That afternoon, Ze'ev sat on the enclosed balcony that had been turned into an uncomfortable study and marked exams. He could continue following the goings-on outside from there. Policemen came and went. One of them, a short bald man, appeared to be the senior officer on the scene. He was agitated, constantly on the phone, and sometimes raising his voice. 'Take him back. I'm not to blame that the fools didn't get the message,' Ze'ev heard him shout. 'It can't wait. I've been trying to reach her all morning and can't wait any longer. Get her out of the meeting,' he then shouted into the telephone.

A short while later, the officer went into the front yard of the building, almost tripping over a rock. He was looking for something among the bushes, but when he emerged his hands were empty. There was something clumsy about his movements. He lifted his head, seemingly to meet the gaze of another policeman standing on the third-floor balcony. Ze'ev didn't know what the officer had been looking for, or if he had managed to catch a glimpse of his eyes peering out through the narrow opening in the shutters on the second floor before he backed away quickly into his study. Hannah Sharabi came down to the pavement outside the building for a few minutes, surrounded by three policemen. She explained something to them, gesturing with her hands to illustrate her point. She appeared to be directing them somewhere. If Ze'ev had opened the window properly, he would have heard them. Other neighbors too were watching from their windows, from the adjacent buildings. He didn't see Hannah Sharabi's husband or the children.

He tried to focus on the exams. The grammar exercises were easy to check, but the short essays required attention. The topic was 'What will the world look like in twenty-five years?' It was intended to test usage of the future tense, and also tied in with a discussion Ze'ev wanted to raise in class after their reading of a few pages from Aldous Huxley's *Brave New*

*World*. Between each exam, he searched through news sites and Google News for reports related to the city of Holon or the name Sharabi.

Elie had been sleeping for more than two hours – a lot longer than he usually slept in the afternoons – and Michal had had time to bathe and dress. There was a moment, while she was in the shower, when both of them seemed not to be at home, a brief moment of deep inner silence. Then she came out to the balcony and kissed Ze'ev on his cheek. 'How are you getting along?' she asked, and he replied that he'd be done in time. He made himself a cup of tea with milk.

Elie woke shortly before three, crying as usual. Ze'ev hurried to complete checking the last essay and relieved his wife, who went out onto the balcony to sit at the desk he had been sitting at before and prepare her lessons for the following day. He and Elie played with building blocks on the carpet in the living room. He would build a low tower with the colorful blocks, and Elie would knock it down, looking at his father with satisfaction and pride. Ze'ev then tried to get him interested in two colorful children's books, one with a mirror – and managed to hold his attention for a short while. He was tense, but it was a good kind of tension, primed for action. He fought the impulse to put Elie in the trampoline seat in front of the television and go check what was happening outside. The infant obviously sensed it, and he whined and tried to crawl over to his mother. 'I think I'll take him out for a walk,' Ze'ev said to Michal. 'Do you need anything from the supermarket?'

The first sign Ze'ev noticed was on an electricity pole outside the building. Ofer's face, somewhat blurred, in the center of a standard white A4 sheet of printer paper that had been stuck to the concrete pole with clear tape. Dark-skinned, very thin, sunken black eyes, a small nose, and thin lips that were showing signs of a black mustache that needed shaving. He looked very serious in the picture. No smile, staring straight into the camera. Ze'ev thought back to the last time he saw his face, up close and serious. He thought the picture didn't convey any of his softness. It looked more like a 'Wanted' poster than the image of a missing youth.

The large bold print above the picture read '**MISSING**' – and below that were some printed lines of text:

*Ofer Sharabi went missing on Wednesday, May 4, in the morning. Age: 16. Build: Very thin. Hair: Short, black. Height: Average. If anyone has seen him, please contact the family or the police.*

There was a telephone number at the bottom of the page.

Ze'ev wondered who had put up the posters; he didn't think it was the police. They were posted the entire length of their street, on electricity poles and road signs, and he thought about tearing one off without being seen and taking it home. He might need it at some point. Had Ofer's mother made the posters herself?

Across from the retirement home, an elderly man pushed his face up close to one of the posters until his nose was almost touching it. He was wearing an old checkered shirt and carrying a light-brown leather bag in one hand. Elie was restless and was struggling to free himself from the straps of the stroller. They turned right onto Shenkar Street and walked to the kiosk at the corner, where Ze'ev bought Elie a small packet of peanut-butter snacks and placed it on his lap. Across the street, he could see the first-floor neighbor tearing off a piece of Scotch tape with her teeth and sticking up a picture of Ofer at the bus stop. He turned for home again. The police station wasn't far away.

The police knocked on their door early in the evening, sooner than he had expected. That was the first surprise. Ze'ev and Michal were getting Elie ready for his bath. Ze'ev opened the door to two police officers – the short clumsy one he had seen from the window in the afternoon, and a younger woman he hadn't seen before.

'Sorry to disturb you,' began the male officer, 'but you must be aware that your neighbor's son has been missing since yesterday. As part of our search, we are interviewing all the neighbors, and we'd like to ask you a few questions. Is this a good time?'

Michal stepped out of the bathroom with Elie in her arms, undiapered, and the officer looked embarrassed. He didn't switch on the light that had gone out in the stairwell and stood there in the darkness. 'Perhaps you'd like us to come back a little later,' the officer said. 'We can talk to the other neighbors in the meanwhile.'

Ze'ev invited them in. Elie fixed the police officers with a serious stare, like he always did when guests arrived. The policewoman's name was engraved on the silver tag on the pocket of her shirt – Liat Mantsur. Ze'ev felt the same inner explosion he had felt that afternoon when he returned home and saw the patrol cars. The other person inside him tensed in anticipation. Perhaps this is the beginning, he thought. He must remember every detail.

★

The police surprised him again. Ze'ev hadn't expected them to question him and Michal separately, and couldn't understand why the senior officer decided to sit in the kitchen with his wife while he sat in the living room with the junior officer, Liat Mantsur. A small, blue plastic plate with the remains of Elie's vegetable mash was still on the kitchen table. Scattered around the plate were bits of moist bread and crumbs.

'Would you like something to drink?' he asked the policewoman.

'No,' she replied, and rested a dark plastic clipboard on her knees. A black pen had been used to divide the sheet of paper on the board into three columns, each with a few lines of text at the top. He sat on the sofa, with the policewoman sitting opposite him, on the armchair.

'We are currently collecting information about the missing boy,' she said. 'It would help us if you could tell us when you last saw him – you may have seen him yesterday, or even today – and what your impression of him is.'

They seemed to be working by the book, and procedures most likely dictated that the neighbors must be interviewed and asked the exact same questions, even if nothing helpful came of them. The policewoman didn't look around the room, not even at the solitary picture – a reproduction of van Gogh's *Bedroom in Arles* – hanging on the wall across from the sofa, above the rickety sideboard; or at the old and ugly brown sofa, draped in a black-and-white-striped sheet to cover its stains and protect it from more; or at the toys strewn across the floor, giving the living room the appearance of a warehouse. So uninspired. She didn't look, but he could see through her eyes just how temporary the apartment seemed, how gloomily lit it appeared when evening fell.

'I didn't see Ofer yesterday, or today,' Ze'ev said. 'As far as my impression of him goes, he seems to be a pleasant, intro-verted boy.'

Already she made notes with a black pen. What the hell did she have to write about?

'I'm taking down notes while you speak, okay? When did you last see him? Do you remember, perhaps?'

'Not the exact date. At some point this week, I'm sure. In the stairwell. I teach at a high school, so we leave home at the same time, and sometimes we cross paths.'

'And did he appear the same as usual, or was there any-thing unusual about his behavior? Did you notice anything?'

Ze'ev was frustrated. He wasn't able to make out the con-versation between Michal and the senior investigator, only Elie's crying as he sat on his mother's lap, wrapped up in a dry towel and getting more agitated with every passing moment. The boy was tired and wasn't at all happy with the fact that two people were speaking to each other and not to him.

'Are you sure you won't have something to drink?' Ze'ev asked, hoping for an excuse to go into the kitchen. He wasn't quite sure yet about when in the conversation he would sur-prise her. Or perhaps he should save the surprise for the senior investigator, he thought.

'No, thanks, we're fine,' she replied. 'Okay . . . is there anything you know about the missing boy or his family that you'd like to share with us? Do you sometimes hear any fighting or arguing coming from there?'

So that's why the senior officer had chosen to speak to his wife, Ze'ev presumed to himself. He probably assumed that she was at home most of the time and would therefore know more about the goings-on in the building.

'Not at all,' Ze'ev said. 'We hear some noise sometimes; they have three children and live above us. But I think we are actually the ones making most of the noise in the building lately.' He smiled and wondered if she understood what he had meant. Her head was tilted toward the plastic clipboard on her lap and her gaze was fixed on the piece of paper, like a short-sighted student taking a test. 'We moved in here just over a year ago, before Elie was born. We used to live in the center of Tel Aviv, and I still work there. I teach at the Ironi A high school, next to the Cinematheque, if you know where that is.'

'And what was your general impression of the missing boy? Was he a good kid, or have you had any run-ins with him in the past?'

It was terrible. She wasn't even listening to the answers he gave to her routine questions. 'Not at all. Like I said, I got the impression that he's a pleasant, if slightly introverted, child.' He hesitated for a moment, again glancing over toward the kitchen, and then added, 'My acquaintance with him was a lot closer than neighborly ties.'

She didn't lift her head and continued writing. 'What do you mean?'

'I mean that I gave him private English lessons for four months.'

'And how was he?'

'What do you mean by "how was he"? How was he as a student?'

'As a student, as a person. What was your impression of him?'

Her repetition of the word 'impression' was ridiculous.

'I got the impression that he's a child who takes his studies seriously, but that English is not his strongest subject. He is a

27

gentle and pleasant young boy, introverted – like I told you. As I'm sure you can imagine, I meet many young people, but Ofer was unusual. I think we formed a strong connection.'

'And he didn't say anything to you about plans to run away, suicide perhaps, problems at school?'

'Not a word. We spoke mostly about his English, and he didn't say anything about suicide or running away in English.'

'So, you're saying he had no problems?'

'I didn't say that at all. I said we didn't speak about such things. And may I ask you why you are speaking about him in the past tense? It's unnerving.'

'I'm sorry, it's just a manner of speaking,' the policewoman replied, getting up from her chair and adding, 'Just a moment, I need to check up on something.'

She went to the kitchen. It was an odd moment: he wasn't sure if he was allowed to stand up in his own home. A moment later she returned with his wife and the senior policeman, but the three of them walked over to the door. That was the third surprise. Ze'ev stood up and joined them.

'I understand from your wife that you gave private lessons to Ofer,' the policeman said. 'So I may come by later to ask a few more questions. Thank you very much for your help.'

The stairwell was dark and quiet, as if the investigation had been wrapped up. They stood on either side of the threshold – two police officers on the one side, in the dark, a man, a woman, and a baby on the other, and an open door between them once again. Where was Hannah Sharabi? Was she at home? Alone? Did she have policemen with her?

'You're welcome anytime,' Ze'ev said. 'Although I don't know if we have been of much help. I'll be happy to help more – if you need help searching, for example. I don't know what your plans are. Do you intend to go on with the search through the night?'

The senior policeman looked surprised, as if he hadn't considered the option of searching at night. Ze'ev felt for the light switch on the wall next to the door, and with the stairwell lit up, he could see the policeman's name was Avi Avraham. He had taken a pack of cigarettes out of his pocket and was playing with it between his fingers.

'Thank you,' Avraham said. 'Some searches may be carried out, but we don't yet know exactly where or when. If we do mount searches, we'd be happy to have help from you, and the other neighbors too.' He continued to address Michal more than Ze'ev.

'Do you have any ideas about where Ofer might be?' Ze'ev decided to ask.

Avraham was on edge. 'Not yet, unfortunately. We are hoping to find him as quickly as possible.' And he suddenly turned to Ze'ev. 'Do you, perhaps?'

The light in the stairwell had gone out, and he turned it on again. For the first time since the police had come in, he felt like someone was actually speaking to him. 'I wish I knew' was all he said.

Their front door was the only one in the building that did not have a sign bearing the family's name – only some advertising stickers for locksmiths, plumbers, and electricians, along with a triangular magnet from Pizza Centro. And the policewoman hadn't even asked his name.

'So what did they ask you?' Ze'ev offhandedly asked Michal as they bathed Elie.

He was angry. Why hadn't she asked him the same question first? And why hadn't she told him what she and the senior officer had spoken about? His disappointment with Avraham's decision to speak with Michal hadn't abated; instead, it had become more bitter as a result of his brief, provocative exchange with the senior policeman at the door.

'Probably the same questions they asked you,' Michal said. 'How well I know Ofer. If I had noticed anything out of the ordinary. If I had seen any of his friends here or people he hung out with who looked offbeat.'

'And what did you say?'

'That I hadn't. That you gave him some private lessons at the beginning of the year, in their apartment. That he hadn't come here, and that he and I never exchanged anything more than hello and good-bye on the stairs. I may have once asked him how he was doing with his English or something like that. I told him that I think I heard a fight or argument coming from there this week, in the evening, maybe the evening before he disappeared, but that I have no idea who was involved or what it was about, or if it even had anything to do with Ofer. It may have been an argument between the parents.'

That was the final surprise. Ze'ev was stunned.

'Did you really hear them arguing?' he asked, and Michal laughed. 'What do you think – that I'd say something like that to him for no reason? Didn't you hear it?'

He couldn't remember. 'I may have been asleep already. Perhaps it was from their TV?' he asked, and Michal said, 'You know what? You could be right.'

They ate a light dinner in front of the television, watching a reality show, after Michal had put Elie to sleep. There was nothing of interest on the news. Michal returned to the balcony to continue working, and Ze'ev opened Ian McEwan's *On Chesil Beach*, an elegiac novel, very short, about missing out on love in an instant owing to reticence. He had been reading it for a few days, in small doses, welling up with sadness every time. He took note of the economical yet precise eye for detail of the British writer, whom he had not been familiar with beforehand. Elie was whimpering in his bed, and Ze'ev went to his room and put the pacifier back in his mouth.

He put off drinking his last cup of tea for the evening. He was waiting for Inspector Avraham and planned to offer him a coffee and drink one with him. The day had fulfilled less than it had originally promised. And he felt like he had so much to say. He heard sounds from the stairwell, people going up and down, but he couldn't know if they had anything to do with the search for Ofer or simply life itself. Neighbors came and went. A doorbell rang and someone said, 'It's me.' Doors slammed shut. The light went on and off. There were few cars on the street outside. After 11:00 p.m., the building was cloaked in silence. Avraham wasn't coming. Ze'ev returned the two clean mugs he had left out on the counter to the kitchen cupboard. He went into the bathroom to change clothes, brushed his teeth, and got into bed.

Michal came shortly afterward. She laid her pajamas out on the bed, undressed, and slowly put on her nightclothes in front of him, watching him as he continued reading. His eyes didn't budge from the page, as if he didn't see anything at all while she took off her bra. There was something unseemly in the room. She was undressing in front of someone else, someone she didn't even know.

'Are you thinking about Ofer?' she asked.

'Yes,' he said.

'What are you thinking?'

'That perhaps we'll join the search if they're still searching on the weekend. We'll leave Elie with your mother, or we can take him along in a carrier.'

'Do you think Ofer's run away from home?'

'I don't know. He doesn't give the impression of being independent or strong enough. Running away like that takes a lot of guts. This will be the second night since he disappeared, and he needs to sleep somewhere.'

His words shook her. 'His poor mother,' she said. 'I can't even begin to imagine how she must be feeling right now. To go through two nights without knowing where your son may be, it's terrible.'

Ze'ev fell asleep before her, dropping off into slumber quickly. One moment he was awake, and a moment later his eyes were closed. She watched his quiet breathing, then went into Elie's room to make sure he was covered. Babbling in his sleep, the infant sighed and stretched out his arms toward her as she wrapped the blanket a little tighter around his small body.

# 3

He was awoken on Friday morning by a long buzz on the intercom. It was late, a lot later than his usual waking hour, even on his day off.

'A delivery for Avi Avraham.'

In his mouth was that dry, bitter taste that's left behind by too brief a night after a long day, and almost three packs of Time. The flower-delivery boy was dressed in a green uniform. His helmet was still on, and he was hidden behind a large bouquet in shades of pink, white, and purple – lilies, lisianthus, and gerberas, interspersed with an abundance of green foliage. He tore off the greeting card and read:

> Dear Avi,
> Happy 38th birthday.
> Wishing you lots of health, happiness, and continued success through life, wherever it may lead you.
> Love,
> Mom and Dad

He didn't call to say he had received the flower arrangement, which he placed on the kitchen table, not yet in a vase with water. The daylight shining in from the kitchen window was too strong. He placed a finjan with water and enough Turkish coffee to make two cups on the gas stove. The rumbling of the engine of a delivery truck outside the building shook the floor. It was all so different from the quiet he usually woke to.

He generally rose before six, without the need for an alarm. He'd brush his teeth while traipsing around the palely lit apartment, boil water in the kitchen, and go into the living room, where he'd open the shutters and continue brushing as he looked out at the dark street. There'd be hardly any traffic, only frozen cars parked in lines on either side of the road. Sometimes he'd see someone leaving early for work, sometimes he'd even hear the chirping of a stray bird.

Perhaps the noise wasn't coming from the street, but from somewhere within him. He had woken restless, as if the delivery truck had dumped all of yesterday inside him the moment he heard the buzzer of the intercom. All the images, all the conversations. The uncertainty, Hannah Sharabi through the dusty glass door, the endless ringing of his cell phone, the sense that things were getting out of hand, the neighbors looking down at him from the balconies, the drive through the city at night, alone, aimlessly.

Hannah Sharabi had popped into his mind the moment he woke the day before, too. It was 5:50 a.m. He checked his phone and saw that he hadn't missed a call during the night. He couldn't be sure if that was good news or not.

He decided to forgo the walk, instead driving his car to the station. He wanted to be mobile during the day if the need arose. He walked into the almost empty station just before seven thirty. The duty officer informed him that no reports about a missing boy had come through during the night, and that no one had asked him to call any mother in the morning to find out if her son had returned home.

The following two hours were a nightmare. Nothing happened. He sent out e-mails, completed a personal questionnaire he needed to pass on to the human resources department because of his trip to Brussels, read the headlines on the *Haaretz* news website, and browsed through the Kintiev file to prepare for the next stage in the investigation. The sheet of paper on which he had jotted down short sentences from his conversation with the mother the night before was still on the desk, where he had forgotten it, neatly folded into a small square.

The records from the night between Wednesday and Thursday revealed nothing related to Ofer Sharabi. There had been a fire at an insurance agency and the firefighting crew suspected arson. A scooter had been stolen just a few dozen yards from his apartment. He could have called the boy's mother to ease the uncertainty, but a dull feeling inside of him told him not to tempt fate. The fact that she hadn't called might be a sign that all is well, and he didn't want to break that with a phone call. And if not, if a tragedy loomed, it would be best to wait rather than hasten its arrival.

After a while, he left his office to make a cup of coffee and use the copying machine behind the duty sergeant's desk. The station was already a-buzz with the morning's activity. Civilians stood in line at the front desk. Two traffic policewomen were in conversation at the entrance to the station. And then he saw her. She was standing outside the station and he spotted her through the dusty glass door. She was in the same clothes he had seen her in the night before – just as he had thought she would be. The shabby leather bag was hanging off her shoulder by its thin strap, and she was clutching the cell phone in her hand, as if she hadn't let it go since they parted. The pain he felt on seeing her took him by surprise.

Ofer hadn't returned.

Avraham froze for a moment – and then left the copying machine and hurried over to her. He thought about placing his hand on her shoulder but then noticed that she wasn't alone. He looked over at the man she was with and quietly asked, 'He didn't come home, did he?'

'I'm Ofer's uncle,' said the man at her side. 'My brother called me at six this morning and told me what's happening. Are you the policeman who spoke with her yesterday?'

Avraham didn't respond. He turned to Hannah Sharabi and asked, 'You haven't heard a thing?' But she remained silent, as if the presence of the uncle had made her presence unnecessary.

'Nothing,' the uncle replied. 'You told her that you would begin searches in the morning.'

Avraham quickly ushered them to his room, without anyone noticing.

They remained at the station until late in the morning. His hand hardly let go of the telephone. Again he made calls to the hospital emergency rooms, went through the reports and incidents from the night before, and received updates from the intelligence coordinators in the police district. He left the room a few times to try to get hold of Ilana, but her cell was switched off and the secretary at the Investigations Division told him that she was in meetings at the National Headquarters in Jerusalem. He wanted to consult with her, but mostly he wanted to be the first one to tell her the story.

The mother was even quieter than she had been during their talk the day before. He asked her if she'd like something to drink, and she shook her head to say no. Even when he asked her direct questions about Ofer, the uncle answered instead. Only when he inquired about Ofer's height and the uncle responded, 'Five feet four inches,' did she intervene and say, 'Five feet six inches.' He weighed around 130 pounds.

With the help of the mother and uncle, he put together a brief announcement about the missing boy. They gave him permission to post it on the police website and Facebook page, and he explained that the same announcement would also appear in the media. The mother then placed a plastic sandwich bag on the table and took out six photographs of Ofer. That moment haunted him later that night, before he fell asleep. He hadn't had time to examine the pictures, and knew that night that he had made a mistake. Could he have seen something in them? Perhaps. And even if not, she had wanted him to look at Ofer, to say something about him. He asked which was the most recent and took them all to be scanned. On his way back to his office, he remembered that Igor Kintiev was supposed to arrive at the station at 1:00 p.m. from the holding cells at the Abu Kabir facility and he called to cancel the interrogation. His remand was for another four days, and the questioning could wait.

The thing that surprised him throughout the morning was that no one had blamed him for anything – neither the uncle nor the mother. They hadn't attacked him for his decision not to begin a search, nor had they reminded him that the night before, there hadn't been a policeman in Israel who knew of Ofer's disappearance, apart from him. The fact that they hadn't blamed him only seemed to heighten the sense of urgency. He managed to put together a temporary team around noon – five officers, including a young policewoman from the Traffic Division who had completed her shift and volunteered to stay for a few extra hours. They were also joined by an investigator from the IT Division who accompanied him on the short drive from the station to Histadrut Street.

This must be the first time Hannah Sharabi has been in a police patrol car, Avraham thought to himself when they got in the car. He looked at her in the rearview mirror as she buckled up in the backseat.

From then on, he felt that things were getting out of control, that he wasn't able to manage his temporary team, his situation, the way he wanted to. And it was all Ilana's fault – at least that's how he felt at the time. Her absence prevented him from thinking things through, and he wasn't quite sure why. In any event, it was scandalous – a Special Investigations Division officer disappearing in the middle of the day and impossible to get hold of.

He tried nevertheless to begin the investigation in an orderly and rational manner. It was his hard-and-fast rule. He wanted to sit down for a quiet talk with Hannah Sharabi, but it was simply impossible. The apartment was a hive of activity. His officers came and went, neighbors came up, and the uncle brought over more relatives and didn't leave the mother's side for a moment, sticking to her like a bodyguard. And the telephones didn't stop – a different ringtone every second, or the same ringtone and three or four people fumbling for their phones in their respective pockets, thinking the sound was coming from there. He instructed the traffic policewoman to restore some order and to stop anyone else from entering. He was sure that was the key. If he could only sit down with the mother for a few minutes and ask her a question he hadn't yet asked and still wasn't aware of, everything would become a lot clearer – a question that would evolve out of the conversation and elicit a piece of information she wasn't aware of having. She'd remember something Ofer had said, a friend she had forgotten to mention, and they'd know where to begin looking. It had been only a little more than twenty-four hours since Ofer's disappearance; anything was still possible.

He sat in the car to think. A call from the station informed him that Igor Kintiev had arrived for questioning. And for the first time that day, he raised his voice, shouting that he had called two hours earlier to cancel the interrogation and giving instructions for Kintiev to be returned to the holding cells. A woman he had seen earlier in the apartment came over to his car and asked if she could put up posters along the street.

He hung out around the building, smoking, trying again to get hold of Ilana. Rinat Pinto, who had been sent to carry out initial inquiries at Ofer's school, returned empty-handed. They met up at the entrance to the building and she asked Avraham if she should question additional teachers and friends. And Ilana remained out of reach. The investigator from the IT Division presumed he had gone back to the station and called him from upstairs. His initial check through Ofer's e-mails and text messages had revealed nothing of any importance, and he asked if he should get the family's go-ahead to remove the computer's hard drive for further examination. 'Wait just a moment, I'm coming up,' Avraham replied, returning to the apartment and asking if it would be okay for him to smoke on the balcony.

It was past three when Ilana eventually called. She sounded aloof. Her tone was official. He could hear sounds in the background, coming perhaps from a radio. Was there someone in the car with her? He went out onto the balcony to be alone while they spoke, and lit a cigarette, placing the lighter and pack on the open windowsill. The lighter fell down to the yard. He gave Ilana an update on the start of the investigation without mentioning the mother's visit to the station the previous evening. She said he seemed to be doing all the right things at this stage in the investigation and didn't see any cause for deviating from standard search procedures.

'As far as I understand things, there's no special urgency, right?' she added, and he wanted to roar back, 'What do you mean, no special urgency? We have no idea at all where the boy spent the night,' but instead he just asked, 'And what about tomorrow?' wondering if she could notice the tension in his voice.

'What do you mean, what about tomorrow?'

She hadn't noticed.

'Tomorrow's Friday. If I want an extensive search, I'll need to bring in personnel.'

'Until you have a concrete lead to follow, Avi, there's no point. And from what you've told me so far, you don't have one for now, right?' He had already told her that he didn't have one, and couldn't understand why she was repeating and loudly stressing the question in the presence of the person sitting next to her. 'The moment you have a lead, we'll bring in more personnel; it won't be a problem,' she said.

'Will you be in the area today, by any chance?' he asked.

'I don't think so. I'm on my way back from Jerusalem and have meetings at district headquarters all afternoon. But call me if something urgent comes up. Keep me posted on your progress in the investigation, in the evening and over the weekend too if something new turns up. Okay?'

She was speaking to him in that manner only because of

the person or persons sitting beside her. She was with someone important, he thought – the district commander perhaps, or maybe the deputy chief of police. This conversation with her had been useless.

Only evening brought quiet to the building on Histadrut Street. Everyone had been released from duty or was done for the day. He asked Liat Mantsur to join him for some questioning of the neighbors. They went from one apartment to the next, but nothing significant came from any of their conversations. No one had heard a thing, no one knew Ofer Sharabi beyond polite small talk on the stairs – everyone apart from the neighbor who had asked his permission to put up posters in the street. She said she was 'close to the family,' and that Ofer was a 'wonderful boy' – and she cried.

Avraham went up to the Sharabis' apartment one last time before they all left the building. He knocked softly on the closed door, thinking in the few seconds that passed before it opened that every knock had the potential of driving the mother over the edge. 'It's Inspector Avraham,' he called out in a loud voice through the door. 'Can you open for a moment?'

A woman in her fifties opened the door – the uncle's wife, ready for bed. She had assumed command of the situation. The mother was sitting on a leather sofa in the living room, a young girl of around Ofer's age beside her. On the table in front of them were small plates of salted snacks, an open bottle of Diet Sprite, cups with the remains of coffee – like during the shivah after a funeral. The TV was on, Channel 2.

Avraham stood in front of her in the living room, between the sofa and the television. 'That's it,' he said. 'We're done here for now and I'm going back to the station. You should get some sleep.'

'In a little while,' the mother replied, but her eyes asked him if he really thought she was going to go to bed.

'I'll come by tomorrow morning,' Avraham continued. 'And let me know at any time if something happens during the night. You have my cell number, right?'

The aunt accompanied him to the door, whispering that she and her daughter would be spending the night.


He dropped off Liat Mantsur at her place, but instead of heading home, he drove around for a while longer, aimlessly.

He had no reason to return to the station.

His failure of the night before had been compounded by another one. He hadn't acted like the commander of an investigation. He hadn't paused to think. He hadn't looked. He hadn't listened. Whatever happens with Ofer, wherever he may be, there was a story here that had started telling itself. And he hadn't listened to the story. Not only did he not know how it would end; he couldn't say how it had started, either. He didn't have a clue who the characters were. That's what he'd have to do tomorrow, to listen to the story – to get to know Ofer Sharabi, and also his mother and his father, who was on a cargo ship somewhere on the way to Trieste, as well as his brother and sister, whom he hadn't yet seen.

Slower, slowly, he whispered to himself again, just as he had done on the way home the night before.

He drove up and down Sokolov, Holon's main commercial street, his eyes on the crowds of young people who filled it. Thursday, 11:30 p.m. – the cafés were packed, with lines stretching outside. The street belonged to the adults during the day, the shopkeepers and the shoppers; but at night the youth ruled. He slowed down almost to a standstill. When he was young, there wasn't a single café in Holon – only one or two ice cream parlors, a few small, failing pizza stands that opened, closed, then reopened under different names, and a confectionery store where he worked one summer. For now, he had no way of knowing whether the cafés or one of their customers were part of the story he needed to listen to.

He stopped off at Struma Square to buy a falafel, parking his car up on the pavement. Despite the late hour, there was a long line. A group of young boys and girls were crowded around a man whose face he thought he recognized from the sports section of the newspaper. He bought half a portion; it was late to be eating, and he didn't want to spend all the cash he was carrying. He ate standing up, close to a group of young people who were leaning against a red BMW, trying to listen to their conversation. He was so much older than them. In fact, as it was past midnight already, he was exactly thirty-eight years old. How long had it been since he last went out at that time of night? He got back into his car and continued to drive, slowing down when he saw someone walking along the pavement alone, stopping alongside a parked car in which a couple were sitting in the dark.

It all reminded him of a different time, and evoked a strange sense of duplicity. He was he, and also someone else that was no longer there. He parked his car below his building on Yom Kippur Street after 2:00 a.m. He turned on the light in the apartment, stared at the silent television set, and then went into the kitchen to pour himself a glass of water. Was this his way of celebrating? The thought amused him. It took him a long time to fall asleep.

*

The buzz of the intercom was followed thirty minutes later by a phone call. By then, Avraham was dressed in civilian clothing – a clean pair of jeans and a wide mustard-colored polo shirt, one of the only ones in which he felt comfortable. 'Are you up?' his mother asked, as if she was used to him sleeping at that time. 'We wanted to say *mazel tov*. You do remember it's your birthday, right? And that you're coming to our place.'

She didn't mention the arrangement of lisianthus and gerberas. And he too said nothing, although he could have thanked her. She passed the phone to his father, and he wished him well with practically the very same words that were on the card, as if he were reading from a piece of paper: 'We wish you only health, wherever life may lead you.'

Did she know no one else would call to wish him happy birthday, and so she did so twice, once with the card and once by phone? Or perhaps she thought he'd get dozens of calls and messages and wanted to be the first?

Before leaving the apartment, he placed the pink, white, and purple arrangement in a jar he had found in the kitchen and filled with water. He left the bouquet still wrapped in the noisy cellophane in which it had arrived.

Unlike most of his colleagues, Avraham liked going into the station on Friday mornings. He had nothing else to do.

The station was quiet, as it was every Friday. The morning shift's duty sergeant, David Ezra, appeared cheerful. He was speaking to someone on the phone and moved the mouthpiece aside to whisper to Avraham, 'Have you come in to work on the missing-persons case? Wait just a moment, then,' and he handed over a short list of calls that had come in overnight about the young boy, along with the names of the callers, their

44

numbers, and a few words on the information they wished to pass on.

'Is that all?' Avraham asked.

Ezra nodded and continued his conversation.

Because of the urgency and the presence of the mother and uncle in his office, he had forgotten to turn off his computer when they left for the building on Histadrut Street the previous day. It was still on. He went through the list of callers, marking a few with a blue asterisk. He then opened the missing-persons section on the police department's Facebook page, and was surprised to see the very small number of responses to the report about Ofer's disappearance. And they were all insignificant – good luck wishes to the police, two offers to help with the search, and one that linked the deteriorating state of the youth in general to the hallucinatory drugs that were being sold at late-night kiosks and the police's inefficient handling of the matter.

He didn't know why he was at the station at all. He could have waited at home for some concrete information to come in. But he wanted to be active. The more time that went by since Ofer's disappearance, the less chance they had of finding him. He sensed he needed to take the initiative, to make things right, to attack, that something would happen in the coming hours. He had promised himself the day before that he would start listening to the story. He jotted down a few questions he planned to ask Hannah Sharabi.

He then called one of the telephone numbers. There was no reply. His fourth call was answered by a child.

'Hello, this is Inspector Avraham Avraham from the police. You left a message regarding a missing boy, Ofer Sharabi,' he said.

'Just a moment, I'll call my mom,' replied the girl. Her childish voice was soon replaced by the deep voice of a man.

Avraham repeated himself.

'Good of you to call,' the man said. 'My wife and I saw the missing boy yesterday evening.'

The man went on to say that he and his wife had seen Ofer at a gas station on the road to Ashdod. They had stopped to fill up their tank and buy a cup of coffee at the adjacent convenience store. They had seen a young boy sitting alone at a table outside the store, smoking. The man and his wife had sat at the table next to him for almost ten minutes. The boy had looked familiar, but the man couldn't place him and had simply stared at him until he got up and left. Only afterward, when they were back in the car, did he remember seeing a picture of the boy earlier that afternoon on the missing-persons page of the police website. Avraham didn't ask him why he had opened the police website's missing-persons page in the first place.

'Was he carrying a black bag perhaps?'

'A black bag?'

'Yes. Did you happen to see if he had a black bag with him?'

'I don't remember seeing a bag.'

'And do you remember what he was wearing?'

'Uh, no, not really. A white shirt maybe? My wife would remember.'

'Can you go to the Ashdod police station and make a more detailed statement?' Avraham asked, and the man said, 'Ashdod? But we live in Modi'in. We were on our way to a wedding.'

'To the Modi'in police, then.'

'On a Friday? Will someone be there? Can't we just do this over the phone?'

'I'd like you to have a look at some photographs, but Sunday morning would be okay too,' Avraham said, knowing all too well that the man had no more information to share anyway. The important thing was that if he had seen Ofer and could positively identify him, that would be a sign of life.

The building he arrived at that afternoon felt strangely like home already. He parked his car in the same place he had parked it the previous day, across from the entrance, but on the other side of the street. The building was an old tenement structure from the 1950s or '60s that had been renovated at some point since, yet still looked neglected – a ship that had run aground and had been left in the sun to rust. Plastic blue-and-white flags still waved in the wind from some of the balconies – leftovers from the Independence Day celebrations a week earlier. He had spent almost the entire day there yesterday, and although he hadn't made an effort to take in the details, some of the familiar decor had sunk in.

The door to the building was closed, and he received no answer when he buzzed the intercom. He suddenly realized that none of the family had called him since the night before. Was there no one at home? He waited a moment and then buzzed the neighbor from the first floor. They went up to the third floor together and knocked. 'Hannah, the police are here,' the neighbor called out, and the mother opened the door. She said she hadn't heard the intercom, and Avraham suddenly wondered if he had in fact rung after all.

She was alone in the apartment, which looked clean and tidy – no dishes on the living-room table, no visitors. The neighbor looked disappointed when Avraham asked her to leave them alone. He had been waiting for this moment since yesterday, and he didn't know how much time he had before the family returned.

They sat at the counter between the kitchen and the living room. The mother had changed her clothes and her hair was wet. He said yes to a cup of Turkish coffee, with one sugar, and alongside the mug she placed a small plate of pretzels.

'Any news? Have you heard anything?' he asked, and immediately regretted doing so. She should be the one asking him for news, and he should be the one updating her, not the other way around. He had to convince her – himself too, perhaps – that they were doing everything possible, that he was firmly in control of the investigation.

She shook her head.

'Where's everyone?' he asked, and she said, 'I needed some quiet. They'll probably come back.'

He tried to sound official, despite feeling they had known each other for a long time. 'I came to update you on the investigation and ask a few more questions,' he said.

'Okay.'

'We are currently conducting the investigation on a number of levels at the same time. The first level is a more passive one. We have started to receive information from people who saw Ofer or say that they saw him, and we are trying to verify this information. I was at the police station this morning and checked out a few things,' Avraham said, wondering if he should tell her about the call from Ashdod – or, rather, Modi'in. 'Random information like this very often leads us in the right direction. The second level of the investigation is a more active one. We are questioning Ofer's friends, and we are doing an in-depth examination of his computer. A team of investigators was dealing with this yesterday, and we will continue over the weekend. Something is likely to come up from that too, because every action leaves behind a trail – and certainly an action that has been planned, such as running away. In addition to this, there is the ongoing intelligence level, with the intelligence coordinators receiving updates on the situation, and they, of course, are under orders to pass on to me any relevant information they receive.'

'So you aren't searching for him? With police forces?' she asked.

'All these operations, ma'am, are being conducted by the police. But if you mean searches out in the field, then no, not yet. We still don't know where to look.'

He wanted to tell her that it was impossible to simply send police officers out into the street to call out, 'Ofer, come home! Your mother's worried sick about you!' as she would like them to do, but he didn't. She waited for him to continue.

'I'd like to speak to Ofer's brother and sister,' Avraham said. 'Where are they now? I didn't see them yesterday either.'

'At my husband's parents.'

'Why?'

'I can't look after them now on my own. I don't have the strength. Maybe I'll bring them home on Sunday,' she answered, and suddenly burst into tears – perhaps because of her thoughts of Sunday and the fact that the weekend would go by without Ofer. Her whimpering was soft, stifled, fragmented, like that of a dog that has been left outside the house and is trying to get in.

'And are you in touch with your husband?'

'I haven't spoken to him today. He's in touch with his brother, who keeps him updated. He'll be back on Sunday.'

Avraham waited for her to calm down.

'I know I have asked you this a number of times,' he continued, 'but we have some peace and quiet now, and perhaps you've had more time to think. Are you sure that nothing happened that could be linked to Ofer's running away?'

Why had he asked about Ofer running away as if he already obviously had?

'I've told you everything. And you have the names of everyone he knows.'

'Look, ma'am, I'll try to explain why I keep going back to this. It is unlikely for a teenager to run away without help. He doesn't have a credit card, and you told us that he didn't have cash. And he doesn't have his cell phone with him. He can't get far without help, without someone who perhaps gave him money, or a place to sleep.'

Did he believe what he was saying, or was he simply trying to paint a soothing picture, one of Ofer sleeping under a roof somewhere and not alone?

'Do you know if he knows anyone in Ashdod?' he suddenly asked.

'Ashdod?' She thought for a moment. 'He has been there often, with his father, at the port. But he doesn't have family there. Why Ashdod?'

'Just a routine question,' Avraham said, and then added, 'Tell me more about Ofer.'

She looked up at him and thought for a moment, wondering perhaps where to begin.

'I told you yesterday. He's a good student. He studies the sciences. He doesn't go out, doesn't have many friends. He goes to school and comes home, plays with his sister and brother, helps a lot around the house. He doesn't talk much – not to me, and not to his father, either . . .'

He interrupted her: 'Does he surf the Internet?'

'He's on the computer a lot. I don't know what he does with it.'

'Does he have a girlfriend?'

She hesitated before answering. 'No, I don't think he goes out with girls.'

'What does he plan to do in the army?'

'He hasn't said anything about it, although he has received his draft papers. What can he do in the army? He isn't a boy with many friends.'

'Do you think he was afraid of the army? Did he ever say anything about it?'

'I don't know. Maybe he was scared.'

How could she not know anything about her son? Avraham wondered. He was about to complete eleventh grade, so how could he not have done anything worth speaking about, not have said anything, not have spoken to anyone about anything? Yet this is what everyone had been telling him for the past twenty-four hours.

'May I see his room again?' he asked.

The mother stood up, and Avraham followed her to the room he had gone into several times the day before. She stopped at the doorway. It wasn't the typical teenager's room that you see in advertisements, but rather a random collection of unrelated pieces of furniture. The shutters were closed and the room was dark. No one had slept there that night.

Avraham switched on the light. In front of the wall to the right of the door stood a large wardrobe finished with a mousy-gray Formica surface. A plastic basketball hoop was stuck to it at the top, and under the brown single bed Avraham could see the orange sponge ball used for shooting baskets. There were two posters on the wall above the bed, opposite the door – one from one of the *Harry Potter* movies, and the other of a young man he didn't recognize. The posters looked old, like they had been hung up there maybe two or three years ago. A desk unit with a black Formica surface stood to the left of the bed – four not very full shelves with textbooks, notebooks, dictionaries, a few computer-game packages, an alarm clock, a handful of teen novels, and a lamp. All surprisingly neat. Uncharacteristic for a teenager. Next to the lamp were a computer screen – a black flat-screen monitor – and a silver mouse that wasn't connected to anything, as the computer itself had been taken away for examination. The five-year-old brother's things, although similarly few in number, appeared more prominent in the room, he thought. In the right corner of the room, next to the child's bed, was a low shelf unit displaying plastic cars, books, and teddy bears. Some other toys were scattered across the floor, next to the bed and underneath it. But they were more colorful.

Avraham sat down on Ofer's bed. His mother remained in the doorway. But when he began opening the drawers, after asking her permission, she came in and sat down too, a small distance from him. He liked the fragrance of the soap she'd used in her bath.

The top drawer in the small cupboard contained an old Discman that appeared to be broken, batteries, rulers, a math compass, a cell-phone charger, an empty leather wallet, and a set of keys. In the second drawer, he found documents and papers, a health-insurance card, the draft papers Ofer had received from the army, and a printed schedule of classes. The third and largest of the drawers was filled with notebooks and tests, from previous school years most likely.

Avraham removed the class schedule from the second drawer and the keys from the first, closing them all afterward. If Ofer had gone to school on Wednesday, he would have had algebra class from eight to ten, then English, sociology, and literature. He also had an hour of PE.

'I don't see Ofer's ID card here,' Avraham said. 'Does he usually carry it with him?'

'I don't know,' she answered. 'I know he has one.'

'And what about a passport?'

'His passport is old. I think my husband has it.'

The set of keys was resting in his open palm, and he appeared to be estimating its weight. 'Is this the key to the house?' he asked. 'Didn't he take a key with him?'

'I think that's an old key,' the mother replied. 'We changed locks. I can check.'

Avraham stood up – and she followed his lead. 'Ofer's a very tidy boy,' he said.

She looked around the room and he thought he could see a sense of surprise in her eyes. 'I didn't know he was so tidy,' she said. 'I've never opened his drawers.'

He left Hannah Sharabi that afternoon without knowing a thing about Ofer he hadn't known beforehand. He got into his car and began driving home. This time, however, he stopped at the mall, parked the car, crossed the street, and sat at a table at Cup o' Joe, outside. The café was almost empty. He picked up a pile of weekend newspapers and ordered a double espresso and a piece of carrot cake. My birthday celebration, he thought.

The truth was, he had no idea what his next step should be. He didn't have a single lead and, for some unknown reason, was pinning all his hopes on the call from Ashdod. He had left the mother alone in the apartment. Ilana hadn't called all morning. It was a Friday just like any other Friday, the eve of the Sabbath, when, as the hours passed and the day drew to a close, so too did everyone else, gradually closing up their homes and affairs.

The articles in the local newspapers were ridiculous. Most were about people younger than him. There was, however, an interesting piece in *Haaretz* – a serious report about the battle for the post of chief of police that very accurately described the infighting among the police top brass. The article also alluded to a sex scandal involving one of the candidates, whom Avraham had never met but knew well by reputation.

He went over to his parents' at exactly 6:00 p.m. Like always, they were in the middle of an argument. His mother opened the door and kissed his unshaved cheek, calling out to his father: 'Okay, enough already, Avi's here and we can sit down to eat.'

'No, I want you to check on the Internet,' his father said, brushing aside the checkered woolen blanket that was covering him and getting up from his easy chair to shake Avraham's hand. He was dressed in a dark pair of tracksuit pants and an old white undershirt.

'What do you need to check?' Avraham asked his mother, and his father replied instead: 'If there are mosquitoes. She says there are no mosquitoes before July, but I was bitten the entire night.'

'It's not mosquitoes. He closes all the windows, puts the air conditioner on at sixty-five degrees, and lies under a blanket.

And I freeze. Why must I feel like I'm in a hospital? Do you know how good the air is outside? What do we have all these windows for? Avi, tell him about the air outside.'

What could he say about the air?

'One would think we were in Switzerland,' his father retorted. 'It's hot outside, and that's why there are so many mosquitoes.'

'Okay, there are mosquitoes. Just do me a favor and get dressed already. It's Avi's birthday. You can't sit at the table like that.'

'Why not? Are you all dressed up? What's wrong with what I'm wearing? Avi, is it okay with you if I sit down like this? He's not a stranger.'

Because they were only three, his mother had set the small table in the kitchen and not the large one in the dining room. But she had covered it with a white cloth and had taken out the plates usually reserved for guests. The cutlery was laid out on folded red napkins. The centerpiece was a bottle of red wine that they wouldn't open. She was fuming. 'Wear whatever you like. Don't change – sit there at the table in the smelly clothes you sleep in. I don't have the strength to fight with him all day.'

His father went to his room to dress.

When he was growing up, the room had been Avraham's, but a few years after he left home and clearly wasn't returning, it became a storeroom, and in recent years, since his father's return from the hospital after his stroke, the storeroom became his room. They fitted an air conditioner and slept in separate rooms – and not only because of the temperature differences.

Avraham took his seat and placed his pack of cigarettes and cell phone on the table beside him.

'You still smoke?' his mother said. 'No wonder you don't feel well.'

'I feel fine,' he responded.

'Did you get the flowers?'

'Yes. Thanks. They arrived early this morning.'

'And you don't say anything? Do you know I called to shout at them this afternoon for not making the delivery? They may have sent you another arrangement. The first has probably withered already because I'm sure you didn't put it in water.'

His father returned wearing a brown sweatshirt over the white undershirt. He was still in his tracksuit pants. The conversation took its usual turn. His mother asked him questions about his life, and he evaded answering them.

'Have you heard about the big mess with the police?' he asked.

'It's absolutely terrible,' his mother replied. 'I'd be ashamed to work in a place like that. Tell me something, does everyone there mess around with young policewomen, aside from you? No wonder there's no security in the country.'

She took out an open bottle of white wine from the fridge and they raised a toast and wished him happy birthday again, with the same words – success through life, wherever it may lead you. His father gradually became withdrawn. It had been that way since the stroke, despite his recovery, which had astounded the doctors. He'd lose focus, get confused, speak incoherently, and, finally, as if he were aware of his regression, he'd go almost completely quiet and withdraw into his plate of food, eating very slowly. They waited for him to finish his soup. The only thing that could perk him up was a conversation about Iran and the likelihood of an attack on Israel in the near future.

Avraham's mood turned gradually more somber. His mother brought out the main dish she had prepared specially for his birthday – fried chicken livers with onions, mashed potatoes, and a spicy tomato salad. He had stopped hearing her questions and laid into his food very quickly. He had two theories regarding his parents' influence on the career he'd chosen – one related to his mother, and the other to his father. According to the first, he became a detective when he returned home from school as a child and tried to read the telltale signs of his mother's moods. He developed an extreme sensitivity to signs and signals, facial expressions, changes in her tone of voice. While still on the stairs, he'd try to smell what she had cooked that day to know if the meal would end in a beating. If she had made something he liked, the meal would generally pass quietly. But if she had made something he couldn't stomach, for reasons he never understood, it would end badly. The smell of stuffed cabbage in the stair-well, for example, was a sure sign that a severe beating was in store.

According to his second theory, he became a detective while out for the day with his father, especially on Saturdays. They had a game his father had made up. 'I think I see a woman dressed in a blue coat,' his father would say. And the three- or four-year-old Avraham, in his stroller, would scan the street excitedly, until he too spotted her and pointed. The game turned more subtle as he grew older. 'I think I see a man who is late for an appointment,' his father would say, and Avraham would scan the street until he spotted an unshaven man crossing the road against the lights, and would point him out. His father, whose hand he'd be holding, would say, 'Exactly' – and it would make Avraham so happy.

He broke the silence and turned to his father. 'How are you feeling?' he asked. But his father didn't hear the question.

'Shlomo, Avi's asking how you feel,' his mother said. 'What's wrong with you? Have you gone deaf now too?'

They had finished eating and his mother had loaded the dishwasher when his cell phone rang.

'Inspector Avraham?' inquired the voice on the other end of the line.

He left the kitchen. 'Speaking.'

'It's Lital Levy from the station,' said the policewoman, who was young and just a few months out of the police academy. 'You're in charge of the missing-persons file that was opened yesterday, right?'

'Yes, Ofer Sharabi.'

'Yes, Sharabi. We just received an anonymous call that may need following up.'

'Can you give me the details? Did you take the call?' Avraham asked, hoping she couldn't hear the anxiety in his voice.

'It was short and I didn't really understand it. But he said we should look for the boy on the dunes behind the H300 building project. "That's where we'll find the body," he said.'

# 4

He ended up being the last one who joined the search – and on his own, initially feeling an outsider among the other searchers, who wouldn't have been there had it not been for him.

He woke first. Elie was still asleep; Michal too. He peered out through the shutters of the balcony. It was the third day. All appeared quiet outside, with no signs of activity in the building or along the street. Two elderly men carrying blue-velvet prayer-shawl bags were walking along the pavement. Ze'ev was unaware of a synagogue nearby.

Saturdays belonged to Michal – or to him, in fact. They were her days for sleeping in, his days to get up for Elie. And every moment that the infant slept felt like a sweet, stolen one. He was a flurry of emotions. He had yet to digest what had happened to him over the past few days, what he had never imagined being able to do just an hour before doing it. Unfamiliar, contradictory feelings coursed through him with an intensity he had never before experienced. He was so filled with shame and pride that he felt he would explode.

Elie woke to the sounds of the kettle boiling and shaking – as he usually did. Ze'ev listened to his son's crying from the kitchen, where he prepared a bottle of warm milk for the boy and a cup of tea with a slice of lemon and brown sugar for himself. He lifted Elie out of his bed, and the infant looked at his father and around the room in surprise, still half asleep.

They said good morning to the spotted furry dog, the wooden horse, the goldfish that swam back and forth in the tiny bowl. Ze'ev carried the small warm body to the living room, sat in the rocking chair, and fed him his bottle. The tea was left to get cold.

An hour or so later, he took Elie out for a walk in his stroller.

The city was deserted.

He followed their regular route, along Histadrut Street, holding back the urge to head immediately toward the dunes.

He had taken along his copy of *On Chesil Beach* in case Elie fell asleep in the stroller, but Elie didn't. And he wouldn't have read anyway. When they lived in Tel Aviv, before Elie was born, he would go out on Saturday mornings to a café, usually somewhere near the beach, with a book or a pen and note-book. Sacred hours – the only time almost when he wasn't a high school teacher, when he could still be anything else, any-thing he really wanted to be. Now he was different again, ever since Thursday. And again he was on the verge of writing, after a period of desolation of more than a year.

Michal was awake and dressed in her robe when they returned. She was in the kitchen, drinking coffee and eating a piece of toast with butter and plum jam. 'How was the walk?' she asked, and then remembered and added, 'Our neighbor was here earlier. They're organizing a group to help with the searches.'

How had he managed not to tell her? Nothing amazed or saddened him more than that. He had kept at least two secrets from her over the past few weeks. He hadn't planned to conceal the writing workshop and Michael Rosin. He simply hadn't told her the first time he went there – and the secret had grown since; it was impossible to speak about it now. And he certainly couldn't speak about the events of the past few days, not until he understood them himself. He felt he was keeping his very essence from her. Yesterday evening he had told her he was going to a certain place despite knowing that he was going somewhere else. And when he returned, his blood racing, she was asleep. He had undressed and got into bed, and she had turned over in her sleep and kissed him with her eyes closed.

'When was he here?' Ze'ev asked, and Michal said, 'Fifteen minutes ago. I was in the middle of such a strange dream. I was dreaming we were on a luxury cruise ship heading for Istanbul. And suddenly I couldn't see you, and Elie and I were looking for you on the deck and starting to go from cabin to cabin inside the ship. And then I suddenly found my mother in one of the cabins . . . Now I don't know if we would have found you in the end.' She hugged him and nuzzled her face into his neck. 'It must have something to do with what's going on.' She liked telling him her dreams.

Ze'ev nodded. 'And where are they searching?' he asked, despite not needing to. He knew.

The area in which the search was taking place was relatively small, less than a square mile, and the police had divided it into two sections. The first, the northern section, covered the area between Golda Meir Street to the north and Menachem Begin Street to the south. It included the courtyards and parking lots of the occupied buildings, as well as the buildings still under construction. The second section was the extensive sandy area farther to the south, which was all dunes, and then more dunes – small hills of soft sand and dry bushes that stretched all the way to the next city.

Ze'ev went there on foot. It took them a while to decide that he would go alone and Michal would stay with Elie, and then he had hung back at the apartment for a little longer. He changed his clothes and shoes, looked for the keys to the motorbike, then decided to do without it, and wondered if he should take along his wallet or only some cash. Would anyone ask him for his ID card?

He wasn't familiar with the neighborhood he came to, and walked a few dozen yards before seeing something that looked to be part of a search operation. An empty police car parked alongside a brown trailer, the sales office for the residential development that was going up there. He could see familiar faces in the distance, faces he recognized from the street on which he lived. Among them was the neighbor who had been at his apartment that morning to tell them about the search. His heart was pounding with excitement. He decided not to take the black notebook out of his bag. It would be best to remember and make notes only when he got home. This wasn't how he had pictured the search for Ofer the night before. There were no uniformed police to be seen anywhere, and Avraham wasn't there.

Ze'ev's random encounter with Avraham on the stairs yesterday afternoon was probably what gave him the whole idea in the first place. Avraham wasn't in uniform last night, so perhaps now too he should be looking for him among the people in civilian dress, he thought to himself. The fact that he knew the name of the officer who appeared to be in charge of the investigation surprised him, although the explanation was a simple one. Avraham had been at his apartment on Thursday evening. He had sat in the kitchen with his wife and child, in his chair. And then they had passed each other on the stairs the next day.

The neighbor who had come to notify them about the searches was standing with a small group of people who were talking among themselves. They all knew one another. Ze'ev wondered if he should introduce himself to anyone. Were the police keeping a record of who was participating in the search? Were they dividing people into groups with specific tasks or could he simply join the search and wander around the area? He approached the neighbor and they shook hands.

'Have you been here for long?' Ze'ev asked, and the neighbor said, 'An hour, hour-and-a-half.'

They had never exchanged more than a few words. The neighbor, who owned a building supply store, was a few years older than him. He drove a white Toyota Corolla, and he and his wife had two children. A short while after Ze'ev and Michal's move to Holon, the neighbor had knocked on their door to ask if the scooter standing in the building's parking lot was his. He had asked Ze'ev if he could please park it elsewhere, as it was blocking the path to the garbage room. Since then, Ze'ev had parked his motorbike opposite the building, on the pavement. Now there seemed to be an air of unfamiliarity and embarrassment between them – but closeness too, almost a brotherhood. He could still feel the dry sensation of the neighbor's palm on his own skin.

'Where are the searches actually taking place?' Ze'ev asked.

'They told us to look here, in the neighborhood,' the neighbor replied. 'The police are searching the dunes at the back.'

That's where he'd probably find Avraham, who, the previous evening, hadn't even stopped for a moment on the stairs to greet him – or to apologize for not returning on Thursday night to finish off their conversation as he had said he would. When Ze'ev realized that Avraham hadn't recognized him and simply continued up the stairs, he too pretended not to notice the person who had just rushed past him.

'And do we know what to look for?'

'They didn't say. Things that appear suspicious, I imagine. Clothes. Bags.'

Ze'ev had no control over the tremor he felt deep inside, but he showed no signs of it as he spoke. 'The question is, why here of all places? Do you know if the police received specific information about the area in which the searches are taking place?'

'I've no idea,' the neighbor replied. 'It's what the family asked for.'

He could see a group of teenagers a short distance from them, a few of Ofer's classmates probably. One was kneeling down and looking under the cars that were parked along the street. Ze'ev wondered if any of the teachers from Ofer's school were there.

'Is there anything I can do? Perhaps I could join you?' Ze'ev asked, and the neighbor said, 'We're waiting for them to open. They've asked the contractor to open the construction sites in the neighborhood.'

Ze'ev stuck close to the neighbor until he felt sufficiently at ease to go off on his own. Logic told him that someone from the family was managing the volunteers, but he couldn't see any of the family members. Ofer's mother was certainly nowhere in sight. Had the police chosen not to update her about the information they had received and the decision to begin a search in the area? There weren't many women there, and he was pleased Michal had decided not to join him.

After the contractor arrived, six or seven of them, all men, walked through the huge concrete building shell. They maneuvered their way over sloping segments of cast concrete to which wooden beams had been attached with nails. The smell of damp filled the air. Wet sand and stone. Making their way between iron poles and over broken bricks, someone behind him said, 'Careful, guys, we're not insured for this.' Ze'ev's shoes and the cuffs of his trousers were rimmed with dust.

He was sent to the sixth floor out of the nine that had been built so far. The neighbor went onto the fifth floor and Ze'ev made his way up alone, one floor higher, pausing at the entrance to an immense maze of walls.

The completed building would have three apartments on each floor; at this stage, however, they were still wide open, joined to a single expanse without any doors – only tall and wide openings in bare brick walls through which one could see more rooms with more openings in the walls and other rooms. He recalled climbing up the stairs of his apartment building on Thursday, when it all began. The open doors. And he found himself in the same room over and over again.

It would have been easy to get the wrong impression and think that he was engrossed in the task of searching, but Ze'ev was the only man on the construction site who knew they wouldn't find anything in the empty rooms. A few pairs of old work shoes were arranged in a row under a wide window in a very large room. Hanging on a strand of wire that seemed to be growing out of the bricks like a piece of ivy was a plastic supermarket bag filled with empty tins of canned food. Half a loaf of stale bread and an almost-full bottle of Coke lay on the sandy floor. The stench and rags in another of the rooms seemed to indicate that this was the workmen's toilet.

Ze'ev stopped looking. He was sure of himself now. He walked over to a north-facing window and stood there, looking out over the city, the sparse traffic on the roads, the handful of volunteers downstairs, below him. He could see the back of the building where he lived, and also the police station, not too far from there. He then found a south-facing window that overlooked the dunes. From up on the sixth floor, the blue figures of the policemen appeared tiny. A few of them were leading what seemed to be miniature dogs on leashes.

A woman dressed in tailored black slacks, a light-colored silk blouse, and shiny shoes that were not suited to searching through dunes stood with her back to the street in conversation with Avraham. Ze'ev waited a short distance from them, pretending to be searching. The woman looked to be in her forties and was a head taller than Avraham. A senior commander who had stopped by in the area for a short while to oversee the searches on her way to a family lunch perhaps? Had she been a volunteer or family member who had joined the search, she would have been wearing more comfortable clothes, and different shoes surely.

Ze'ev was almost certain that he hadn't mentioned the name of Inspector Avi Avraham when he made the call to the police. He had intended initially to ask to speak to him – that had been the objective of the call. But then he changed his mind. Amid the storm of thoughts that raged through his mind last night, there was a moment when he suddenly fixed on the idea that the officer's full name must be Avraham Avraham. And with that thought, the policeman's entire world opened up to him, as if he had caught a glimpse of the man's bedroom. But although he had prepared for it well, repeatedly rehearsing in his mind the brief things he wanted to say in their conversation, he was thrown off upon hearing the young female voice that answered his call – and he almost hung up. He recovered somewhat, and then said things he hadn't intended to say, hanging up frightened and agitated by the words that had come out of his mouth.

The conversation between Inspector Avraham and the women in the silk blouse dragged on. Ze'ev couldn't see any police tape or anything else to indicate that the area had been cordoned off. He was again astounded by the lack of proper order, and made a note to himself that this was a detail of some significance. He had freely entered an area in which a police search was taking place. No one had taken any notice of him. There were no more than five or six uniformed policemen there, apart from Avraham, with a number of people in civilian dress walking around among them. Some may have been policemen and others volunteers like him. Two of the policemen were maneuvering a black device that looked like a vacuum cleaner or metal detector across the sand. There was an air of amateurism and disorder about the entire scene. Ze'ev recalled a French film he had seen at the Cinematheque a few years earlier. Hundreds of policemen were searching through a forest for an escaped criminal. They were standing alongside one another in a long line, their hands linked, and moving forward as a single entity so as not to miss a single piece of ground.

The smartly dressed woman who had been speaking to Avraham got into a car parked at the side of the road. This was his chance.

*

Ze'ev tapped Avraham on the shoulder from behind. 'Excuse me, Inspector Avraham. Can I speak to you for a moment?' he said, breathing heavily as if he had just run a marathon.

Avraham turned to him, surprised both by the light touch on his shoulder and the face he saw in front of him.

'Do you remember me?' Ze'ev asked, adding immediately, before Avraham had a chance to respond: 'I'm the neighbor from Ofer's building. You spoke with my wife on Thursday and said you would come back to see us. The second floor. I was Ofer's private English tutor.'

'Yes, yes, I know. I wasn't able to return, as we were over-loaded with work that afternoon. We may call you in this week to continue the interview.'

Ze'ev wasn't sure if he did indeed remember. Just as he did on Thursday, Avraham appeared stressed and agitated – on top of being very tired now too.

'I've come to help with the search in the meantime,' Ze'ev said. 'I've been here since the morning. First we looked through the building sites, presumably based on your instructions. You're in charge of the investigation, right?'

Avraham ignored the question. Was someone else in charge, or was he not allowed to divulge such information? 'And did you find anything?' he asked.

'No,' Ze'ev said. 'But I'm not sure we knew exactly what we were looking for.'

'Anything that could be related to Ofer.'

'I understand, but how are we supposed to know what could be related to Ofer and what isn't?'

Avraham appeared not to know what to say or how to respond to the person who had tapped him on his shoulder. He began to walk away, and Ze'ev escorted him. They walked side by side across the sand, like acquaintances – or commander and deputy, shoulder to shoulder, just as Ze'ev had imagined they would when the notion to call had lit up in his thoughts. But Avraham seemed to have no intention of asking Ze'ev anything at all, and if he himself didn't speak up, their conversation would dry up then and there. One of the policemen or volunteers could turn up at any moment and claim the inspector's attention, and then it would be impossible to renew the dialogue in the same natural way it had started.

'Do you have any breakthroughs in the investigation?' Ze'ev asked. And Avraham again looked surprised, as if he hadn't noticed that Ze'ev was walking along with him.

'No, not for the moment,' he replied.

'So why, then, is the search taking place here? And, as I asked before, what are we actually looking for?'

'Nothing special.'

There was more than just a touch of impatience, even rudeness, in Avraham's tone, and in the fact that he kept on walking. Ze'ev continued, nevertheless: 'I'm just curious to know how the commander of an investigation decides where to conduct searches. Aren't searches in a particular area usually based on solid information?'

Avraham stopped again. 'We have nothing concrete at the moment, just some general information that he was seen hanging around here,' he said.

As he did on Thursday, Avraham again surprised Ze'ev. What was that about hanging around here? Did the policewoman he had spoken to not hear what he had said? Or was Avraham lying? It was exactly what Ze'ev had planned to say when he called – that Ofer was alive, that he knew Ofer was alive and knew where to look for him. In the end, however, without meaning to, he had blurted out that the police needed to look for a body – and then hung up. Had his speech been so rushed that the policewoman hadn't understood him?

Nothing that had happened the previous evening had gone according to plan.

Initially, he intended to use the public telephone on Shprintzak Street, which ran between the Cinematheque and the school where he taught in Tel Aviv; but then he decided that wouldn't be very wise. He headed into Tel Aviv after all, stopping at four different kiosks before finding one that sold calling cards for public phone booths. He thought he'd be able to find a public telephone somewhere in the south of Tel Aviv, close to the old Central Bus Station, which now played home to African refugees and foreign workers. But the darkness of the empty streets had frightened him, and he continued farther north. He stopped and parked his motorbike on Allenby Street, taking off his helmet and placing it on the seat. The telephone was out of order. He returned to the center of the city and found a working phone alongside the Gat cinema house, at a very busy intersection. He would have liked to have found one on a quieter street, but it was now or never. And then, just before he again picked up the receiver to make the call, he heard someone call out his name. He froze in fright.

Orna Abiri, a young math teacher from the school, walked up to him and kissed him twice on the cheek – not the usual greeting she gave him when they were at work. She introduced Ze'ev to her two friends and asked what he was doing there. He was embarrassed, at a loss for words, and finally blurted out something about having just seen a movie. Luckily, she didn't ask him about it. Although they had no particular relationship at school, she asked him if he'd like to join them at a bar nearby. Ze'ev declined, apologizing and saying he was on his way to see some friends.

'Do you need a phone?' she asked before they parted, and Ze'ev, thinking she was offering him her telephone number for some reason, said, 'What?'

'You appeared to be about to make a call from the public telephone. If you need to make a call, I have a cell phone.'

Ze'ev laughed. 'No, I've just finished a call. I forgot to take the address and left my cell phone at home.'

He managed to make the call only after 10:00 p.m., from a pay phone near the beach.

'What? Ofer was seen wandering around here?' Ze'ev asked Avraham, unable to conceal the astonishment in his voice. 'Does that mean you have information that he is alive?'

'Why shouldn't he be alive?'

Ze'ev was flustered. 'No, I meant to ask if you know where he might be,' he said.

'We don't know anything for certain. We try to check all the information we receive.'

'And what makes you trust this information?' Ze'ev asked, continuing to probe. 'Surely you don't carry out searches after every phone call you get.'

Avraham peered at Ze'ev in wonderment. 'We try to follow up on everything,' he said.

A young policewoman approached them. She was carrying a rag that was once a pair of brown corduroy trousers. 'Excuse me now, I need to go,' Avraham said impatiently. 'Thank you for joining the search, and I promise someone will call you to make arrangements for a second interview. What's your name again?'

'Ze'ev Avni,' Ze'ev replied, hurriedly adding: 'And it's

good that you asked. The policewoman who interviewed me on Thursday didn't ask. I'll be happy to speak to you about Ofer. I don't know what you have learned about him so far, but I have lots to say. I think I got to know Ofer well during the months I tutored him.'

Inspector Avraham made a signal with his hand and the policewoman put the corduroy trousers into a large black plastic bag. 'At the very least we're cleaning up the dunes. We've turned into the nature conservation authority,' Ze'ev heard her say.

He didn't return to the searchers after parting company with Avraham. He was satisfied to a certain extent with the wealth of detail he had gathered, but it was diluted by the bitterness and disappointment he felt from his too-brief talk with the inspector. He had pictured them in his imagination speaking for hours, exchanging information and ideas about the case. He wanted to go home and suddenly regretted coming without his motorbike.

On his way home he could feel a sense of gloom spreading through him and didn't at first know why. Was it because he had suddenly understood the seriousness of his actions? Or was it because of Avraham's impatience, the fact that he hadn't remembered him when he introduced himself? He hoped he hadn't called for nothing. Nevertheless, Avraham appeared to have listened to him for a short while, and he did genuinely seem intent on calling him in for another talk about Ofer.

And then it dawned on him.

His legs shook, and he had the feeling he was frozen to the spot, although in actual fact, without sensing it, he had picked up his walking pace.

In one of the questions he had asked Inspector Avraham, seemingly off the cuff, he'd said something about the fact that the information based on which the searches were being carried out had been received by telephone – though Avraham hadn't mentioned it. Perhaps he could explain knowing this by saying he had heard one of the policemen say something about it?

Ze'ev couldn't remember how he got home. He hoped Michal would be there, but when he opened the door, the apartment was empty. He lay down on their bed and forced his eyes closed, like children do.

He was sure a policeman would be knocking on the door at any minute.

# 5

Pressing his palm down on the metal door handle to Ilana's office was one of those moments in his work that Avraham lived for. One moment he'd be at Tel Aviv District Police Headquarters, and an instant later, when the door closed behind him, he'd be entirely somewhere else – at home. Sometimes she'd be waiting for him at the door as he stepped inside.

And it's not like the office on the second floor of the new building on Salame Street was very different from other police offices. In the center stood a wide desk of dark wood, and on it, a flat-screen Dell monitor. Framed police diplomas and certificates of merit hung on the walls alongside pictures of the president and prime minister. A large photograph, of spectacular beauty and breathtaking color, showed Vancouver's Lions Gate Bridge at sunset; Ilana had spent a number of years there on official duty, with her family, and she always said that a part of her had 'remained in that cold city and didn't come back.' Two smaller photographs were of Ilana herself – one with a former Supreme Court president justice and the other, taken many years ago, with a pop star. Ilana was young at the time, and her hair was long and brown, without the interwoven gray strands she had had since they first met. The most precious photograph of all stood on the desk, framed in black – a family picture taken in front of the Church of the Sacré-Cœur in Paris, on a trip ahead of the enlistment of Ilana's eldest son,

Amir. The soon-to-be-soldier towers joyfully above his younger two brothers and sister in the center of the picture, as tall as his father and mother, who embrace him on either side. A training accident took his life a few months later.

'You can come in,' Ilana said, leaving Avraham feeling deflated on realizing that Shrapstein had got there before him. They were in the middle of a conversation and Ilana was laughing out loud.

'Come in, Avi,' Ilana continued. 'Eyal is updating me on the results of yesterday's searches.'

'You mean the lack of results,' Shrapstein interjected, with Ilana replying, presumably continuing the talk that had started before his arrival, 'A leather jacket isn't too bad. It can be cleaned up and worn. I read somewhere that leather is coming back.'

'And don't forget the corduroys,' Shrapstein added with a laugh.

Right away Avraham felt under attack. He had been puzzled the previous evening by the decision to assign Shrapstein to the investigation team. Why had she thought he needed another officer on the team? 'He's available, and you know he's brilliant, Avi, if intolerable at times. You are the senior investigator, you head the team. Use him as you please, he'll be of value to you,' Ilana had said, trying to justify her decision.

'When is Eliyahu coming?' Avraham asked.

'He's on the way. He'll be here in three minutes,' Ilana replied. 'Eyal, you know you owe Avi some good wishes. He had a birthday on Friday.'

She had wanted to make him happy, but instead he cringed in his seat.

'Congratulations! How old are you?' Shrapstein asked.

And Ilana, who felt the uneasiness she had aroused, answered for him: 'Not yet forty. Still a kid. So, Avi, you have two more years as a "promising young investigator." The title remains valid until forty.'

'So I have almost ten years left, then,' Shrapstein said.

Eliyahu Ma'alul came in, dressed, for some unknown reason, in a gray Windbreaker, and greeted everyone with his standard opening line: 'I see I am upping the average age but lowering the average beauty in the room.' He placed a hand on Avraham's shoulder and bent over to whisper, 'It's good to see you,' before sitting down in the chair alongside him.

'Okay, let's get started,' Ilana said. 'I'm short on time. Give us the briefing, Avi, and try to make it as detailed as possible.'

Avraham placed the thin investigation file on the desk and removed the three pages he had printed out and stapled together that morning at the station. 'So this is what we have,' he said. 'Ofer Sharabi, a resident of Holon, born December 1994, no criminal record, missing since Wednesday morning. He left for school as usual on Wednesday, before eight a.m., but never got there. We found no note or anything else to indicate he has run away. His cell phone was left at home, so cellular tracking is not an option. The complaint to the police was filed on Thursday morning by his mother, Hannah Sharabi – '

Shrapstein already cut him short, raising his hand and beginning to speak immediately – a self-confident student who doesn't need a signal from the teacher to interrupt his lecture. 'That's more than twenty-four hours after his disappearance. A little late, don't you think?'

'Not exactly. The mother learned that he hadn't been at school only on Wednesday afternoon, when he failed to return home,' Avraham responded. 'In fact, she showed up at the station Wednesday evening, but wasn't definitive about filing a complaint.'

Ilana remained silent, but Shrapstein didn't relent. 'What do you mean, she wasn't definitive? Who spoke to her?'

'I was the duty officer,' Avraham replied. 'She arrived in the evening and wasn't sure about filing a complaint.'

Ilana stopped Shrapstein from continuing. 'Let's move on,' she said. 'These details are irrelevant for now. If they turn out to be important, we'll get back to them at a later stage. Let's move ahead.'

'As I was saying,' Avraham continued, 'the investigation opened on Thursday, with notifications in the media and on the Internet, along with initial questioning of the family, friends, and neighbors. We also conducted a preliminary search of the boy's room, as well as an examination of his computer and cell phone. There have also been the routine calls to the intelligence coordinators. Relatively speaking, however, we have received few responses and reports from the public – perhaps because the media didn't run news items but only announcements. Of the reports that did come in to the call centers, none provided any concrete information to forward the investigation – '

'Apart from the anonymous call that had us wandering around for half of Saturday, cleaning up the sand dunes,' Shrapstein interrupted again.

Eliyahu Ma'alul appeared confused, finding himself behind the curve of the conversation. 'Which dunes?' he asked.

'I was just getting to that . . . okay, I'll cover it now,' Avraham pressed on. 'The divisional call center received an anonymous tip Friday evening that the body of the missing boy could be found on the dunes behind the H300 building project. I had no way of confirming the information, but decided nonetheless to carry out limited searches in the area yesterday morning to rule out the possibility – and also to ease the slightest concern that the missing boy might have been there, alive but injured and unable to move himself, or even unconscious.'

'If there was such a concern, putting things off from Friday evening until Saturday morning sounds unreasonable,' Shrapstein commented.

'You're right, but night-time searches require special equipment and budgets, and you all know how complicated that is,' Avraham said.

'It was a decision Avi took with my backing,' Ilana added.

'And do you feel you've ruled out that possibility entirely?' Ma'alul questioned.

Ma'alul's stern and quiet demeanor reminded Avraham of his father before the stroke. He was a short man, thin and dark-skinned. His somewhat sunken eyes were large and patient, and his questions, which were always frank and never double-talk, encouraged the respondent to pour his heart out, even when simply asked, 'How are you?' His decision to specialize in juvenile crime investigation, which he made some twenty-five years earlier, had stemmed from a sincere desire to help teenagers, whose direction in life could still be altered. At heart, he was more a social worker than a policeman, but Avraham viewed him as an investigator with whom it was a pleasure to work. No one ever called him brilliant, but he did his work thoroughly, modestly, and without a fuss.

'Not with absolute certainty,' Avraham replied to Ma'alul's question. 'But I believe so. We did not do any digging with heavy machinery, but we covered the area well. We came across a few items of clothing, which the family confirmed as not belonging to the missing boy.'

Ma'alul nodded.

'And we didn't get anything from the public telephone from which the call to the police was placed, right?' Ilana asked.

'Nothing so far,' Avraham replied.

Avraham removed some papers from the investigation file. 'I've made copies of the summaries of the interviews,' he said, handing them out. 'Ilana has already seen them; they don't contain anything significant. The missing boy wasn't very active on the computer. He has a single e-mail address and very few contacts. Most of the mail he receives is advertising material, and his last message was sent out about a week or so ago. He doesn't have a Facebook page.'

'Porn sites? Dating sites? Gambling sites?' Shrapstein asked.

That same question had been asked in almost every investigation in recent years – as if surfing the Internet was the source of all crimes and the principal avenue for solving them.

'There seems to be some porn history on the computer, but nothing special,' Avraham said. 'There's only one computer in the house – in the room the missing boy shares with his younger brother – and I don't think he had too many opportunities to look at pornographic material. I asked the IT Division people to check the history for travel sites, travel agencies, but they found nothing. Most of the Internet browsing history is related to computer games and gaming sites.

'The interviews with friends and family also failed to yield any real information that could give us a lead in the investigation,' he continued. 'None of the people we questioned had any prior knowledge of the possibility that he might run away, and we are unaware of any history of emotional or behavioral disturbances. We do know that the missing youth ran away from home twice before, following arguments with the parents. He did so for only a few hours, but it may hint at the possibility of another attempt.

'The missing youth is coming to the end of eleventh grade at Kugel High School, and he's a pretty good student. He has been described as a quiet boy, not very popular, but no social issues either. There's no evidence of him suffering any abuse or harassment from other students. And I don't know if I mentioned it already, but we have no information linking him to any criminal activity.'

Avraham lifted his head from the papers and looked at Ilana. She sighed.

They had sat like this in her office for hours on end so many times over the past four years, since her appointment as head of the Tel Aviv District's Investigations and Intelligence Wing, poring over each and every detail, reading to each other from the transcripts of the interrogations, trying to understand first one way and then another, building fact upon fact in an effort to arrive at a hypothesis. If there was a place where investigations that appeared to be heading nowhere ultimately ended in success, it was there, in that very room, and thanks to such talks.

'In short, we don't have a lead,' Ma'alul commented.

'No,' Avraham replied, 'although I believe we are dealing with an attempt to run away from home that may have gone wrong somehow – or, in the worst case, a suicide.'

'Why?' Ma'alul asked.

Avraham hesitated for a moment under the gaze of Ma'alul's soft, beautiful eyes. 'Primarily because the missing youth has no criminal background and we have found nothing to link him to any criminal activity, but also in light of the information about him that we have collected. In addition, there is something about the family that I just can't put my finger on. He comes across as a boy with hardly any friends, extremely introverted, doesn't share things with his parents. From my experience, these are behavioral characteristics that can point to runaway attempts or suicide – unless you think differently.'

'It's possible,' Ma'alul responded, and Ilana asked, 'And what do you mean when you say "may have gone wrong"?'

'That perhaps he planned to disappear for a day or a few hours, but got caught up in something unexpected,' Avraham replied. 'I honestly don't know.'

'I disagree,' Shrapstein said.

Ilana and Ma'alul turned to look at him. 'Why?' Ilana asked.

'Because I don't believe that a youth of – How old did you say he is? Fifteen? Sixteen?' Shrapstein said.

'Sixteen-and-a-half,' Avraham responded.

'I don't believe that a sixteen-and-a-half-year-old teenager just disappears without leaving behind a trail that we'd be able to pick up on in three days of investigation – even if it wasn't the most comprehensive investigation in the world,' Shrapstein continued. 'He must leave some trace. He has to draw out money before or after he disappears, doesn't he? And even if he did get caught up in something unexpected, what are the chances that we don't learn of it? And even if he wants to commit suicide without anyone's knowledge, he has to do it somehow, right? He has to steal a gun from someone, or pills from his parents' medicine cabinet, a knife from the kitchen, something or other. In general, people who kill themselves actually want to be found; that's what I've been taught.'

Ilana turned to look at Avraham, seemingly inviting him to respond to the challenge laid down by the young and 'brilliant' inspector she had brought onto his team. 'You can buy pills at a drugstore,' Avraham said.

'So what are you actually telling us – that he bought two boxes of headache tablets at a pharmacy without telling anyone, and then went and swallowed them on the dunes?' Shrapstein continued. 'That doesn't make sense.'

The young officer looked over at Ilana and she nodded her head. 'So you believe we are dealing with a crime?' she asked. 'What kind of crime?'

'As far as I'm concerned, the investigation hasn't started yet and all options are open,' Shrapstein went on. 'Clearly, we haven't acted fast enough thus far. Even if he did run away from home – and I don't believe that is the case – he got farther away from us with each passing night. And I still don't know anything about the missing boy – that's what troubles me. Anything is possible – a kidnapping, involvement in a crime and an escape, anything. Even murder. It doesn't make sense for a sixteen-and-a-half-year-old to run away from home for five days and not be in touch with anyone at all.'

Avraham was momentarily befuddled by a burning sense of anger and defiance that Shrapstein's words were evoking in him. After all, there had been moments when he had thought the same. How many times in the past few days had he asked himself that same question: How can a sixteen-year-old boy disappear from home without anyone knowing a thing about it? Perhaps the defiance was sparked by Shrapstein's adamant tone, his attempt to convey the sense that everything he said had to be right. 'Perhaps he has made contact with someone we have yet to get to,' Avraham said, as if to himself, not directing his comment at anyone in particular, to which Shrapstein responded quietly, 'Well, that's a different matter.'

Ma'alul remained on the sidelines of the conversation until Ilana addressed him, asking him if, based on his experience, he thought they were dealing with a runaway. As always, he took his time before responding. His brown eyes closed for an instant, and then opened again, while his stubby fingers ran lightly over his bald head. 'Based on what we have heard so far – no,' Ma'alul said, looking over at Avraham slightly apologetically. 'I'd like to be cautious here,' he continued, 'but when it comes to planned disappearances at this age, there are usually warning signs. Truancy or dropping out of school, mixing with street gangs, criminal records related to alcohol or drug use. The fact that he has no history of any of these, if I am to understand correctly, adds to my concerns that something has happened to him – and not the contrary, as Avi has presented things. And, again, I'm saying this with caution. I also agree with Eyal that we need to act quickly, to put as much effort as possible into the investigation over the coming days. Five days without a sign of life is much too long.'

Ilana took off her glasses. Over the past weeks, Avraham had come to believe that she would wear the rectangular-framed glasses when she wasn't looking at anything in particular, and would remove them when she wanted to study something in earnest. She looked over the pictures of Ofer that were scattered on the desk in front of her. The lateness of the hour dictated that the meeting would be a short one.

'I'm pleased you have different gut feelings,' Ilana said. 'It could benefit the investigation. What I'd like to ask of you, however, is not to race ahead with your hunches and get too attached to any one theory, because it's pretty clear that we don't have anything solid to go on right now. We are at a very preliminary stage of collecting material and findings, and we cannot approach the matter with any foregone conclusions at this point; we'll only end up missing certain details and focusing too intently on others. I know it's the hardest thing for us all to do, but we have to accept the uncertainty, to remain with it and try to understand it. A lack of information can also tell us something – just as Eyal and Eliyahu have seemed to imply – although I am not sure exactly what. I want us to be attentive to both what we have and what we don't have, and not to lock in on just one option.'

She was looking at him. Then she asked, 'Avi, have you requisitioned the records of the calls made from Ofer's cell phone over the past weeks?'

'No, not yet,' Avraham replied. 'I'll do it right away.'

'I already ordered them – from a year back,' Shrapstein cut in. 'I spoke this morning to his service provider and, as usual, it will take a day or two, but I have some good contacts there and I'm trying to speed things up. I'll go over the printouts when they arrive.'

The mood in Ilana's office had taken on the energy and decisiveness that typified the start of an investigation, with each member of the team assigned certain tasks and each one eager to fulfill them, and only Avraham feeling a sense of profound weariness – an overall depletion of body and soul that would usually overcome him at the end of a case, or on vacation. He thought he should ask Ilana to take him off the case, and hoped she could sense his waning spirits.

Shrapstein continued. 'Aside from that, this morning I started going through the criminal reports from the area in recent weeks,' he said. 'I'd also like to check if any of the residents in the neighborhood has a criminal background. I think, too, that we should check for any criminal reports related to the school. They may turn up nothing, but it's worth a shot.'

'Excellent, good thinking,' Ilana said. 'Just make sure you coordinate everything with Avi so we don't end up doing the same work twice. And go through the material we get from the IT Division. Make sure they pass on as much information as possible. Just sit yourself down and read through it all. Eliyahu will return to the school and reinterview Ofer's classmates, and, if need be, we'll bring in another investigator from Juvenile. Divide up the ongoing questioning of the family among yourselves.'

Shrapstein asked Eliyahu if it was possible to look into the criminal backgrounds of all the students at the school. Everything's possible, the veteran investigator replied, jotting down something in a small notebook he had taken out of an inside pocket of his Windbreaker.

'We should consider what we want to do about the media,' Shrapstein suggested. 'It may be worth initiating a report for one of the news broadcasts; they won't take it upon themselves to approach us.'

There wasn't a single member of the police district who was unaware that Shrapstein's sister was a producer for *Channel 10 News*, and that he could turn any trivial investigation into an item on television.

Avraham switched off. He had been full of adrenaline when he arrived early that morning at the station, feeling sure that the meeting in Ilana's office would breathe some life into the investigation, which had come unstuck in the dunes. He had even momentarily toyed with the idea that it would all be over that same day. But something had gone wrong since.

'We'll wait awhile with the media,' Ilana said. 'I want us to be careful about releasing information we don't know the significance of. Ah yes, and one more thing – the father; he returns to Israel today if I'm not mistaken. He's a member of the local Labor Party branch and the Workers Council Union of Zim Shipping Lines. I've already received calls from "people" inquiring about our progress in the case and what we are doing to bring his son home. I'm sure I don't need to explain things to you . . .'

The three investigators stood up. 'To work, then,' Eliyahu Ma'alul said.

Avraham asked him why he was wearing a Windbreaker. 'What do you mean, Avi?' Ma'alul responded. 'Against the wind.'

Ilana opened the large window facing the street and placed a small glass ashtray on the desk. The sudden rush of air into the room restored his spirits somewhat, and the noise of the bus traffic along Salame Street lightened his mood as well.

'You look shattered,' she said to him.

'I'm tired,' he replied, lighting a cigarette.

'Because of Wednesday night?' she asked, her voice sounding closer with just the two of them in the room now.

'I don't know,' Avraham replied.

'Don't be too hard on yourself about Wednesday evening,' Ilana continued. 'You made a decision that may or may not have been the right one but can certainly be understood and justified in the broad context of police work. In any event, there's no point in wallowing in it. You have a complex investigation on your hands and now need to manage things quickly but also in a focused and clear-thinking fashion. Would you like a coffee? We have ten minutes.'

He looked at her, bemused. 'A clear-thinking fashion?' he said, repeating her words.

'Yes, a clear-thinking fashion. What's wrong with that? You can't conduct an investigation out of a sense of guilt, particularly without knowing if you have any reason to feel guilty. We've been working together long enough for me to know you can do it.'

'Of course there's a reason. Even if it turns out to be insignificant, I shouldn't have sent her home from the station without doing anything. And on top of that, I gave her a lecture about being worried for no reason and how Ofer would come back that same night.'

'About mysteries and why there are no detective novels in Hebrew?' Ilana questioned. 'I thought you had vowed to stop with that.'

She tried to placate him with her smile and a further softening of her voice. They had known each other for almost nine years. Before her promotion to chief of the Investigations and Intelligence Division, she was Superintendent Ilana Lis, one of the most highly regarded investigators in the Tel Aviv Police District. A few months after Avraham completed his officers' course and joined the division, he was assigned to a team she was leading in an investigation of a lawyer who had stolen millions of shekels from his elderly clients. The frankness with which she had spoken to him about the investigation had stunned him; she hadn't made any effort to conceal her feelings or concerns, and she had listened to his thoughts.

Together, they had come up with the strategy that finally broke the lawyer down after many exhausting hours of questioning. He had been thrilled by her ability to create trust among her colleagues. He had never before met anyone like her, in the police or elsewhere. She had invited him into her old office to celebrate the victory with red wine in plastic cups. It was almost three in the morning. She told him he had played a huge role in the success of the investigation, that she had enjoyed working with him, and that she planned to make him a part of any investigation team she would be heading in the future. And in the years to follow, before her promotion, they did work together continually, and grew close to each other. He had met her husband, too, on a number of occasions – at family events and ceremonies. He had been sitting in her office when the Israel Defense Forces representatives came to inform her of the death of her son, and he had held her when she collapsed and passed out, before driving her to the IDF training base. She was probably the one person closest to him, despite the fact that they spoke almost exclusively about work.

'Do you know what the hardest part of investigating missing persons is?' Ilana asked. 'You only know if you did what you should have done once they are found. There's no way of knowing for certain beforehand.'

'That's not it,' Avraham responded. 'The hard part is not knowing if you are investigating a crime or not. We know how to investigate crimes, and we know how to break down suspects in an interrogation, but when it comes to missing persons, you usually have no idea whether or not a crime has been committed. You go out into the world suspecting people, neighbors, friends, family members, the missing person himself, people who care about the missing person just as you do

– or even a lot more so. And you have to suspect them; you have no choice. And in most cases, at the end of the investigation, it turns out that no crime has been committed and that no one hid anything. For all we know, Ofer Sharabi could be stretched out on a beach in Rio de Janeiro, without anyone knowing or being guilty of anything.'

'Nonsense. You know he isn't in Rio de Janeiro. And why Rio, of all places?'

'How do I know he isn't there? I don't know anything.'

'You can find out. You check with Border Security if he has left the country. He didn't get on a plane with a false passport. He's not a Mossad agent, he's a schoolboy.'

Avraham sighed. Thank God she had opened a window to let some air in. 'Okay, you win,' he said, 'he's not in Rio.'

'And I also managed to get us off the subject of your guilt and restore some of your strength and drive,' Ilana said, looking him directly in the eye, which always pained him. 'I don't understand how you still sometimes crack so quickly,' she continued. 'Every little Shrapstein seems to be able to get you down, as if you were the one who joined the force just yesterday and not he, as if you weren't one of the best investigators around.'

Ilana was good at speaking about things he didn't dare mention, out of shame, in a manner that didn't cause him embarrassment. Only once in all the time they had known each other had he dreamed about her resting the palm of her hand on his – no more, just a cold hand. He had come to forget over the years if it had been a night vision or a daydream, and he forbade himself to ever think of it again.

'It kills me to think that Ofer Sharabi will become just another missing boy who was never found,' he finally said.

'That ten or fifteen years will go by without us knowing anything about what happened to him – if he's dead, if he's living somewhere.'

The image of Ofer again appeared in his mind. He could see him as he walked down the stairs with his black bag on his shoulder. He stepped out onto the street and turned right, heading for school. People passed him by and no one noticed anything. And what if he didn't turn right but went left instead? There was a neighborhood grocery store not far from the building where he lived, in the opposite direction to his way to school. Without knowing why, Avraham had stopped there that morning on his way to the police station. He had shown the owner a picture of Ofer and had asked her if he had been in the store on Wednesday, the day he disappeared. She didn't need the picture; she knew Ofer well. Everyone in the area was talking about his disappearance and they all wanted to help with the searches. Ever since he was a young boy, Ofer would come in almost every morning to buy milk and fresh buns, the store owner had told him. She was almost certain, however, that she hadn't seen him that Wednesday morning, and her husband had concurred. 'Wait a moment, I can check,' she had suddenly said, opening a thick notebook in which she recorded the debts of her regular customers. 'Sharabi – May third. That was Tuesday. They haven't bought anything since then,' she had added excitedly, as if they had just located Ofer thanks to her help. Ofer's most recent purchases came to a total of 44.60. He had signed his name in green ink alongside the amount.

'He won't end up just another missing child who was never found,' Ilana said. 'Did the interviews with the friends and neighbors really give us nothing?'

'Practically nothing. There's an odd neighbor in the building who also came yesterday to help with the searches. He insists he knew Ofer better than anyone else. I'll be bringing him in for another interview – tomorrow, when I'm done with the father.'

'Good idea. And shouldn't you be getting ready for your trip? When are you off?'

'Next week. But I'm not sure if I'll go. I'm thinking about canceling.'

'What do you mean, canceling? It's a six-day work trip, and even if we're not done by then, the investigation can go on without you – if it's still in our hands.'

He couldn't believe what he was hearing – and this just moments before she would be chasing him out of her office as she hurried to leave.

'Still in our hands?'

'We all hope the investigation will be over in a week, right? And you know that if the case goes bad or we believe it is no longer merely a missing-persons investigation but something else, like a murder inquiry, we may be forced to set up a special investigation team and hand the case over to them. Especially if there's pressure from the family. It won't be up to me. The case could be handed over to the Serious Crimes Unit. For now, just don't let it get in the way of your investigation. It's a missing-persons case and it's yours. If and when it turns into something else, we'll have to think how best to deal with it. There's time.'

Just then, as he was beginning to feel the fresh air and the clarity of thought she had been talking about before, he felt his dejection return.

He looked her in the eyes as directly as he was capable of doing and implored: 'Ilana, please don't take this case away from me. Just half an hour ago I wanted to ask you to hand it over to someone else, but we both know it would kill me. This is my investigation. It has been mine from the moment Ofer's mother walked into the station, and it has to stay mine until I find the boy and bring him home.'

He had a week. Ilana had made no bones about it. Barring a breakthrough in the investigation before he left on his trip, he would return from Brussels to find the case in strange hands. And even if they didn't set up a special investigation team headed by a higher-ranking officer, or even if the case wasn't handed over to the Serious Crimes Unit, who knew what Shrapstein was capable of doing in his week's absence, if he wouldn't take that opportunity to steal Ofer away from him. Avraham was terrified by the thought that the case could be wrapped up while he was in Brussels.

He drove back to the station via Jaffa, stopping for a moment at the Abulafia bakery to buy himself a pastry with cheese. El Al flight 382 from Milan would be coming in at 22:50. He could wait for Ofer's father in the airport arrivals hall and drive him directly to the station for questioning, or allow him to spend the night with his family and call him in for an interview in the morning. Perhaps he would simply show up and knock on the door to their apartment. He wanted to see it again, to be in the last place Ofer had been before he disappeared, and he wanted to get a look at the mother and the father there together. He hadn't seen Hannah Sharabi since Friday. Perhaps she would be less anxious in the company of her husband and would be able to tell him more about her son. And he wanted to see the father's face and picture Ofer at the same age. He wanted to go into Ofer's room with him, sit next to him on the bed, open the same drawers with him that he had opened on Friday. Would the father's face reveal more details about the son and his life than the mother's had? Isn't that always the case? And if he was to interview the father in his home, he'd be able to work in a quick visit to the odd neighbor. He needed to remember to get in touch with him first to make sure he would be at home.

His cell phone rang just as he pulled into the station parking lot. It was an unlisted number.

'May I speak to the esteemed Chief Inspector Avraham Avraham?' asked the voice on the line.

He hadn't heard the voice for at least six months but recognized it immediately – and was sorry he had answered the call. 'Yes, speaking,' he said.

'Hi there, Avraham Avraham, this is Uri Uri from security security service service,' the voice said. His childish giggle was confusing. 'I'm calling about the investigation into the MIA MIA.'

Avraham drove his car to his usual parking place and remained in his seat.

'Are you there?' came the voice again. 'Don't be offended. You know I horse around with you only because I feel we have a good bond. The Israel Police investigators have become awfully sensitive ever since female officers started taking up the senior command posts, don't you think?'

Though they had never met, Avraham detested him. They had spoken on the phone some six months earlier about an investigation into a car thief from a village near Nablus who had been apprehended in the south of Tel Aviv. The Shin Bet security service had appropriated the case from the police because the young Palestinian was also suspected of crossing over into Israel illegally and being a member of a terror organization. His brother, some ten years his senior, had been sentenced to a number of years in prison for being involved in security-related offenses. Back then, 'Uri from the service' had spoken to him like the owner of a restaurant would speak to his lowliest dishwasher, despite probably being his junior both in age and in rank. Avraham hadn't dared to put up a fuss when asked to send over the file and evidentiary material he had collected over many days of hard work.

'I wanted to let you know that at this stage, we have no interest at all in the investigation into the missing boy,' Uri continued. 'We have run our checks and we aren't dealing here with a hostile act of terror. But if at some point in the investigation even a single Arabic letter turns up, you'll let me know immediately, right?'

'I will,' Avraham spat out.

'Great. That's what we call cooperation between the various security branches.'

Where was he calling from? Avraham wondered. Where, in fact, was the office of 'Uri from the service'? He thought for a moment that Israel had another police force about which he knew very little – a special police force, only for Arab-related matters, without stations, without published telephone numbers.

'Is that it? Is there anything else you need?' Avraham dared to ask.

'Yes, there is one small thing, in fact – a surprise I prepared especially for you,' replied the youthful voice. 'Are you ready? A little birdie told me that you were interested in the question of why Israel doesn't produce detective novels. Is that true? Am I right or not?'

Avraham felt a shudder go through him. Surely the Shin Bet doesn't bug police interview rooms or tap the phones of police investigators. That's impossible. Someone from within the police must have told him.

'What?' Avraham asked. 'I didn't get that.'

'Yes, a songbird. So listen up. We held an urgent team meeting to discuss the matter, and we have an official answer for you. Would you like to hear it?'

No, Avraham said to himself. I don't want to hear it.

'The answer is that the police in Israel are responsible for trivial investigations that no one would bother reading or writing a book about, and also because most of the police investigators aren't particularly bright. The Shin Bet handles the important investigations, and no one knows anything about us. And those who do know aren't allowed to breathe a word. Did you get that get that?'

# 6

The elderly woman's voice trembled as she came to the end of her story.

She described her mother getting off an old bus on a Jerusalem street and the heavy rain washing over her face. From time to time she would stop reading in midsentence and sigh, in an effort, perhaps, to ease the tension in her voice. She might have been hoping that they'd think her emotion stemmed from the content of the story and not the fact that she was reading out loud, standing up, in front of all the other writing workshop students.

Ze'ev couldn't remember the name of the elderly woman, who appeared so nervous that she was about to choke on her words. When he first saw her before the opening class of the workshop, he wanted to run away and give up on the whole idea. She was sitting on one of the ten or so chairs that had been arranged in a circle in the small room, and looked like someone who'd be more suited to a bridge group. He decided to stay only when, a minute or two after his arrival, a man who looked his age walked in, followed by two young women.

As expected, the elderly woman's story ended with the death of her sick mother. She sat back down, looking distinctly relieved. No one clapped – they had agreed on that in the first lesson – and not a single hand was raised. They knew Michael Rosin wouldn't say anything, yet all the students turned to look at him. He was sitting there on his chair in his usual listening position, slightly hunched over, his elbows resting on his knees, his clenched fists supporting his forehead, and his face hidden. They were all trying to guess what he thought, in order to say something similar. There was silence in the room and Michael respected, even prolonged it. 'Silence is an important response to a story,' he had told them in the first class.

'The content is certainly touching, but as a literary text the story misses the mark.' As in the previous classes, the silence was broken by a man of around his age, Avner, who had introduced himself as a journalist when they all first met. He had taken on the role of the bad boy of the workshop from the outset and appeared to take an excess of pleasure in the ridiculous argumentative stance he always adopted. 'I am not convinced by the character's last-minute turnaround; it's too optimistic,' Avner continued. 'The protagonist is angry with her mother throughout the story, and then suddenly she softens, for no apparent reason.' His customary response. He could never understand how people changed, and he viewed every emotional upheaval as sudden and mechanical.

How would he explain the change Ze'ev had undergone, what had happened to him since last week? Now more than ever before, Ze'ev had doubts as to whether deep emotional change could be understood at all.

That morning, at 7:45 a.m., he had called the school secretary to report he was ill. Following his conversation with Inspector Avraham Avraham on the dunes, he had stayed in bed for the entire day yesterday, and was burning up with a fever when Michal and Elie returned in the afternoon from her parents'. He slept, and might have mumbled a few words as he did. He woke in the middle of the night and made himself a cup of tea with milk. He sat in the living room and waited. He slowly came to realize that more than twelve hours had passed since his talk with Avraham and his slip of the tongue, and no one had shown up to arrest him, and no one probably would. He could have prepared his lesson but decided instead to take the day off work. The thought of policemen coming into the classroom terrified him. He could picture himself being led through the school courtyard in handcuffs, with all the teachers and students watching him from the windows above. It was past 5:00 a.m. when he finally went back to bed. He had spent most of that day in Tel Aviv, and had caught a British period drama at the cinema. He didn't want to be at home; his mother-in-law looked after Elie on Sundays.

One of the young female students quickly came to the defense of the elderly woman. 'What are you talking about?' she addressed Avner. 'Of course there's a reason for her change. She remembered what happened on the bus.'

'And she couldn't remember it before? So why does she remember just then? There should be some textual justification, shouldn't there?'

Michael Rosin remained silent, as did Ze'ev. Ze'ev hadn't yet spoken during the workshop, and hadn't written any stories. He would just observe and occasionally write down comments in a black notebook, and was under the impression that his silence made the other students even more curious about his opinion of their stories. It might have also piqued the curiosity of Michael, who, during their talk in the car after the previous lesson, had gently urged him to read something of his own at one of the upcoming classes. That was a week ago – before Ofer, and before Ofer's mother, and before Inspector Avraham, and before the call to the police, and the searches.

He had yet to decide if he would say anything to Michael on their ride home that evening. They had met only four weeks ago, but Ze'ev felt they shared a sense of quiet affinity, which was almost always a sign of a close friendship in the making.

The discussion in class was becoming repetitive and dreary. Ze'ev knew what Michael Rosin was thinking, and he waited.

'I was very moved by the story,' Michael said, lifting his head and speaking in a soft voice. Somewhat taken aback by the choice of words, Ze'ev tried to read the teacher's eyes, to ask them if he had indeed been moved. Michael's piercing gaze was focused on the elderly woman, who was still trying to catch her breath.

The class went silent, and Michael continued: 'I think you have a wonderful talent for depicting a complete scene in just a few sentences. In just two-and-a-half pages you have created two emotionally credible characters. Aside from that, you have successfully created two story planes, which are set far apart from one another, without using any specific time points, and only with the help of place references, the modern hospital ward and the old bus.'

Michael's voice remained soft even when the tone changed. 'Nevertheless, in my opinion your story could have been even better and more powerful than it already is – and it is a wonderful story, I want to stress that – had you not done what I have been speaking about since the first meeting; that is, had you not written literature,' he said. 'The pain in your story is still alive, and it seems to me that when it becomes unbearable, you escape into literature, so-called literature – in other words, into analogies and symbolism. In reality there are no analogies and no symbols, like the rain that washes over the mother's face or the moment at the end when the daughter closes the mother's eyes and says to her in Polish, "Forgive me, my darling," repeating the words her mother had said to her on the bus.'

Ze'ev could not resolve the profound contradiction between Michael Rosin's provocative appearance and the softness and sensitivity of his voice. His beard was wild and unkempt, and his eyes were red. As they sat alongside each other in his car a week ago, his black sweatshirt had reeked of cigarette smoke and sweat, and alcohol too, perhaps. He tried to picture Michael's apartment, his study, and his mind conjured up images of ashtrays overflowing with cigarette butts and piles of books and half-empty bottles of wine on the desk. Michael wouldn't be inviting him in this evening, after their ride home together, but it could happen over the coming weeks, before the workshop ended.

Michael's soft, comforting gaze remained fixed on the elderly woman.

'You wanted the story to come to a harmonious conclusion,' he continued, 'and so you ended it with the daughter's repetition of the mother's words. We are all under the impression that literature, and beauty in art in general, is harmony, and that anger isn't literature. But I think that it doesn't matter what literature is. As I said in our first meeting, I can't and don't want to help you to write literature. I want to help you to write.'

'What's wrong with writing literature?' the young student asked. 'Everyone can write.'

'There's nothing wrong with it, Einat. It's simply using someone else's words and patterns. And I don't agree with what you said about everyone being able to write. Remember what

I read to you in the first class, that excerpt from Kafka's letter?' Michael closed his eyes and quoted from memory: '"I think we ought to read only the kind of books that wound or stab us. If the book we're reading doesn't wake us up with a blow to the head, what are we reading it for? We need books that affect us like a disaster, that grieve us deeply, like the death of someone we loved more than ourselves, like being banished into faraway forests, like a suicide. A book must be the ax for the frozen sea within us. That is my belief."'

Michael's gaze moved over the faces of the students, stopping to focus on Ze'ev's eyes.

Could he see what Ze'ev had yet to grasp, that at that particular moment his writing began? Or was it perhaps a little later, during the ride home together, when the words they had exchanged were closer and more intimate, and Ze'ev had felt that Michael was trying to tell him something, as if he already knew?

Michael was held up in class. He must have been speaking to some student who had approached him. Ze'ev waited for him in the library courtyard. Evening had fallen and upper-middle-class couples were streaming into the adjacent Cameri Theater and the Opera House.

'Are you waiting for me?' Michael asked when he came out a few minutes later with the young student and noticed Ze'ev.

'I thought you might like a ride home,' Ze'ev said.

Michael lit up a cigarette he had removed from a crumpled pack.

They stood facing each other on the steps leading up to the library. Michael was a tall man, and his eyes were a fiery red. 'Oh, thanks,' he said, 'but I'm off to visit a friend.'

Ze'ev quickly composed himself. 'No problem,' he said. 'I'll drop you off wherever you need to go.'

'It's completely out of your way,' Michael replied. 'She lives in the south of Tel Aviv.'

When Ze'ev had waited for him last week and offered him a ride, he had told Michael that he lived in north Tel Aviv, not far from Michael's apartment, at the northern end of Ben Yehuda Street, where he and Michal had indeed lived before Elie was born. 'Don't worry about it,' he said. 'I'm happy to make a detour.'

They made their way toward the lot where Ze'ev had parked his old Daihatsu. Michael walked like someone who owned the city, and Ze'ev got the impression that Michael was looking at the traffic and streetlights like a child who was seeing them for the first time. That morning he had asked Michal if he could have the car for the day purely for this ride home. He had dropped her off at school and had come into Tel Aviv with the car and not his bike.

Ze'ev cleared away the books and CDs that were strewn across the passenger seat and lying on the rubber mat on the floor, apologizing for the mess. 'Wow, you have an entire mobile library in here,' Michael laughed.

The sounds of a Shostakovich string quartet filled the car soon after Ze'ev started the engine, and he removed the CD. 'I'm not in the mood for that right now,' he said, as if to himself. The eight o'clock news was on the radio. Elie's car seat was in the back. Michael had noticed it the last time and had asked him how many children he had and their ages. 'Just one,' Ze'ev had responded. 'He's almost a year old now, and I am not quite used to it all yet.'

After asking Michael the best route to take to the south of

Tel Aviv, Ze'ev turned left onto Ibn Gabirol Street and headed for Yehuda Halevy.

'That was a tough class, wasn't it?' Ze'ev said. 'She didn't understand a word you said.'

Michael looked at him, surprised. 'I actually thought it was a good meeting,' he replied. 'She impressed me. She wrote a very nice story. I hope I didn't give the wrong impression.'

Ze'ev turned at the wrong intersection, instead of heading straight onto Yitzhak Sadeh. 'Never mind,' Michael said. 'You could do a U-turn somewhere, but that'll take you far out of your way; you can drop me off here.' Then he asked Ze'ev, 'And when are you going to read something for us? I don't call on you in class because I don't want to pressure any of you into reading.'

Ze'ev felt a burning desire to tell Michael that he was finally so close to writing – so close, and after so many years. He could picture Ofer's face as he had seen it the last time, and had thought about how he would describe his features, the trace of a mustache, his embarrassed laughter. For three days now, he had known what he would write, but had yet to capture the precise words. They were still forming in his mind.

'I think I'll write this week,' Ze'ev said. 'I believe I've found my topic – thanks to you.' But Michael was too cautious and remained silent, not asking him anything, so Ze'ev added, 'And what about you? Are you writing anything at the moment?'

They were stopped at a red light. Michael sighed. His long legs were a tight fit in the small car.

'I always write. But I think it's been months since I have produced something that I can stand behind and publish. That's why I agreed to give the workshop. I am hoping it will help me with my own writing too.'

Michael's sigh and ensuing confession appeared to bring the two men in the car a little closer. Ze'ev had read his last book, published some two years earlier – initially in envy, sparked by the writer's young age, and then in wonder and admiration. Michael had published three books, two collections of short stories and a short novel, and although they hadn't sold all that well, they had won praise. Michael's red T-shirt was giving off that same pungent smell that had come from the black sweatshirt the week before, and Ze'ev wondered if it was Michael's body odor.

'Do you go through some long periods when you don't write?' Ze'ev asked, and Michael said, 'I'm always writing something. But there are times when I don't write anything worth reading.'

'Who decides what is good or bad?'

'I do.'

Ze'ev laughed, but Michael remained stern-faced, as if there hadn't been a hint of humor in his reply.

'How in fact did you begin writing?' Ze'ev asked, and Michael said, 'I don't even remember. I do remember myself writing as a child in elementary school – sitting in class, not listening to a word the teacher was saying, and writing poems.'

Ze'ev hated that sort of answer when it appeared in newspaper interviews with writers. He hadn't allowed himself to miss a word the teachers said, and the thing he remembered best from elementary school was his fear that the teacher would call on him with a question.

Michael turned the radio down. 'Since when have you been writing?' he asked. 'I somehow got the impression that you're not a workshop kind of person, that you know pretty well what and how you want to write.'

Ze'ev was stunned by Michael's words. Had he managed to deceive him, to hide the truth from him, or had Michael, with his sensitivity, perceived something that Ze'ev wasn't able to discern in himself, seen in him an inner truth whose existence he was too frightened to believe in?

'I don't write at all. Who told you I write?' Ze'ev asked jokingly, in an effort to conceal his emotions. 'Truth be told, I joined the workshop purely by chance. I hadn't planned on it. I was passing by the library, saw the notice, and decided to come in – not to learn how to write, but more to see what it's all about and what others write about. I wasn't sure about staying but was very impressed by what you said in the first lesson and got the sense that I'd have something to learn from you. And I think I have learned something already; I can feel it coming.'

Ze'ev was on the verge of confessing at that point in their conversation. But then Michael seemed embarrassed, perhaps unsure about how to take the compliment, and silence fell again. They had reached the southern neighborhoods of Tel Aviv, and Michael's red eyes were peering through the window. 'This is a pretty good neighborhood,' he said. 'I'm thinking about moving here. The rent here is a lot lower than in our area,' and Ze'ev immediately blurted, 'Yeah, prices in Tel Aviv are crazy.'

The intimate moment passed.

'We're thinking about moving too,' Ze'ev continued. 'Our landlord wants to raise the rent, and we need a larger apartment in any case – with a room for the kid. It's tough these days to rent an apartment in Tel Aviv on the salary of two teachers.'

'Where will you move to?'

'Holon, perhaps. Although we're a little hesitant to do so. It would be very hard for us to leave Tel Aviv – for me, at least.'

'I'd move to Holon,' Michael said. 'It seems like the right place.'

'The right place?' Ze'ev asked, surprised.

'The right place to live and write in. I'm sick of writing about Tel Aviv. I think I'm looking for a way to write more simply, and perhaps to write simply, one needs to live a simple life among simple people. I'm sick of overly sophisticated literature. But I'm not sure, maybe it's naive of me to talk like this.'

It was Ze'ev's turn to feel Michael's sting. 'You really do hate literature, don't you?' he said.

'No, no. Oh God, I get the sense I have been horribly misunderstood today. Perhaps I came in feeling on edge and that's what you've picked up on. I'm going to have to correct that impression at the next meeting. I'm simply trying to help you to free yourselves from worrying about what is literature and what isn't, and to express what you have inside you in your writing. The most powerful text ever written – in my opinion, at least – wasn't composed as a literary text. Do you know Kafka's *Letter to His Father*?'

Ze'ev was afraid to admit he had never read the letter, and even more so to claim he had read it and then get caught in a lie. Had Michael asked him the question because he had already placed him in the category of those simple people who lived simple lives? He could have said something nonspecific, like 'I read it ages ago; I don't remember it word for word' – but decided to say he hadn't.

'Okay, that's excellent,' Michael said, 'I'll bring it to class next time – just an excerpt, though, because it's pretty long.

And there's even a new translation. It's a letter Kafka wrote to his father in 1920, I believe; or it might've been 1919. Anyway, it was written a few years before he died, and his father never received it. Think about it: one of the greatest literary texts in history wasn't composed as a piece of literature but as a letter intended for a single reader, who never even read it. It blows me away every time I think about it. That's how I'd like to write, as if my text is addressed to a single specific reader whom I wish to terrify. It begins with the words "You asked me recently why I maintain that I am afraid of you." Wonderful, isn't it?'

And just then, the first words appeared. And the idea, which still, that afternoon, had yet to express itself, like a baby learning to speak, suddenly came together in lucid sentences that needed only to be put down on the page.

The hours that followed were very different from those just before and after the call to the police on Friday. This time, there was no panic or confusion in his actions. He acted with a sense of inner peace. There wasn't a hint of the fear that had gripped him yesterday afternoon, and that hadn't completely abated when he woke in the small hours of the morning and sat in the living room, enveloped in silence. Everything felt right, just as he had imagined the writing would be.

Ze'ev didn't drive straight home after dropping Michael off. He called Michal to ask if it would be okay if he were a little late. He told her he wanted to catch a movie, and only then remembered the English film he had seen that morning and thought he would be able to tell her about it without lying. He found a window seat at a café in Masaryk Square and ordered a cup of herbal tea.

And there, in his black notebook, the first words were written, as if on their own:

*Father and Mother,*

*I know you've been looking for me for a few days now, but I suggest you stop looking because you won't find me, and neither will the police, not even with tracker dogs.*

*The notices you posted in the streets say I disappeared on Wednesday morning, but all three of us know that isn't true. We all know that I disappeared long before then, without you even noticing, because you didn't pay attention, and that I didn't disappear in a single day either, but it was a gradual process of disappearing, at the end of which you thought I was still at home only because you never even tried to look.*

*I ask myself why are you looking for me now? Why now have you gone to the police? Why didn't you do so in the months and years in which the writing was on the wall? I used to think it's because you were too caught up with yourselves and your lives, but that was a passing, childish thought, because I realized that the real reason was simply that it was hard for you to get close. Because all people are scared of truly seeing what others go through, and what your child goes through, in particular – especially when he is different, different from you, someone you can't understand, a strange bird.*

*I know this letter will cause you pain, but maybe I want you to hurt like I did. You could have prevented it but you didn't. You remembered me when it was too late.*

*You must be asking yourselves where I am now and where am I writing from – and I can only say that I am writing from somewhere far away, somewhere all good.*

*No longer yours,*
*Ofer*

Ze'ev sat at the café and read through the letter several times. He wasn't filled with a sense of joy or satisfaction, only hunger for precision, hunger to find the right words and to erase the wrong ones. He added and deleted sentences, weeding out anything in the letter that a boy of Ofer's age wouldn't write, anything that wouldn't ring true as Ofer's voice.

'How are you feeling?' Michal asked him when he returned home.

'Great,' he replied.

They sat together in the living room and Michal cut up a melon, the first of the summer.

He told her about the English film, and she told him about her day at school and the evening with Elie, who had been crankier than usual and hadn't stopped whimpering and looking for his father. At half past eleven Michal said she was going to sleep and asked if he was coming to bed. 'Not yet,' he said. 'I think I want to write something.' He smiled, and Michal looked at him in surprise.

'It's about time,' she said.

Ze'ev sat down at the desk on the enclosed balcony, but only after peeking into the bedroom to make sure Michal was asleep did he remove from his bag the surgical gloves he had bought at a drugstore on the way home, and also a sheet of blank paper from a new ream for the printer. He slowly copied the text he had written at the café, rounding and spacing his usually dense and sharp-edged script. He left out the words '*in which the writing was on the wall,*' because they seemed too clichéd, and also the expression '*a strange bird*,' which Ofer surely wouldn't have been familiar with. He added '*To be continued*' at the bottom of the letter, underneath '*Ofer*,' and then folded the page using a ruler and slipped it into a medium-size brown envelope.

When he came in earlier, Ze'ev had noticed that Michal had already emptied their mailbox, and now he went to the letter basket in the kitchen to fish out an unopened electricity bill. In his other hand, he carried a garbage bag – a good explanation for the gloves, if anyone happened to see and ask, which of course no one did. He put the bill into their mailbox and then took it out again, in the same movement stuffing the brown envelope into the Sharabis' mailbox.

The edge of the envelope jutted out. It couldn't be missed.

He removed the gloves and put them into the garbage bag, which he then threw into the large communal bin. He then went back to the balcony and sat down at the desk again. The shutters were open and the computer was on. Strangely, he remained at ease. The sharp anticipation he felt was both his and not his, all at the same time.

The chances of seeing anyone entering or leaving the building at that time of the night were slim, but he was too keyed up to go to sleep. Was this similar to the feeling of a young writer waiting to see his first story appear in the morning newspaper? It suddenly dawned on Ze'ev that someone from the building could go downstairs to the mailboxes and remove the letter without him seeing. He grabbed the keys to his bike and went down to look for something in the compartment under the seat. The envelope was in its place.

He surfed the Internet for a while, and ate the rest of the melon. Moments before turning off the computer, he heard a car pull up outside the building. The front passenger door opened, as well as the trunk, and a man stepped out.

It was Ofer's father.

Ze'ev watched as the father removed a small suitcase from the trunk and then went around to the driver to shake his hand through the open car window. Carrying the suitcase, he then walked up the path to the building and disappeared into the stairwell.

It was 1:30 a.m.

# 7

In hindsight, that was the day the investigation altered course.

It hadn't dawned on him at the time. A number of days went by before he realized that the case was moving in a direction he had never imagined it would take – and by then he was already in Brussels.

Nevertheless, when he returned home, Monday evening, on foot, following the same path that linked Fichman Street to Kiryat Sharet, Avraham realized that Ofer was no longer a complete mystery to him. He could see Ofer's face as it appeared in the photographs he was given, he could sense the sound of his voice, he could imagine his thoughts.

It was 7:30 a.m. when he spoke by phone with Ofer's father, who had landed at the airport after midnight, and asked him to come in for an interview. He then called Ze'ev Avni, the neighbor he had put off calling the day before. He had missed him by just a few minutes. Avni's wife told him that he had already left for work, and she passed on her husband's cell-phone number. He tried calling but got no reply – as the wife had expected. She had told him that her husband was teaching for a few consecutive periods and would be able to take a call only during one of the short breaks between the lessons. Avraham didn't leave a message.

In the meantime he returned to the Kintiev case; he wanted

to close it before sending it off to the district prosecutor. The day before, because the team meeting had left him paralyzed, and because Ilana had instructed him to focus on the missing-persons case, he had suspended the remainder of the Kintiev investigation; it wasn't that urgent, anyway. On Wednesday, the prosecutor would file charges and request that Kintiev be remanded to custody until the end of the proceedings against him. He continued with his summaries of the statements and the rest of the evidence. The more he read the transcripts of the talks with Kintiev, the stranger they appeared. He decided to dedicate a separate section of his summary to Kintiev's confessions regarding crimes that were not part of the case, the arson and the story about his attempt to electrocute an elderly family member in order to get control of her money, adding a note that this material should be passed on to the relevant Northern District police station for further investigation. Avraham's attention was particularly drawn to an odd expression that Kintiev had repeated over and over again: 'If you're my friend.'

'If you're my friend, I speak to you.' 'If you're my friend, I help you end the investigation.' 'If you're my friend, I tell you things you don't know.'

Avraham had responded to these odd statements only once. 'Yes, I'm your friend,' he had said, and Kintiev had laughed out loud, responding, 'If you're my friend, you let me go now and I come to your house.'

He tried calling Ze'ev Avni again at 10:45 a.m. – and again got his voice mail.

Eliyahu Ma'alul called when Ofer's father was already sitting in his office.

'Can it wait an hour or two?' he asked Ma'alul.

'It's better if it doesn't.'

Apologizing to Ofer's father, Avraham left the room.

As they had agreed, Ma'alul had returned that morning to the school to speak with Ofer's classmates and teachers. He had asked to use the guidance counselor's room and questioned the students in her presence. He thought it might make them feel less insecure and encourage them to talk. 'Certain students are more fearful of the familiar and very tangible authority of school figures than they are of the abstract authority of the police,' he explained.

Ma'alul was breathing heavily, as if he were speaking while walking briskly. 'You've got it wrong, Avi,' he said. 'He didn't run away, and he didn't kill himself. I'm sure of it now.'

When they had spoken the previous evening to prepare for the day's course of action, Avraham had again tried to explain to him why he believed that Ofer's disappearance had in all likelihood been voluntary.

'Did you come up with anything?' he asked.

'Not exactly . . . Actually, you know what? Maybe I did. On Friday evening, two days after his disappearance, Ofer had a date to see a movie with some girl. And as far as I've learned, this did not happen very often. Maybe never. A friend by the name of Yaniv Nesher told me. They're in the same class, and I believe he's Ofer's closest friend – although I don't know how much he really knows. On Sunday, three days before his disappearance, Ofer told him he was supposed to be going to a movie Friday evening with a girl he had met through him.'

Avraham would hear the word 'movie' later that day again – in a different context, and from someone else. He'd recall the movie that Ofer was planning to see on Friday evening and would make a connection between the two movies, between the two conversations.

'What do you mean by "through him"?' he asked, and Ma'alul explained: 'Through his sister. Ofer was at the friend's house, to exchange some computer games, or maybe to play some, and the friend has a sister a year younger than them. The sister had a friend over, and she liked Ofer. Ofer was informed of this and got her number. Looks like it took him a while, but he called her last week. Never mind, the details don't matter. What's important is that they made a date to see a movie last Friday, two days after he disappeared.'

Don't matter? The details mattered, and how! The information didn't appear earth-shattering, but it did show a different Ofer from the one he had been told about over the past few days, the one who never left the house, the one who didn't discuss his life with anyone. All of a sudden, he's visiting friends, he's planning to go out to a movie, he's caught someone's fancy. Avraham hadn't thought anyone liked him at all.

'And did you speak to her?' he asked.

'No, she goes to Kiryat Sharet High School; I'm on my way there. Besides all this, I didn't know they had a handi-capped daughter.'

'Who has?' Avraham asked, wondering what Ma'alul was talking about.

'Ofer's parents. The friend told me that Ofer has a sister with Down's syndrome.'

Avraham had had no idea, and couldn't decide whether to admit as much to Ma'alul. He had been telling himself since Friday that he was trying to hear a story and 'get to know the characters,' yet five days of investigating had gone by and he was completely unaware of that detail, which certainly must have been of significance in Ofer's life.

'I didn't know she had Down's syndrome. I haven't seen her,' Avraham said. 'The brother and sister have been at the grandparents' since Wednesday or Thursday. That explains why the mother couldn't cope by herself with the children while the investigation was going on.'

'It also explains Ofer's introversion,' Ma'alul responded. 'The friend said that he has never been to Ofer's home. Ofer never invited him over, and that must have something to do with the sister.'

Avraham hadn't gone into the sister's room when he was at the Sharabi home – neither on Thursday nor on Friday. The door to that room was closed and he had felt that Hannah Sharabi wanted to keep it that way. He hadn't been in the master bedroom, either. He suddenly recalled the foolish thought he'd entertained that first evening, on his way home, after the mother's visit to the police station – the age difference between the children. Two years after Ofer was born, Hannah Sharabi had a daughter with Down's syndrome. After that, she and her husband didn't want another child – for almost ten years.

He thought for a moment and then asked, 'But what does that give us?'

'Some sort of direction, right? Maybe the girl Ofer was supposed to go out with has a boyfriend who wasn't happy about it all? And it's seeming more and more unlikely to me that he ran away. Does it make sense for him to decide to run away two days before he has a date with a girl for maybe the first time in his life? And who knows, maybe he said something to the girl. Perhaps he has been in contact with her since

Wednesday. She may be the one person we have been looking for, the person whom Ofer has contacted and whom we have yet to come across.'

'Why wouldn't she tell anyone about it?'

'Look, Avi, I really don't know. I'm on my way to see her now. I'll update you after I've spoken to her.'

Five days, and he didn't know – not about the girl Ofer had been in touch with, not about the sister. Bringing Ma'alul into the investigation was undoubtedly the right decision. He felt a burning desire to return to his office and get everything he possibly could out of the father about Ofer and his life, even if their conversation went on late into the night.

Rafael Sharabi was nothing like what Avraham had expected. His stature, his tone of voice, his choice of words. Perhaps because he knew he was a sailor and a member of a workers' union, he had been expecting a heavyset man, tough and loud. He had expected him to speak harshly, to complain about the delay in opening the investigation, to threaten. If he had understood Ilana's hints correctly, a little pressure from Rafael Sharabi and the case would be handed over to a special investigation team under a higher-ranking officer, or to the Central Unit.

'Sorry about that,' Avraham said. 'It was an update from an investigator in the field.'

'Anything new?' the father asked.

'Nothing for now,' Avraham replied, shaking his head. 'We'll see a little later.'

There was something soft about the father's build and facial features. Almost feminine. He was a chubby man, in his mid-forties. Short, curly hair, silvery-black. He was only an inch or two taller than Avraham. There was gray stubble on his round face, as if he were in mourning. Avraham recalled the appearance of the apartment on the first day of the investigation: family members and friends, soda bottles and plates of snacks on the living room table. The father was on a ship bound for Trieste.

Rafael Sharabi didn't threaten, and he didn't say a word about the delay in the start of the investigation. He quietly and patiently listened as Avraham brought him up to speed, then offered any help that would be needed. Colleagues from work had offered to help too, as well as other family members. Had his wife not told him about the delay? Perhaps she had been afraid that he would have thought it was her fault, but he didn't look like a husband to be feared. When they first sat down in his office, after introducing themselves and shaking hands, Avraham had said that it must have been difficult for him to have been so far away, without the option of returning home immediately. 'Yes, it was. But what could I do? I returned the moment we docked at the port,' Rafael Sharabi replied, as if he had been accused of something.

Avraham thought about the sea – whether it was calm or stormy, whether the sailors spent the entire voyage belowdecks or whether they would go up on deck for a breath of fresh air when they had some free time, whether the sea itself was a presence in the lives of the sailors or if the ship was simply a regular workplace, an office tower of sorts that one never stepped out of. 'The toughest part of the investigation for me so far is the sense that I don't know enough about Ofer,' he said. 'That's really the help I need right now. It was difficult for your wife, and I understand that. But I'm having trouble building up a profile, and this complicates the process of establishing a line of inquiry, especially when we don't have any physical evidence.'

The father nodded and remained silent. He might have still been far away at sea or struggling with the feeling that he hadn't been at home when they needed him.

'I understand you are absent from home for long periods,' Avraham continued. 'Can you explain to me how that works? How long are you away for? How often do you travel?'

'I usually do short routes – Cyprus, Turkey – trips of a few days. Once every few months I do longer runs, like Koper or Trieste. I spend at least a few days at home after each trip, sometimes up to two weeks. Every now and then there's ship maintenance work to do at the port.'

Where's Koper? Avraham wondered to himself. Probably a port city on the Mediterranean or some other sea. Every time he came across an unfamiliar detail during an investigation, he felt he was on the right track. He was stepping outside of himself, going beyond his knowledge. And unlike the mother, the father appeared willing to talk, willing to open the door for him – even if, for the moment, it was just a ship's door. When Avraham visited their apartment on Thursday and on Friday, the mother had accompanied him to Ofer's room; she had opened closets and drawers with him, and had sat down beside him on Ofer's bed, and yet he sensed her unwillingness to allow him into their home.

'What's your job title?' Avraham asked.

'Chief engineering officer.'

'Is that a senior position?'

'Senior? I don't know. It's a position you reach after twenty years on the job.'

'And how did you get into this line of work?'

Rafael Sharabi looked at him in surprise, as if the answer was obvious. 'I served in the navy. After my discharge, I did a course in mechanical engineering at the Naval Training Institute in Acre, and went to work for Zim from there.'

'So you're in command of the ship? Are you the captain?' Avraham asked. He was not certain that a ship even had a captain.

'No, the chief engineering officer is responsible only for the mechanical operation of the ship. A captain needs to go through a professional training course. He's responsible for the entire ship, including the logistics of the cargo delivery, the loading and unloading.'

'What type of ships do you work on?'

'Mostly medium-range ships because I don't do the long routes anymore. Small or medium-size feeder ships.'

'What are those?'

'Oh, you asked as if you were familiar with them,' Rafael apologized. 'It's a size class of container ships. Not the biggest. Ships that carry between a thousand and three thousand standard-size containers.'

Avraham made notes on a sheet of paper like the one he had used on Wednesday evening. The day before he had looked for that particular sheet – with the terrible drawing he had unconsciously scribbled at the bottom – but could not find it. 'Isn't it a difficult job – I mean, with a family and all?' he asked, hoping not to sound accusatory, and the father replied drily, 'It's my profession.'

Should he ask him how much a chief engineering officer earns in a month? Avraham wondered. Five thousand? Ten thousand? Thirty thousand? He had no idea. And that's what he wanted to speak to him about – about things he didn't know. That was always the key.

'What did your wife think about it?' he asked. 'How did you meet?' And Rafael Sharabi said, 'She accepted it. She didn't really have a choice, did she?'

So there was something harsh concealed behind his soft roundness after all. The impatience of someone who wasn't used to being asked personal questions and having to answer them. He was accustomed to issuing orders on his boats in a brusque, professional tone – and probably at home too.

'And how did you meet?'

'Hannah served in the navy too. During the tough times, after the children were born, I tried to spend more time at home. As I said, thanks to that job, I can sometimes be at home for two weeks in a row without having to work.'

Was he surprised that the conversation was focused primarily on his work and his absence from home? Avraham hadn't intended to take it in that direction. He had a feeling the father wanted to speak about it. 'How old were you when you got married?' he asked.

'How old? I was twenty-six and Hannah was twenty-one.'

He pictured them at the wedding. He could imagine the father in his twenties – thinner, with a slightly more upright posture, yet still round and soft in appearance, just as he was today, only less confident. He couldn't imagine Hannah as a twenty-one-year-old. It must have been in the early 1990s. 'And when was Ofer born?' he asked.

'I was busy with my apprenticeship when we got married. I was doing the long routes then and was sometimes away from home for more than a month, so we waited. We decided to have Ofer only after I had qualified and got the job with Zim. He was born so small.'

'And how did he take it?'

'Who?'

'Ofer.'

'How did he take what?'

'The fact that you would often disappear.' Now Ofer's disappeared, just like you, Avraham thought, but didn't say it.

The father's hands were large and hairy, and he looked down at them as he placed them on Avraham's desk.

'It was hard for him when he was little,' he said. 'One time I returned from a long trip and he didn't remember me. He insisted I wasn't his father and for several days called me "uncle." But it was okay once he grew up. He helps Hannah a lot when I'm not around. He stays at home, helps around the house. We've been waiting for him to turn seventeen and get his driver's license. Hannah doesn't drive. But maybe it wasn't easy for him, after all.'

'What do you mean?'

'Maybe we put too much on his shoulders, maybe he got fed up.' The father paused for a moment. 'I grew up in a home with financial difficulties and went out to work at a very young age. I wanted my children to live well and to study, and Ofer was a good student. But we also expected a lot from him, to help around the house, to study hard. Maybe it was too much.'

He had yet to say a word about the sister.

'Would you say Ofer had a rough time at home?'

'I don't know, maybe it was hard for him. I thought it was natural. I hadn't thought about it in this way until he disappeared, and he never said anything. Before starting high school, he asked if he could go to the Naval Officers Academy. It's a boarding school in Acre. I wasn't opposed to the idea, but Hannah didn't want him to go. She wanted him at home.'

'Do you have clear rules at home about when and with whom he's allowed to go out?' Avraham cautiously asked, and the father said, 'No, on the contrary. We were very flexible when it came to that. We encouraged him to go out at night, to do whatever he wanted with his friends. Hannah needs less help in the evenings, after the other children go to sleep. We just put too much responsibility on him. Especially when I wasn't there.'

Avraham was sure the father had no idea about Ofer's plans to go out to a movie that Friday night with a girl who liked him – perhaps his first such date.

And he was right.

'What about friends? Girls?' he asked, and the father said, 'I don't think he went out with girls. But that's pretty natural, no? I was shy too at his age. I've always thought the army would do for Ofer what it did for me, open him up.'

'Did he talk about the army?'

'He wanted to join the navy, and I encouraged him – although I wouldn't want him to be a sailor after his military service. I can't tell you how proud it made me to see him study, do his homework, work on the computer. He taught me how to surf the Internet.'

They spoke in his office for four hours – from 11:00 a.m. to 3:00 p.m. And as the time passed, Avraham became aware of just how important their conversation was to him. After Hannah Sharabi's lengthy silences, he felt almost grateful to her husband for talking about himself and his family.

At 1:30 p.m., he went out to order them each a tray of food

from the cafeteria, along with two cups of coffee, and he smoked a cigarette in the parking lot while waiting for lunch to arrive. His cell phone rang. It was Ze'ev Avni. He didn't recall leaving his number with the neighbor. Avraham asked if he could come into the station for an additional interview the following morning, and Avni replied that he had to be at home with his son then and invited Avraham to come to the apartment. Avraham hesitated but then suggested that Avni come to the station that afternoon, at around five. Avni agreed, asked how he would find him, and then said, 'Okay, so, see you at five,' as if they were friends arranging to meet for coffee.

Eliyahu Ma'alul's cell phone was switched off. Perhaps he was busy speaking to the girl from Kiryat Sharet High School. Reluctantly, Avraham also called Shrapstein, who wasn't in his office. He finally answered after ten rings and said he was 'exploring an interesting direction.' Unlike Ma'alul, Shrapstein hadn't called to update him, though Avraham was certain he had called Ilana.

'What "direction"?' Avraham asked.

'It's not clear yet; I'll update you if I get anything concrete,' Shrapstein replied. 'In a nutshell, a resident of the neighborhood who has a history of sex crimes and violence involving youths is out on parole. It's mostly harassment, but you know how these things escalate. For now, I'm collecting information, and we may bring him in to the station for questioning. Do you want to participate in the interrogation when he comes in?'

Of course he wanted to. What a question.

He considered calling Ilana, but decided to wait until he'd finished his meeting with the father. Shrapstein had again managed to irritate him, but overall he felt better. The investigation was moving forward, even if the direction it was taking remained unclear. The story was filling out with detail. The chronicle of Ofer's life was no longer a blank page. It had a wedding in it, at some point in the early 1990s, and a young father who had completed a course to become a chief engineering officer and was away from home for long periods; it had a sister with Down's syndrome whom the family was too ashamed to mention; it had shipping lines that carried thousands of containers to ports in Cyprus and Koper. Owing to his father's absences and the condition of his sister, Ofer was given a heavy load to carry, but the responsibility he was forced to assume wasn't the kind that strengthened – on the contrary, perhaps. He was not asked to step into his father's shoes during the absences. He was just asked to help. Outside the home, there was a friend called Yaniv Nesher, there were computer games, and a girl who liked Ofer. There was a date to see a movie. And there was the wish to leave home and live at a boarding school, to join the navy. The sea had become an inescapable backdrop to the story. Not the beach, with which Avraham was familiar, just like everyone else, and where he'd go sometimes on a Saturday in the summer, without removing his shirt. This was a different kind of sea, a sea that was also a place of work, a sea that was a distance between father and son, wife and husband. He wanted to look again at the photographs of Ofer that he had in his office, though not in the presence of the father.

As he put out his second cigarette, Ze'ev Avni called again, asking if he needed to bring with him to the interview any form of identification or other documents. Avraham told him to bring his identity card, to which Avni replied, 'My ID card is old and not up-to-date. I haven't amended my residential address – it still says I live in Tel Aviv. Is that okay?'

Avraham said it was fine and hung up, already beginning to regret the time he was going to waste in the company of the teacher. Perhaps he could dump Avni on Shrapstein? He smiled. It was an excellent idea.

For the last hour, they spoke mostly about Tuesday. He asked Rafael Sharabi to reconstruct the twenty-four hours prior to Ofer's disappearance, and to try to remember anything unusual.

'I was preparing for a trip, so I was home for most of the day,' the father said. He woke at 6:00 a.m., and then woke the boys. His wife woke their sister. Still no mention of the disability, as if the sister were a normal child. She gets picked up for school at 7:30 a.m. At this point, Avraham was writing down every word.

'Did Ofer go down to the grocery store?'

'I think so. He goes down every morning. But I don't remember. Is it important?'

He then drove the younger son to kindergarten. Ofer left for school as usual, on foot. He didn't know what Hannah had done.

After his stop at the kindergarten, the father had errands to run; he was at the bank, and then drove into Jaffa to renew the license on the car. After he returned home, they went shopping in the industrial area. He had something to eat while they were out. Ofer was the first of the children to return home – at some point before 2:00 p.m., but the father wasn't sure, as he was napping at the time. He thought Ofer usually ate lunch alone, as his brother and sister returned home later. Perhaps he sometimes ate with Hannah. He couldn't remember seeing him after he woke from his afternoon nap, but was sure that Ofer had stayed at home, just as the mother had said. He was probably doing homework or preparing for an exam in his room. Rafael Sharabi was in the bedroom, beginning to pack his bag for the trip, with the help of his wife. He hadn't heard Ofer talking to anyone over the phone. The younger son returned at 4:00 p.m., driven home by the mother of another child from the kindergarten. The daughter got home after 5:00 p.m.

Avraham couldn't hold back anymore. 'So late?' he asked. 'Where does she go to school?'

'What? She's at a special school,' the father quietly responded, looking Avraham in the eyes.

'Why?'

'She has a mental disability. It's a good school, with a long school day and lots of help.'

Now that the father had told him about her, Avraham felt he had nothing more to ask, as if all he had wanted was for them to stop denying her existence. 'So she lives at home, then, not in an institution?' he asked nevertheless.

'No, Hannah wouldn't have that. She barely agreed to send her to school. She wanted her to stay at home and to look after her herself. That's how things were until she was seven. That's why she gave up her job. She used to teach kindergarten.'

'And how did Ofer take it?'

'I thought we should consider a boarding school for her — for the sake of the other children. No, it wasn't easy for him. But he helped out a lot — both Hannah and his sister. It was more difficult when he was little. He was ashamed, and would tell everyone at school that he was an only child. This was before his brother was born. But in recent years he's been really good to her.'

Avraham put down his pen and thought about the silent mother. She had left her job to stay at home with the daughter in order to protect her from any harm out in the world, and inside the home from the father, who wanted to send her to an institution – because of the children, or in other words, for the boys.

'What's her name?' he asked, and the father quietly said, 'Ofer was the first to learn sign language, because she has a severe hearing problem. It's part of her condition. Her name's Danit.'

Avraham picked up his pen again, and they returned to that Tuesday. The family had eaten at around 7:00 p.m. – everyone together. The father bathed the younger son and put him to bed. Ofer was watching TV in the living room. The wife helped Danit bathe herself and get into bed. Ofer went back to his room after his brother had fallen asleep, presumably to play on the computer, with the volume turned down. The father didn't think he had seen him writing e-mails and hadn't noticed if he surfed the Internet, so wouldn't know which sites he may have visited. He didn't hear him talk on the phone. At 9:30 p.m., he and the wife had gone out, like they did before every trip. They went to meet some friends, another couple, at a café in the center of town. He had no idea what Ofer did that evening, and only remembered that when they returned home, relatively early, 11:00 p.m. maybe, he was asleep. There was nothing unusual about that; he thought that was the time Ofer normally went to bed.

'Did you have a fight that evening?' Avraham asked.

'Who?'

'You and your wife – or perhaps between the two of you and Ofer.'

'Not that I recall. Why?'

'Just asking.'

'Not that I remember. Things are a little tense sometimes before I go away, but I don't recall an argument before the last trip.'

'And the next day?'

'I left home at five a.m. I was up already at four fifteen. Hannah also got up and we had coffee together. I then drove to Ashdod and left the car at the port, as always. As far as Hannah told me, Wednesday morning was a regular one too, no different from any other day.'

But on the morning of that Wednesday, Ofer had left for school and didn't get there, and hadn't been seen since. The father hadn't gone into the boys' room before he left. Nevertheless, he was certain they were both sleeping at the time. He hadn't heard any sound coming from their room.

Avraham tried to remember if he had asked all he wanted to. 'While you were out Tuesday evening, could Ofer have taken any money or a credit card from somewhere in the house without you noticing?' he asked. 'Maybe from a drawer in which you hide some cash?'

'I don't hide any,' the father replied. 'There's always some cash in the inner pocket of a jacket in my closet, and Ofer knows where it is. When I'm away, he and Hannah take money from there. He doesn't have a credit card. And he didn't take anything. It was one of the first things I asked Hannah to check.'

Avraham remembered she had told him.

'And you haven't noticed anything missing from the apartment since your return, right? Something he may have taken with him?'

The pages in front of him were filling up with his handwritten notes – diagonal lines of text in blue ink. This time, however, his fingers were clean. He said, 'Is there anything you'd like to tell me that I haven't asked about?' and the father shook his head to say no.

He hadn't dared to with the mother, but he felt that Rafael Sharabi was up to it, and so he said, 'Tell me, what's your gut feeling? Where do you think Ofer might be? What could have happened to him? Try to imagine where he might be right now.'

The father's response was unexpected. 'I have no idea,' he said. 'I'm angry with him. Do you have any idea what I'd give to know? I told Hannah I thought he decided to run away for a few days. Just to scare us. Maybe we did something to him, hurt him in some way. But I am also angry about what he is putting us through, Hannah in particular. She doesn't believe me. She thinks something has happened to him.'

Avraham hadn't expected the father to speak of anger. Maybe it was his way to avoid contemplating the worst, a way to imagine seeing his son again and talking to him as before. Had this anger ever turned into violence? he wondered. Had he ever hit Ofer? Avraham's eyes were once again drawn to the father's large hands.

'How is your wife doing?' he asked, and Rafael Sharabi said, 'She has dreams, nightmares. And she had to cope alone until yesterday. She's barely sleeping.'

Ilana had been briefed about Shrapstein's 'interesting direction' and thought it was a good idea to bring the suspect in for questioning.

'What suspect? Who thinks he's a suspect?' Avraham tried to remain calm.

'We do,' she replied. 'Bring him in. Let's rule out any possibility we can.'

Neither his conversation with Rafael Sharabi nor the picture that was emerging made any impression on her. She was more taken by Shrapstein's arbitrary shift in action. Avraham knocked on his door, but there was no answer. He then called him on his cell phone and asked if he could return to the station to handle the Ze'ev Avni interview for him. Shrapstein refused. His inquiries were progressing and he had received important information from the parole officer about the suspect who lived in the neighborhood. Apparently he hadn't been in touch with her the previous week, contrary to what was required of him.

Avraham had no choice but to wait in his office for Ze'ev Avni.

Perhaps Ilana was right. Despite the open talk he had with the father and the filling-in of some details, he still didn't have a clear notion of the nature of the relationship between Rafael Sharabi and his son – aside from the absences. When he had asked him if he knew who Ofer's friends were, the father had shrugged his shoulders and replied, 'I don't think he has many friends. Don't know.' Apart from pointing out the fact that Ofer had taught him how to use the Internet, there was nothing in his words that spoke of closeness, only of responsibility and duties and mutual assistance. The mother looked after the daughter, and the father, when he was home, helped with the younger son, taking him to kindergarten in the morning and bathing him in the evening. But what about Ofer?

Avraham stared at the walls of his office, with neither a window nor a picture, and thought about Igor Kintiev, who was waiting in a detention cell for his indictment. Suddenly he wanted so much to fly to Brussels. A plane took off from Ben-Gurion Airport and turned westward, flying over the sea, where tiny cargo ships sailed.

Only a few more days – unless something unexpected happened, and unless he canceled the trip at the last minute. What was he going to do for a week in the company of Jean-Marc Karot?

The crazy Belgian police officer who would be hosting him in Brussels had stepped out into the arrivals hall at Ben-Gurion Airport dressed in a black suit and tie. He looked thirty years old, maybe a little younger. He was as tall as a basketball player and as elegant as a movie star. And Avraham stood there like an idiot, carrying a sign that read 'Jean-Marc Karot' and dressed in a formal police uniform. It was back in late March, in the afternoon, and the weather was mild.

'Excellent! So let's drop off my suitcases and go out and find some hookers' were the first words out of the Belgian's mouth after Avraham had told him that he would take him to his hotel in Tel Aviv and that the exchange program didn't start until the next day. Avraham was sure he was joking. He subsequently learned that that was the entirety of what Jean-Marc Karot planned to do in Israel. He was married and had two children. Advanced training courses and police exchange programs were of zero interest to him, and he even hinted to his host that he was welcome to join him in a threesome.

Avraham remembered he hadn't checked to see if his passport was still valid. If it had expired, he'd have to cancel the trip.

There was a knock at the door.

# 8

It was his first time inside a police station.

He had of course seen the precinct house from the outside a number of times; to him, the gray building – short and flat-topped, compressed, as if someone had squashed it – had always represented everything ugly about Holon. From afar, it looked like a handful of trailers that had been joined together in a sandy wasteland. Not an ounce of splendor – a building typical of a city whose inhabitants expect nothing from life other than basic survival. Perhaps because he had never lived among them, Michael Rosin had described them as simple people who led simple lives, Ze'ev thought.

A few years ago, Ze'ev had almost gone to the Tel Aviv central station to file a complaint about a bicycle that had been stolen from a shed in the yard, but was persuaded that the cops wouldn't do anything about it. This time he had been called in. He opened the glass door. To his left, behind a counter, stood a uniformed policewoman. She was eating a rice cracker. The place looked more dingy and grimy than a branch of the Unemployment Services.

He was tense but felt no fear. Had he been called into the police the morning of the day before, he wouldn't have been able to handle it. The time that had since passed had left him stronger. The fear had disappeared by the evening, after the writing workshop and the conversation with Michael Rosin. He had felt liberated enough to write.

'I've been called in for a meeting at five with Inspector Avraham,' Ze'ev said to the policewoman behind the counter. 'Can you tell me where his office is?' and the policewoman asked, 'Is he expecting you?' as if his first remark hadn't implied exactly that.

The police had a single advantage over him: he wasn't aware of exactly what they knew. He was almost certain they knew nothing about the phone call, despite his slip of the tongue on the dunes. Had they known, they would have picked him up immediately. They certainly didn't know about the letter. When he left for the station, the letter was still in the Sharabi family mailbox – despite having been there for more than half the day already, plus the fact that Ofer's father had passed by the mailbox at least twice – the night before, when, standing at the balcony window, Ze'ev had seen him returning home; and in the morning too, because they had met by chance in the stairwell.

There had been something ironic about their encounter. They had gone down the stairs together and had spoken about the searches for Ofer, and because their conversation had gone on until they were outside the building, Ofer's father hadn't had a chance to notice the envelope. When Ze'ev returned later from school in the afternoon, the letter was still there. *I could simply take it out*, flashed through his mind.

Inspector Avraham was waiting for him in a small, dimly lit room in which there was little space for anything other than the desk and the pair of chairs on either side of it. Avraham was in uniform, and didn't get up to shake his hand.

'Is this an interrogation room?' Ze'ev asked as he sat down, and Avraham said, 'It's my office.'

Ze'ev's advantage was that he had spent the past few days thinking endlessly about the police. He had been observing them at work since Thursday, first from the window of his living-room balcony, and then at the search site. He had been preparing for the meeting with Avraham ever since his promise to return to their apartment. He had thought about Inspector Avraham far more than Inspector Avraham had thought about him – of that he was absolutely certain. He handed over his ID card, at Avraham's request, and reminded him that the address had yet to be updated. 'But I'm sure you remember the correct address,' he said and smiled, not entirely sure that the police inspector had understood the remark.

This was their fourth encounter. The first was on Thursday, at the apartment. Avraham had chosen to ignore him and had spoken to Michal in the kitchen. A rank-and-file policewoman was sent to deal with him. He and the inspector had exchanged a few words at the door. On Friday, they had ignored each other on the stairs. And they had met on Saturday too, at the search site, where Avraham was in charge. During all their previous meetings, Ze'ev had tried to attract Avraham's attention, without much success. This time, things were different, although the initial questions he faced were formal and dry, and Avraham did appear somewhat switched off. He was asked how long he and his wife had been living in the building, but wasn't asked where they had lived before then. He was asked about his job and its location, but Avraham stopped him in midsentence.

'What was the nature of your relationship with the missing boy?' Avraham asked, and Ze'ev said, 'I was his private tutor. That's why I'm here, right?'

'You're here because you asked to be here,' Avraham said. 'You said you had information for us regarding the investigation. I'm all ears.'

Michal's text message, which had come through during the break between the second and third classes, had alarmed him for a moment. She had told him that Inspector Avraham from the police was looking for him and wanted to arrange a meeting. She had sent him a number to call. He called during the next break but Avraham wasn't available. When he tried again later that afternoon, from outside the schoolyard, Avraham invited him to the station for what he termed 'further questioning.' Now he was being told outright that he had been called in only because he had asked to be. There appeared to be no reason for any uneasiness regarding his slip of the tongue at the search site – unless it was all an interrogation ploy.

'Not exactly information,' Ze'ev said. 'I simply wanted to tell you a little about Ofer, to give you a better picture of who he is. Maybe it will help your investigation. I'm sure you've spoken to his teachers at school, but I had a very special insight into Ofer's life. I tutored him privately, in his room, and I am also familiar with the entire context, his parents, the home environment. That's a big advantage – in my opinion, at least.'

Avraham asked how he had come to be Ofer's tutor, and he duly described the circumstances, all the while getting the impression that his words were sparking some interest in the policeman. At this stage in their conversation, he was still unable to read and correctly interpret the facial expressions of the inspector, who glanced from time to time at the modest digital watch on his right wrist. Ze'ev wanted to ask him why his parents had named him Avraham; after all, they must have known that his double-barreled name was likely to attract a degree of ridicule – particularly at a young age, from among the other children. He would have gladly asked him, too, about his decision to become a policeman and what he had studied at university. Had he always known that this was what he wanted to do?

Ofer's parents had learned that Ze'ev was an English teacher at a Tel Aviv high school. His wife had probably told them. Ofer's mother had knocked on the door to their apartment one evening, without Ofer, and had asked Ze'ev if he'd be willing to tutor him. It was a few weeks into the school year – still September, probably. The students in Ofer's class had been divided into groups based on their competency in English, and Ofer had been placed in the bottom group. His parents wanted him to aim higher. His mother, Hannah, appeared particularly concerned with the matter. He hadn't been sure about it. He had no experience in private tutoring. He had consented in the end because they were neighbors, but primarily because he had been drawn to Ofer's shyness. He had of course seen him in and around the building. He had offered to begin and see how things went.

'Lessons in return for payment?' Avraham asked, and Ze'ev said, 'Certainly, although I know I didn't do it for the money. I asked for ninety shekels per hour, a lot less than the going rate. Put it this way, the lessons didn't make me a wealthy man. I did it for Ofer.'

Avraham remained silent, perhaps waiting for Ze'ev to elaborate. 'Everything's been reported to the Tax Authority,' he added and smiled.

'How many times a week did you tutor him?'

'Once a week – and sometimes twice before exams. In the

beginning, we worked on grammar. They put an emphasis on grammar at his school – which is obviously wrongheaded. That's not the way to teach children a language, and that's not the way I teach students at my school, in Tel Aviv. But Ofer was a fast learner. He was very organized and systematic in his studies and progressed well, so we could move on to other things – vocabulary, conversational English, reading and writing. Those are the important things, as far as I'm concerned, and he struggled more with them. Would you like me to try to explain to you why I was drawn to Ofer?'

'Yes. Please,' Avraham replied. 'But just remind me first: I believe you told the policewoman who interviewed you that the lessons took place at their home, in his room, right?'

The question puzzled Ze'ev. 'Yes, I just told you, a minute or two ago,' he said.

Avraham looked down at the sheets of paper strewn across the desk in front of him. 'True, true, you did,' he said. 'Go on.'

It was the moment Ze'ev had been waiting for, the moment to begin his statement. He was ready with its prepared and polished opening lines. They had coalesced in his mind already on Friday, when he thought that his talk with Avraham would take place on Saturday, at the site of the search he had initiated, almost solely for his own purposes. Ahead of their current meeting at the station, he had repeated them to himself.

'I've been teaching students of Ofer's age – eleventh- and twelfth-graders – at Ironi High School in Tel Aviv for five years,' Ze'ev began. 'I don't know if you're familiar with this school; many of its students were born with silver spoons in their mouths – children of actors and singers and playwrights and journalists. It's right in the center of Tel Aviv, next to the Cinematheque, if you know where that is. The school offers studies in film, theater, and dance, and most of these kids, not all of them, are kids who are sure that the world belongs to them. They know English – and not only English – far better than their teachers, or so they think. At fourteen they are already movie directors. Little Spielbergs. Some are poets and writers; they form rock bands and work on albums. They derive their confidence not from themselves but from their environment, from their parents, from society, which tells them they can do anything and everything, that they excel at everything. I'm not saying it's a bad thing, although it may sound like it. I'm simply stating the facts. Ofer comes from a different place and was a different child. Do you understand what I'm trying to say? Just to look at him for a second was enough to tell you that this was a boy who didn't believe in himself, who felt he was worthless. But he was sensitive; he had the vulnerable soul of an artist.'

Avraham was becoming more and more drawn in by his words – just as he knew he would be.

'What do you mean by "vulnerable"?' the police inspector asked, and Ze'ev continued: 'Every word I said to him had an immediate effect on him from within,' he said. 'If I had a good word for him, praised him for something he wrote or a grammar exercise he solved correctly, he would glow from within. He didn't show much on the outside. And the opposite too: if he made a mistake, or if I criticized something he wrote or said, he'd be devastated inside. I have to stress that it wasn't anger toward me or an inability to take criticism that would do it. He'd break down inside, purely out of anger at himself. It was like every simple mistake had the potential to overwhelm him with a deep sense of failure and incompetence. And you must understand, it has nothing to do with his true capabilities. It stems from the place he comes from. I like to call it the "social place."'

Avraham listened without making notes – a sign, as Ze'ev knew from experience, that he had finally captured his interest. When students put down their pens and lift their heads from their notebooks, you know they're listening. 'Aren't all kids like that?' he asked, and Ze'ev had a broad smile on his face when he said, 'You don't have children, do you?'

Avraham shook his head to confirm.

He took a liking to the police inspector the moment he saw him from the balcony window, on Thursday afternoon, restlessly scurrying around the building. And Ze'ev knew he'd be able to capture his attention even when Avraham had initially ignored him. In the movies they say, 'They could have been good friends had they met under different circumstances.' In their case, however, it was the opposite. Had they met under different circumstances, Ze'ev probably wouldn't have taken any interest in Avraham at all. They were unlikely to have much to talk about. The current circumstances alone had brought them together and were allowing them to speak like this to each other.

'Not all children,' Ze'ev said. 'It's because of misconceptions like that that I believe policemen – and not only policemen, teachers too, by the way – should be trained in psychology. With most of the children at the school where I teach, compliments are taken for granted – because they're so sure they're the best. Criticize them, and they simply think that you, and not they, are mistaken. To them, it's crystal clear that you're wrong. They just never make mistakes.'

*

Ze'ev was unaware of just how much time had passed – an hour, maybe two. Avraham appeared at ease. He was no longer glancing at his watch and seemed to be thirstily drinking in his words. And the more Ze'ev spoke, the more he felt that his observations were becoming even sharper and more profound than he had initially believed. From time to time, Avraham would jot down a few words on the page in front of him, and Ze'ev suddenly wanted to talk about how all of this was linked with the act of writing. Another letter was formulating in his thoughts. He wanted to write it later that evening.

A few weeks into the private lessons, it dawned on Ze'ev that he wanted to help Ofer with not only his English studies. He wanted to get close to him and help him open up. And Ofer had felt it. To enrich his vocabulary, and primarily in an effort to expose him to different experiences, other than those with which he was familiar at home, Ze'ev suggested that he watch movies and high-quality English-language television shows without subtitles. He lent him a DVD with episodes from the first season of *House*, as well as a Martin Scorsese box set, which included *Taxi Driver*, *Raging Bull*, and *Casino*. Within a week, Ofer had watched them all. During their lessons, he tried to encourage a discussion of the films, in English of course. Ofer was restrained, embarrassed – not because of his English, but because no one had ever asked him his opinion of a movie. Ze'ev subsequently lent him a box set of Alfred Hitchcock films. 'It may sound pretentious,' he said, 'but I honestly believe Ofer discovered the world of movies thanks to me.'

'What do you mean by that?' Avraham quickly responded. 'Do you think he had a special interest in movies?'

He appeared on edge.

'Yes, if you were to ask me, I'd say Ofer would like to try

his hand at acting. In one of our last lessons, we read through a text they had received at school, a passage related to the theater, and we spoke about drama school, acting classes – things that were so far removed from his world, he didn't even know they existed. For him, actors and artists were a different species of people, who were born that way, and there was no chance for him. Do you know that he asked me if one studied acting at university? I tried to find out if he was interested in studying drama – this was all in English, of course – and he said no, and then possibly yes, that he wasn't sure if it suited him. I explained to him that he needn't wait until university, that there were youth drama classes he could attend, probably even in Holon, and maybe even at his school. I thought of speaking to his parents about it, but decided against it; it should come from him. Besides, I don't think they'd let him, anyway.'

'Why? Do you think they were strict with him?'

'No, don't get me wrong, I think they are good people – both of them. The mother is a quiet, intelligent woman who knows exactly what she wants; and the father, too. He comes across as a simple and decent working man. But they weren't aware of this side of Ofer. They never nurtured it – not, in my opinion, out of meanness, it's simply not a part of their world. It took an outsider to notice that Ofer is a different kind of child, with a different soul, the soul of an artist – like I told you before – and to give him a push in the right direction.'

'What was your impression of the home when you were there, of his relationship with his parents?' Inspector Avraham asked. 'Do you think Ofer bore any resentment toward them?'

'No, no, you're missing the point here completely,' Ze'ev replied. 'I think it's a great home. Warm and everything. You probably know that Ofer has a severely mentally disabled sister, and they care for her lovingly – Ofer too. Perhaps they devoted more time to the sister, because of her condition, but that's not the issue. I'm simply saying they weren't able to see that side of Ofer because it's beyond their scope. There are things that certain parents aren't able to give their children, things that someone from the outside has to step in and give.'

'So you don't think they placed too much on Ofer's shoulders because of the father's absences and the condition of the sister?'

Why wouldn't he drop that subject? Ze'ev wondered. And he wasn't sure, either, what Avraham had meant about the father's absences. 'Maybe,' he said. 'But why do you ask? Do you think Ofer has disappeared because things were hard for him at home? I don't think that's the issue here at all. Listen, let me try to clarify my observation for you. The point is not that they treated him badly, but that they weren't able to see that he's not like them. There's a difference. They couldn't see what I saw, which is why I thought it was a shame that we stopped the lessons.'

'Why did you stop? After how long?'

'It's quite ironic. I think they were stopped because they helped. Ofer's grades improved and the school was thinking about bumping him up to a higher group. If you ask me, the lessons were stopped because the parents were unable to cope with the effect they had on Ofer. They told me they were looking for a math tutor in place of the English. I said I was willing to continue for nothing, but they wouldn't have it. They just wouldn't hear of it.'

'And did Ofer want to continue?'

'Of course he did.'

'Did he actually say so?'

'He wouldn't have dared to say anything to contradict his parents.'

'And when the lessons stopped, did your relationship end as well? Did you still see him?'

'Of course I saw him. In the building, obviously, from time to time. I'd ask how he was doing and progressing, and invited him over to borrow more movies. I was under the impression he was avoiding me because he felt bad about the lessons ending. He seemed embarrassed about it, guilty toward me. He shouldn't have.'

Ze'ev was exhausted. When he got home he realized that his talk with Avraham had gone on for more than two hours. Michal was waiting for him to bathe Elie. They had already eaten supper. She asked him how it went, and he said okay. He lay back on the sofa in the living room and she placed Elie in his arms while she went to fill up the blue tub. Elie was clutching an old pair of broken sunglasses and trying to put them on his father's head. Despite his weariness, Ze'ev was happy to have his son in his arms and looked forward to spending the morning with him the next day. He had missed his son's sparkling eyes and sense of humor.

'But what did you say there?' Michal shouted out to him from the bathroom, although she knew how much he hated conversations that were yelled from one room to another.

'The same I said to you,' Ze'ev said. 'I told him about Ofer. Though I don't know how much help it will be to the investigation.'

His exhaustion and confusion, in fact, were the result of the end of his meeting with Avraham – as well as what had happened to him on the way home. He had said what he came to say, but Avraham had continued to ask questions. And as Ze'ev's responses had shortened, so had Avraham's questions. They had moved on to the routine line.

'Did Ofer ever tell you anything that could imply he may be caught up in something criminal or about plans to run away from home?'

'Did you notice anything unusual about Ofer's behavior in the days leading up to his disappearance?'

'Did he ever talk to you about his friends?'

Ze'ev responded tersely and in the negative; he had already answered all these questions on Thursday.

Avraham glanced through the notes strewn out on the desk in front of him. 'In the initial interview we conducted at your apartment, your wife said . . . Let's see here . . . She said she had heard an argument or fight taking place in the Sharabis' apartment, and that she believed it was the evening before Ofer's disappearance. Do you remember any such incident?'

What incident? She had probably heard noises from the television.

'Do you hear everything that goes on upstairs?' Avraham asked.

'Generally, no. You hear things as you would in any apartment building. But, like I told the policewoman who interviewed me, we're probably the ones who make the most noise in the building.'

Avraham asked if he had anything else to add, and Ze'ev shook his head. And then he asked him to say what he thought had happened to Ofer. 'Tell me what your gut feeling is,' Avraham said. 'Try to imagine where he is at this very moment, right now.'

Ze'ev was at a loss for words. Had he been asked the same question at the start of the interview, he would have been better equipped to think of a possible scenario. 'Imagine?' he asked. 'How can I imagine where he might be? I only hope nothing has happened to him, that he's in a safe place.'

Ze'ev was about to stand up to leave. 'May I?' he asked, pointing to his ID card, which still lay on the table, but Avraham had more questions. 'When you gave him the lessons, were his parents always home?' he asked. 'What time were the lessons?'

'How should I remember?' Ze'ev replied. 'I think Hannah was usually home.'

'Do you recall what time the lessons were?'

'It varied. Usually around five or six.'

'Did you ever arrange to meet somewhere else – somewhere other than in the building, I mean?'

The allusion stunned him. 'No. Why would we meet elsewhere? Am I suspected of anything?' he asked, and Avraham said, 'God forbid. I'm simply trying to find out if you ever ran into him elsewhere. I'm an investigator. That's my job.'

On his way home Ze'ev considered whether he should remove the letter from the mailbox. Avraham's final questions were echoing in his mind, leaving him with a dull sense of fear.

The letter wasn't there.

He turned on the light in the stairwell and looked for the brown envelope in the small plastic trash can in the foyer of the building. He then looked around again near the mailboxes.

Ze'ev didn't write another letter that night. He was dead tired and got into bed early – but didn't fall asleep. He lay on his back and looked up at the ceiling. He recalled the scent of Michael Rosin's skin and his long legs, and regretted not taking Kafka's *Letter to His Father* out of the library. Michal was hanging up the washing, and when she came into the bedroom, he closed his eyes and pretended he was asleep. She read in bed – a novel by Haruki Murakami. And at that moment, someone in the apartment above – just ten or twelve feet above his head – was reading his letter. The mother perhaps? Or the father?

He had been trying since yesterday to imagine their response. They were his first readers. Did they read the letter together or separately? And how did they react? He wished he could have watched their faces as they read. Still pretending to sleep, he turned his back toward Michal, who also had her back to him. She was close to him, yet knew nothing. He regretted that.

As always, his sleep was brief and dreamless.

He woke in the early hours of the morning and hurried to the balcony in his underwear, without first brushing his teeth or making a cup of tea. The darkness outside was turning blue and the street was silent as he wrote his second letter.

Avraham sat in his office at the station. The day had finally come to an end.

He was sure that now, after five days of investigation, something was finally moving – out in the world, and inside him too. It was almost 8:00 p.m. and he was hungry and thirsty. He made note of a number of additional questions he wanted to ask Rafael and Hannah Sharabi. He'd certainly ask them about Ze'ev Avni, about the private lessons, and why they decided to stop them. He needed to get a grip on their opinion of Avni and know what Ofer thought of him. His interview with Avni had left him feeling uneasy.

During his talk with the teacher, Ma'alul had stopped by the station to drop off transcripts of the interviews he had conducted that morning with Ofer's schoolmates and the girl he was supposed to take out. Avraham glanced over them. He was familiar with Ma'alul's meticulousness. The veteran investigator had written down every question he had asked and every answer. That he probably documented his arguments with his wife in the same way was the joke around the station.

The girl didn't know much. Ofer hadn't canceled their Friday-evening date, and she had heard about his disappearance from her friend, the sister of Ofer's classmate.

Shrapstein had left a text message on his cell phone informing him that he was 'heading home,' that his line of inquiry was getting hot, and that he planned to bring in the suspect for questioning the following day. 'I'm convinced we're onto something,' he had written. 'My instinct tells me.'

Avraham, too, should have been 'heading home.' But nothing awaited him there. Channel 3 would be airing an episode of *Law & Order* that he had seen at least five times, and he had already picked out all the mistakes the detectives made in their investigation. For no real reason, he reread the second page of the transcript from Ma'alul's pointless talk with Lital Aharon, the tenth-grade student from Kiryat Sharet High School.

> *Question: How many times did you speak to each other?*
> *Answer: Twice, I think.*
> *Question: When?*
> *Answer: Don't know – maybe on Thursday and on*
>     *Tuesday. No, on Monday.*
> *Question: So, on Thursday a week-and-a-half ago?*
> *Answer: Not last Thursday, the one before.*
> *Question: Did Ofer call you?*

*Answer: Yes.*

*Question: Both times?*

*Answer: Yes.*

*Question: And what did you talk about?*

*Answer: He asked if I wanted to go with him to a movie on Friday.*

*Question: This was the first conversation, right?*

*Answer: Yes.*

*Question: What time did he call?*

*Answer: How should I know? In the evening, I guess.*

*Question: And what did you say?*

*Answer: I said sure, but that I had a family dinner so I couldn't go then.*

*Question: And?*

*Answer: He said no problem, maybe another time. I thought he thought I was lying, so I said I could go on Saturday. But then I remembered that I couldn't on Saturday either.*

*Question: So how did you make plans for the following Friday?*

*Answer: I said what about next Friday, and he said okay.*

*Question: If I understand you correctly, he may have thought you were trying to reject him. Do you think he was sure you were going out?*

*Answer: Yes, that's why he called on Monday. We said we'd go see* Twilight, *and he called to say he thought that by Friday it wouldn't be playing at the cinema nearby so we should choose another movie or go see it at another mall. It was sweet that he called just for that. Like he was thinking about it. We agreed he'd call on Thursday and we'd decide then.*

*Question: Did he call from home?*

*Answer: How am I supposed to know? I think so. Maybe. I still have the number in my phone. Maybe it also says what time it was.*

*Question: Okay, please check.*

*Answer: —*

*Question: In any of your conversations did Ofer say anything that may have sounded like he was distressed or in danger?*

*Answer: No.*

*Question: Are you sure? Try to remember. Maybe he said something that made you think he's afraid of something.*

*Answer: Why would he say anything like that? We barely knew each other.*

*Question: That's not the point. Just try to remember. Maybe Ofer said he wasn't sure if he would make it on Friday, that something might come up that would force him to cancel?*

*Answer: No.*

*Question: Do you have a boyfriend?*

*Answer: You think I'd be going out with someone else if I had a boyfriend?*

*Question: Did you have a boyfriend?*

*Answer: Like a steady boyfriend?*

*Question: A boyfriend; a young man you go out with.*

*Answer: No.*

*Question: How old are you?*

*Answer: Fifteen and two months.*

*Question: Why did you ask your friends to give your number to Ofer?*

*Answer: What? I didn't ask them. I said he was cute and
that I'd go out with him. Yaniv said he'd give him my
number, and I said I didn't care.*

*Question: Why did you like him?*

*Answer: What do you mean?*

*Question: Why him out of everyone else? Why did you ask
them to give him your number?*

*Answer: How should I know? And I told you, I didn't ask
them to. He seemed cute. He was quiet. I thought I
wouldn't mind getting to know him and maybe go out
with him, but it didn't mean anything.*


Avraham put down the papers. He admired Ma'alul's pur-
poseful style of investigation.

At this point, no other investigation existed, only the
search for Ofer.

And it meant a lot.

He already knew what he'd pick up from the grocery store
on the way home and what he'd have for supper. He switched
the computer to standby mode, turned off the light in the
office, and left.

# PART TWO

# 9

What am I doing in Brussels?

The question played on his mind all week, from Sunday through to Saturday – well, until Friday evening, at least, when the despair lifted and the days that passed took on a different hue.

Avraham walked out of the terminal into the arrivals hall at Brussels Airport on Sunday afternoon.

Jean-Marc Karot was the type of person one notices on first glance; not noticing him meant he wasn't there. Neither was there anyone holding up a sign reading 'Avraham Avraham' or 'Abraham Abraham,' or even 'Brussels Police.' He waited.

Fortunately, he had prepared a folder containing the confirmation of his hotel reservation. The cab ride took less than half an hour and cost fifty-five euros – five euros more than the per diem allowance he had received in an envelope from the Manpower Division and from which he had hoped to save.

A message from Jean-Marc was waiting for him when he arrived at the Espagne Hotel: 'Sorry for not coming to the airport. Contact me urgently.' He called from room 307. The Belgian policeman answered in French, and sounded agitated. The shouting and police sirens in the background made it sound like he was at the scene of a terror attack or caught up in a revolution.

He had arrived on the worst day possible. Earlier that afternoon, two cyclists had discovered the body of Johanna Getz, a twenty-five-year-old landscape architect, in a potato field on the outskirt of Brussels. She had disappeared exactly a week earlier, and the police had been searching for her ever since.

Avraham felt a chill run through him.

But the circumstances were entirely different. It was clear from the moment Johanna Getz's partner, a graphic designer in his late twenties, reported her missing that she had fallen victim to a serious crime. She had returned on Sunday evening to the apartment she shared with her partner and another roommate in the north of Brussels, and, based on the evidence at the scene, had been forcibly abducted shortly thereafter. Her wallet and purse were found on the table in the kitchen; a dried-out pizza she had been warming up was still in the oven. The Belgian press gave the story extensive coverage. Some newspapers implied that it would be preferable for young women not to walk the streets alone at night, or even remain at home alone, until the mystery of Johanna's disappearance was resolved. Now, with her body found, and with the media in the dark, the fear had mounted – and with it, the pressure on the police.

Avraham turned on the small television set in his room. One of the six stations he could get clearly was showing what appeared to be a report from the field where the body had been found. He couldn't spot Jean-Marc among the numerous policemen who were on the scene, all wearing gloves and special plastic shoe coverings, but assumed he was there, as he had told him. The entire police exchange program appeared to be an exercise in futility, he thought, unless they gave him a full-time interpreter.

The rain caught him only two minutes after he had been out on the street. Dressed in a pair of jeans and a short-sleeved shirt, he was walking down a long, dimly lit street that appeared to lead to nowhere, and the name of which was nowhere to be seen. Brussels was shrouded in darkness, and all the stores were shuttered. Instead of at a local bistro, he opted to have supper at a Subway, where he also took cover from the driving rain. Low-calorie bread, ham, mayonnaise, and a touch of mustard. There was a women's basketball game on the television, on Eurosport 2 – a team from Kaunas against one from Prague. It was exactly 9:00 p.m. when he returned to his small room at the Espagne. His parents had called his cell phone every ten minutes, despite his warning that the calls were expensive. His father wanted to make sure he had arrived safely – as if he would not have heard on the news had the plane crashed or had he been abducted somewhere between Tel Aviv and Brussels. 'I saw on the Internet that it's raining in Brussels,' he said.

Any hope of progress in the investigation that had been awakened in Avraham died out during the days leading up to his trip. It was a slow death, accompanied by spasms and convulsions. Shrapstein's line of inquiry, which had momentarily gripped the interest of the entire team – even Avraham's – turned out to be a dead end. The parolee was called in for questioning, denied any involvement, and claimed he had been in Jerusalem the week Ofer disappeared. His statement checked out. Shrapstein bid a sad farewell to the suspect at the entrance to the station, promising him they would surely meet again, before renewing his search for other known criminals in the area.

Avraham interviewed Rafael and Hannah Sharabi twice more – once together, and then separately. He went back to the fight, or argument, that might have taken place between them, or between the two of them and Ofer, on Tuesday night. They insisted that there had been no fight. He also questioned other neighbors who might have heard the argument, but the ones from the apartment opposite the Sharabi home on the third floor had been at a bar mitzvah that evening.

He also returned to the subject of Ze'ev Avni. Both Rafael and Hannah Sharabi told him they had stopped the private lessons at Ofer's request. He felt he had improved sufficiently and wanted to work on his math. The parents liked the private tutor and appreciated his dedication to their son, but Ofer had adamantly refused to continue with the lessons. Had something happened between them? Had Avni hurt Ofer in any way? Certainly not, to the best of their knowledge. Ofer had simply insisted that he no longer needed help with English and they respected his wishes.

Avraham asked Ma'alul to have an unofficial word with the principal of the school where Avni worked, and Eliyahu met with him on one of Avni's days off. He tried to ease the concerns of the principal, and stressed that the police had no information about any wrongdoing on the part of Avni toward students; but, yes, the talk might have been somewhat damaging to the teacher. It was inevitable. No complaints had been filed against Avni. Two years previously, a student had claimed that Avni had intentionally failed him in an exam, but the kid was a serial complainer. Avni had no history of disciplinary problems, despite not being well liked. 'Do I have anything to be concerned about? Do you think I should suspend him temporarily or keep an eye on him?' the principal asked. 'Not at the present time,' Ma'alul said. 'But one should always keep an eye out.'

The already meager number of calls from civilians with potential information also dwindled. On Tuesday, the Tiberias police conducted searches on the basis of reports that two youths – one matching the general description of Ofer – had been smoking hashish and were involved in a fight at one of the beaches on Lake Kinneret. On Wednesday, Ilana called him in the morning, before eight, to tell him about a youth from Holon who had gone missing during the night. It turned out to be a false alarm. The teenager in question – a punk rocker or goth – was nothing like Ofer. He was found that afternoon at the apartment of a girlfriend, high, and sleeping in the bed of the girl's parents, wearing only boxer shorts and army boots.

The days went by, and concern for Ofer's fate increased.

They had no choice now but to turn to the media. The approach was formulated a week after Ofer's disappearance. Ilana had made the decision, and Avraham spent Thursday on the telephone with television production assistants. No one was very enthusiastic about the story – because there was no story; some of them even told him so outright. One of them asked if he thought they were dealing with a kidnapping or murder, and if he planned to intimate as much in the broadcast – if not, it would be hard to get it on the air. They eventually gave him three-and-a-half minutes on the early-evening news show. The interview was recorded on Thursday but aired only on Sunday, when he was on the plane to Brussels. And all the while, the threat of having the investigation taken out of his hands hung over him like a dark cloud that would clearly rain down on him at some point.

Jean-Marc picked him up from the hotel on Monday morning in a new navy-blue Peugeot. The Belgian policeman was dressed in black trousers and a thin blue sweater and looked refreshed, as if he had slept the entire weekend. He stepped out of the car to embrace his Israeli colleague. The streets were still quite dark, and the road glistened with rain. Jean-Marc Karot drove like a man possessed.

The underground parking garage that swallowed them up was full of police vehicles.

An urgent meeting had been called for 8:30 a.m. at the Division Centrale, the main unit of the Brussels police. More than fifteen investigators and other team members were gathered around an oval-shaped table. Each was holding a steaming paper cup. Avraham sat behind them on a chair whose backrest was propped up by one of the walls of the room. His view through the window showed heavy gray skies. Maps and charts were pinned to a large display board in the corner of the room, and a laptop computer connected to a projector was screening photographs and short video clips from the potato field where the body had been found. Johanna Getz had been found fully clothed. There were bruises on her lower stomach and back; she had been strangled to death.

They took a short break an hour into the meeting.

'Well, what do you think?' Jean-Marc asked him in English, with a thick French accent, and Avraham just said, 'I didn't understand a single word.'

They decided that Avraham would wait at a café across the road from the police station while Jean-Marc looked into the possibility of getting him an interpreter, and also made inquiries as to how the exchange program would continue in light of the urgent investigation. The Brussels police force was entirely focused on that one single matter.

'You came the wrong week,' Jean-Marc observed, not for the first time.

At least the coffee at the small café was excellent. He sat at a large window overlooking the street. The Division Centrale was located in a five-story brown brick building. It was almost 10:00 a.m. and the sun had yet to show its face. The long, narrow windows of the investigators' offices, with their high ceilings, were framed with pale wood, and a warm orange light shone from the rooms. Avraham thought it was difficult to conceive that they were the rooms where investigations into murders, rapes, and drug crimes were conducted. From the outside, the building had the appearance of a university library. Through one window on the first floor he could see a chest of drawers made from antique wood on top of which rested three police hats – blue, white, and black.

Jean-Marc Karot would have preferred it had Avraham said, 'Forget the interpreter, give me the addresses of some brothels in the city and maybe we'll talk later in the week.' That's what he had done in Israel. He stopped by the station for a brief visit and accompanied Avraham on a tour of police headquarters in Tel Aviv, where he met with Ilana. Then he spent the rest of the time sunbathing at the beach, despite the fact that it was still winter, and looking for 'clean and respectable places where a man can have a good time.' After work one day, Avraham took him out to eat at a good restaurant on the Tel Aviv promenade. The guest showed no interest at all in the cases his host tried to share with him, while polishing off two bottles of white wine with his fish.

After about an hour-and-a-half at the café, Avraham's patience wore thin and he went for a walk.

The Division Centrale lay on the corner of two small,

picturesque streets, Rue du Midi and Rue du Marché au Charbon, in what appeared to Avraham to be an old part of the city. The streets in the area were narrow and well-kept, and the centuries-old buildings that rose up alongside them tilted over so that their roofs were almost touching, like treetops arching over a roadway. The stores were high-end ones: antique furniture shops, chocolatiers, and an endless number of small art galleries that displayed abstract, incomprehensible works in their pristine windows – as if the Belgians had forgotten how to paint simple works depicting dark skies or a tree or a young woman lying dead in a potato field. He was shocked to come across Homo Erectus, a gay bar and gallery, right opposite police headquarters, and was even more surprised when he realized that the narrow street led him directly to Grote Markt, the only place in Brussels he knew he had to see. The Internet sites he had browsed through ahead of his trip all said that the city's main square was a must-see attraction. Avraham couldn't understand why writer Victor Hugo had described it as 'the most beautiful square in the whole of Europe.'

And Eliyahu Ma'alul still had not called.

Ma'alul, who would make sure the case did not slip out of Avraham's control, had promised to call him every day to update him with information from their ongoing routine checks at hospitals each morning, as well as any responses to his television appearance. 'Avi, I know what you are afraid of, and you have nothing to worry about,' Ma'alul had said to him before he left for the airport. 'I'm here and I've got you covered, don't worry.'

On Tuesday and Wednesday, he continued to tag along behind Jean-Marc. Without an interpreter.

Use of civilian security cameras in Brussels had increased ever since European Union regulations came into effect and the city was flooded with large waves of immigrants from Eastern Europe and Africa. As a result, the police were in possession of images of Johanna Getz – albeit from strange angles and tinged with a greenish hue – drinking beer at a bar on Sunday evening, a few hours before she was abducted from her apartment. They also had pictures of her buying a frozen pizza, a carton of milk, and cigarettes at a supermarket on the way home. She was also caught by a camera installed on the street in which she had lived. She was tall and thin, with blond hair, and didn't appear drunk.

What's the use of it all? Avraham wondered. After all, you already know she had made it to her apartment. True, the security cameras might have captured someone following her on the way – but they hadn't. They also failed to document the moment she was taken from her apartment. Moreover, the Belgian investigators were all worked up by the fact that her body was found fully clothed, but without shoes, and that one pink sock appeared to be missing. Jean-Marc spoke to him about the missing sock as if he were a character in an Agatha Christie novel. Pictures of the other sock were aired on television. Did they think the murderer had taken a sock as a souvenir? 'We request information from the public regarding anyone who may have been spotted with the deceased's pink sock displayed in their living room!' In any event, the forensic investigators assessed that the body had been lying among the potatoes for several days. Perhaps a raccoon or a rat had pulled the sock off her cold foot? Avraham thought that it was for the best, after all, that there weren't too many detective novels in Hebrew and that Israeli police investigators didn't read the ones that did exist, the way Belgians probably did.

Meanwhile, to ease the fears of the public, the Brussels police hastily brought in two suspects for questioning – Johanna's boyfriend, who had spent the weekend of her disappearance in Antwerp; and the owner of the apartment, an eccentric sixty-two-year-old bachelor who lived on the third floor of the building. A pensioner now, he had worked previously as the principal and teacher at an elementary school. He looked like a madman in the photographs they had of him. The similar circumstances again sent a shiver through Avraham. His host didn't play a part in the interrogation of the detainees, who were questioned by the Division Centrale's two most seasoned and decorated investigators.

Jean-Marc didn't come to pick him up from the hotel on Thursday. He had been called out in the early hours of the morning to the other side of the city. He called at noon to apologize and suggest that Avraham spend the next two days in Brussels as a tourist. Compensation came in the form of an invitation to a family meal at the home of Jean-Marc's parents on Friday evening. Avraham tried to get out of it, but suddenly his host wouldn't take no for an answer. His father and brother were policemen, he said, and the conversation with them, in English, would be just like a true exchange session. He also promised to take him to the best mussels restaurant in town on Saturday, Avraham's last day in Brussels.

The girl behind the reception desk at the hotel tried to explain to Avraham – in broken English, with a Spanish accent – how to get to the center of the city. There was nothing to see around the hotel. He turned left and walked along Avenue Brugmann, which appeared to be the street he had wandered down in the dark on his first evening in the city. He passed by a Polish grocery store, a Thai laborers' eatery, a sushi bar, and a café that served a variety of dishes from the Ivory Coast – and ended up nowhere in particular. The city's main avenues eluded him, and he wasn't able to locate the palaces, pictures of which he had seen on Wikipedia, or the parks, which were supposed to be in full bloom.

Avraham's feet hurt from all the walking, and his trousers were wet. He realized, too, that for the most part he had been holding the map they had given him at the hotel upside down. The rain continued to fall, but he didn't want to waste money on a cab because he assumed he'd have to make his own way to the airport. In the afternoon he found himself at the top of a number of steep, narrow, and neglected streets and passed by several public housing projects and elderly individuals who appeared to be of Turkish origin. Without intending to, he came upon the red-light district, which, to his surprise, lay right at the feet of the shiny skyscrapers of the European Union institutions.

Reluctantly, he continued along Rue de la Prairie – as if he were Jean-Marc. In the windows, behind partially drawn curtains, sat young black women, chubby, pretty, all dressed in negligees with pink scarves around their necks. They smiled at him. A client emerged from one of the houses – a man in his sixties, unshaven, counting the money in his wallet.

Avraham stepped up his pace. He returned to what appeared to be a main street, and again found himself at a Subway sandwich shop. His phone rang. It was Ma'alul, who was calling to inform him that Ofer's bag had been found.

'We've finally got our hands on something concrete, Avi,' Ma'alul said. He sounded excited.

Ofer's black backpack had been handed in to the Tel Aviv police station by a building contractor, who had found it in a dumpster he was using for rubble from an apartment he was renovating not far from the Nokia basketball arena in the south of Tel Aviv. The contractor hated it when residents in the area used the dumpster to discard personal items, as it would then fill up too quickly, and each additional one cost him money. He'd also be slapped with a fine if he dumped waste other than construction rubble at the dump site. He had pasted a sign reading 'PRIVATE' on the dumpster, but to no avail. That morning, he had found the black backpack among the pieces of broken brick and empty cement bags. He had thought initially of throwing it into the building's trash bin, but could tell by its weight that it was full. Without thinking twice, he had opened it to find schoolbooks and folders, along with Ofer's ID card, which was in one of the inside pockets. He remembered the name and the boy's photograph from the television. Based on his statement, the bag hadn't been in the container for more than three days. It had been emptied the last time on Monday.

Avraham put down his sandwich and listened to Ma'alul.

'So someone threw the bag there this week, at some point between Monday and today,' he then said, and Ma'alul replied, 'Most likely on Monday or Tuesday. The bag's not in the best condition – very dusty and full of sand, even after the good shake it got from the contractor.'

'What an idiot,' Avraham said, adding, 'It may or may not have been Ofer who did it.'

He wanted to hold the bag. To turn it over in his hands, to open it and look inside, to take out the schoolbooks and folders one by one.

'No way was it Ofer,' Ma'alul said. 'He would walk around with the bag for two weeks without anyone seeing him and then suddenly get rid of it? He'd be walking around with his books as if he was going back to school?'

Avraham listened to Ma'alul, but his thoughts took him elsewhere. 'The bag may have been lying somewhere else for two weeks, and someone may have found it and tossed it.'

'Perhaps, but I don't think so. Would someone pick up a bag that's lying in the street only to throw it away somewhere else?'

Was Ma'alul irritated? Perhaps he had had enough of updating the head of the investigation team, who was managing things by remote control from a different continent.

'So what are you doing with the bag?' Avraham asked.

'Shrapstein has gone to book it in. We'll send it to National Headquarters, although I'm not sure what we'll get from it, from the point of view of fingerprints or other forensic tests. I haven't seen it yet.'

'Even if we get prints, they won't tell us much.'

'Why?' Ma'alul asked.

'Do you know how many prints we're going to find?' Avraham responded. 'Ofer's, his parents', his brother's and sister's perhaps, maybe even all his classmates' too. Are there any bloodstains, or anything that doesn't look like it belongs to Ofer?'

'Books, folders, an ID card, and a few sheets of paper and a pen – that's all. Oh yes, and two twenty-shekel notes and a handful of coins. No keys. No wallet. Nothing else.'

'And stains?'

'I haven't seen the bag, Avi, I told you. But I don't think so.'

'And have you called in his parents to identify the bag and its contents?'

'Sending it to forensics is more urgent. There's no doubt it's his bag. It contained his ID card, and it's exactly the bag we were looking for.'

Before leaving the station the evening Ofer's mother came to file the report, Avraham had given the duty officer a description of the bag. It had been his first course of action in the investigation. He remembered it – a black backpack with white stripes, a Nike imitation, not new. One large compartment, two side pockets, and a third at the front that closed with zippers.

Ma'alul was silent.

Avraham felt stifled by the despair of his miserable week in Brussels. He had been there for five days already, following – without understanding a word – an investigation into the murder of a young woman that had nothing to do with him. And all the while his investigation – yes, still his – was being conducted without him. And now this bag with Ofer's folders, his things, had slipped through his fingers. They had been waiting for a breakthrough like this, and he had no intention of allowing anyone else to run things.

'Have you called in the building contractor to make a statement?' Avraham asked, trying to hide the tension in his voice, and Ma'alul said, 'Yes, he should be here in an hour or so.'

'And have you brought in a forensics team to check if there is anything else in the dumpster?'

'Yes, Avi, we have.'

'Don't breathe a word about the bag to the media, okay? Ask for a gag order if you have to.'

Ma'alul didn't respond.

'What else are you doing?'

'We'll be doing a house-to-house to question the residents in the area. Perhaps someone in the street saw who threw away the bag.'

Such an operation required the recruitment of additional investigators. Ilana had been updated.

'Good idea. Are there security cameras in the area perhaps?' It was just a thought.

'Security cameras, Avi? We're talking about the southern neighborhoods, not city center.'

'Check it out. There may be traffic police cameras,' Avraham insisted.

'Okay,' Ma'alul said, sighing. 'And you cheer up there a little. You sound terrible. Try to enjoy yourself. It won't be long now. The bag has to give us a lead. We'll stick with it until we get something out of it. We're getting close.'

Getting close? He was in a Subway sandwich shop in Brussels. The closest he could get was via the telephone line in room 307 at the hotel. He assumed the bag would get to the forensics lab only later that evening and that they wouldn't get started on it right away – and might even wait until after the weekend. Was he hoping they wouldn't deal with it till Sunday, when he'd be back in Israel?

He took a cab back to the hotel, tried to get through to the office of the Forensics Department's evidence locker to ensure that the bag would find its way not only to the fingerprints lab but would also be examined for foreign fibers and polymers, both inside and out.

'What are you talking about? What bag?' grunted the desk clerk in the office.

He left her his telephone number in the room. He opened the window, lighting one cigarette with another against the hotel's policy.

Then he tried to get hold of Shrapstein, but got no response.

His cell phone rang, and he found it under his suitcase, which he had lifted onto the bed to find his notebook. Of all the people who could have called, it was Ze'ev Avni.

'I'd like to arrange another meeting with you,' the neighbor said.

Avraham explained that he wouldn't be able to see him before Sunday, perhaps even Monday. 'Do you have any additional information concerning the investigation?' he asked, and Avni said, 'Not exactly about the investigation. It's a different matter.'

'If it isn't about the investigation but is urgent, I suggest you call the station. I'm only dealing with Ofer's case.'

'I don't want to speak to anyone else – only you. And it can wait until Sunday. It isn't urgent.'

Nevertheless, Avni did sound less sure of himself than he had in the office at the station.

The phone in the hotel room rang and he ended the conversation with Avni. The desk clerk at the Forensics Department confirmed that the black bag had arrived and was properly logged in. 'But I can't promise they'll begin working on it today,' she said.

The next evening, when the Forensics Department at police headquarters in Jerusalem was already closed for Shabbat, Avraham sat down to dinner in a villa in Anderlecht, a suburb of Brussels. On one side of him sat Jean-Marc, and on the other, his host's brother, Guillaume, who was similar in appearance, but less flashy and charismatic. The two Belgian giants looked like children next to their father, a former police investigator who now served in an administrative capacity at the national police academy. He sat at the head of the table.

Jean-Marc's wife, Elise, was very beautiful. About five-feet-nine-inches tall, with long, strong arms, she wore a dress that exposed her shoulders. Her every movement was a vision to behold. She and the mother of the Karot brothers were the only ones at the table who didn't work for the police – them and the two children, of course. At least for now. Elise worked as a sales manager for Mercedes-Benz.

Marianka sat two chairs away from him, alongside Guillaume, and there was almost no interaction between her and Avraham despite the fact that both were foreigners.

Her foreignness was unmistakable.

Everyone made an effort to speak in English, but naturally drifted back to French every now and then, particularly because of the children. They spoke about Johanna Getz's murder investigation, about budget cuts in the police force, about the food in Belgium and in Israel, and about Tel Aviv.

'Jean-Marc told me that the beaches in Tel Aviv are beautiful but that he barely had a chance to enjoy them because you kept him so busy with work,' Elise said.

Smiling bashfully, Avraham confirmed.

The first course of the meal consisted of slices of smoked salmon and asparagus done in butter; duck was served as the main course. The head of the household hardly spoke, and when he did, Avraham almost choked. He asked if their guest's family was involved in the diamond and gold business like all the other Jews, in Belgium at least. The father chewed his food slowly, with his mouth closed, and sipped his beer after each mouthful.

Marianka's English was better than the others', yet she spoke very little. Most of the time she smiled, seemed tense, and was trying to pay attention to all that was said around the table, even when it got complicated because everyone was talking at the same time. When they were done with the main course, she offered Jean-Marc and Guillaume's mother help with clearing the table. She and Guillaume had been together for just three months, and it was the second time she had been invited to dinner at the family home. They were both traffic police officers. But Marianka was born in Slovenia and had moved to Belgium as a young girl. She was short, about five-two, and had a slim, boyish figure. Brown, short hair. Brown eyes. She was dressed in black jeans and a gray turtle-neck top, and from time to time, when she thought no one was looking, she would tug the collar up over her chin.

Coffee and cake were served in the living room, where Avraham was asked about his first impressions of Brussels. He had had enough wine to admit he hadn't seen much of the city and hadn't been very taken with what he had managed to see. He told them he had hoped to see more the next day, but that Jean-Marc had had to cancel the guided tour and the meal at the mussels restaurant because a development in the murder investigation required him to work on Saturday.

'So perhaps we can take you on a tour,' Marianka said, looking at Jean-Marc's brother.

Guillaume had other plans.

'Never mind,' Avraham said. 'I only have half a day anyway because I need to be at the airport in the afternoon.'

Marianka said that a lot could be seen in half a day.

She and Guillaume dropped him at his hotel.

★

The half a day in Brussels turned out to be so full that Avraham almost forgot about the investigation and Ofer and the bag that had been found in the dumpster and was waiting for someone from forensics to take the time to look it over. He even almost forgot his empty days in the city, which now seemed very different.

He had waited for Marianka at the entrance to the hotel, having checked out of his room and left his suitcase at the reception desk. It was still dark and very cold outside. She wore the same jeans as the night before, with a black turtle-neck this time, and had a striped beret resting at an angle on her head.

'How did you sleep?' she asked.

She didn't look like a policewoman at all.

They walked down Avenue Brugmann, which this time led to a large square where the city spread out before them at sunrise. Marianka maintained a ferocious pace, and he had a hard time keeping up with her.

Standing in Poeller Square and taking in the view of the rooftops and church steeples painted in blue and orange, Avraham lit a cigarette and suggested they pause there a few minutes, but Marianka said that they had to keep going because they still had lots to see.

He wasn't sure if she was enjoying this little race or simply accompanying him out of a sense of duty.

To warm up for a while, they went into a small corner café in the area of the old city near police headquarters. 'We have only fifteen minutes,' Marianka said.

Two elderly women behind a wooden counter greeted them with a *'Bonjour, les enfants,'* and Marianka kissed them both. The café's first customers of the day – elderly men, most of them with mustaches – were sitting around a few small tables. Avraham took off his coat and breathed in the aroma of the coffee. Sports journals were strewn across the tables.

The thing that subsequently surprised him after returning to Israel and recalling the morning with Marianka was that there had been no awkwardness. He asked and she told him that she had come to Brussels fourteen years ago, at the age of thirteen. This is how he learned that she was more than ten years younger than him. Her father wanted to leave Yugoslavia right after it broke up, but they were forced to wait a few years, until he found a permanent job, in Brussels. She applied for Belgian citizenship six years after arriving in the country, and her request was granted a few months later.

'Is your father a policeman too?' he asked, and she smiled and said, 'Not exactly. He's a karate instructor.'

'Seriously? A karate instructor?'

'Yes. Why not? But he's also a teacher at a theological seminary in Liège. He's a unique man. You'd enjoy talking to him.'

'Does that mean he's a priest?' Avraham asked, and Marianka laughed.

'He can't be a priest. He's married and has children. He dreamed of becoming a priest, but then he met my mother and his plans changed.'

'And do you do karate too?'

'Of course I do; he trained me throughout my childhood.'

Marianka's smile made her face take on a childlike appearance, full of joy.

'Wasn't it difficult for you when you first got here?' Avraham asked.

'No. Why should it have been difficult?'

'Because you left friends and a home behind.'

'Not at all. My home is here. We go there every few years in the summer, and all I want to do is get back to Brussels. There's nothing there for me anymore.'

He asked if she was from Ljubljana, the only Slovenian city he could think of, and she told him she was born and raised in Koper, a port city on the Adriatic Sea.

It was an omen.

'I can't believe it,' he said. 'Now I know where Koper is.'

'Why?' she asked. 'What did you lose there?'

A sixteen-year-old boy, he wanted to say.

He told her about Ofer, that he had left home one morning to go to school but hadn't arrived and since then had been declared missing. He told her about the father who had returned home from a sea voyage, and about the place-name, Koper, which the father had mentioned in their talk, and which for him was the first sign that the picture was filling out with details. Not much had happened since – until Ofer's backpack had turned up two days earlier.

The fifteen minutes that Marianka had allotted for coffee had long since passed. She ordered another for each of them and said, 'I don't think you'll find him in Koper. It doesn't get many tourists.'

'What's it like?' he asked, and she said, 'It's a pretty but provincial sort of city. I mostly remember the port from my childhood. My father and I would take the dogs there on Sunday mornings.'

Three hours later, they had seen all there was to see in Brussels – the statue of the little boy urinating on the Dutch conqueror; the Mont des Arts, with its royal palaces that had been turned into museums; the huge statues of King Albert, on horseback, and his wife, Elizabeth, the two gazing at each other for all eternity from opposite sides of the road. Marianka presented Brussels to him with pride, as if the city belonged to her – and maybe it did. Avraham constantly asked to rest. In lieu of lunch they bought Belgian waffles, which they ate while walking so as to save time. Nevertheless, time moved on and grew short. They had less than two hours left.

Marianka had planned for the tour to end in the area of Avraham's hotel. They sat together on a bench in a small inner-city square surrounded by elegant old buildings, facing a dark square-shaped structure that looked like a ship. He insisted he could go no farther. It was Marianka's church. Only then did he learn that she lived not far from his hotel, in a small apartment with a roommate, a Foreign Ministry employee.

'Do you enjoy working for the police?' he asked.

Her childlike face appeared again.

'Not really. I never thought I'd end up a policewoman.'

'So what did you think you'd be?'

'A dancer – when I was a child. And then afterward, a doctor. I ended up in the police by chance.'

'How do you join the police by chance?'

'A newspaper ad – like any other job. My father saw it, cut it out, and said it would suit me. But I'm not sure I'll stay with it for much longer.'

Guillaume's name didn't come up in their conversation at all.

'What will you do?' Avraham asked.

'I could become a sports instructor. I studied physical education. Or maybe a nun,' she said, pointing at the church.

She then told him she was doing a motorcycle training

course through the police and that if she was accepted into the traffic police's motorcycle unit she might stay on for a few more years.

'I bet you always wanted to be a policeman,' she said suddenly, and she was right.

'True. I don't remember it, but my parents have told me that when I was a child, I had a blue policeman's hat that I'd never take off. I insisted on wearing it to kindergarten. One day my mother threw it away without telling me. She was sick of it.'

'Are your parents still alive?'

'Yes.'

'What do they do?'

'Fight,' he said with a laugh. 'My father was a lawyer and my mother taught literature. They're both retired now.'

They had no choice but to get up and walk slowly in the direction of the hotel along a picturesque avenue at the entrance to which stood a statue of the Argentine writer Julio Cortázar. A young woman in spandex jogged past them with earbuds in her ears. Marianka told him that she would often sit on one of the benches along the avenue and listen to music.

'And what do you do when you're not a policeman?' she asked, and he said, 'I'm a policeman then too.'

It made her laugh.

'Even on weekends? Don't you have any hobbies? Like karate perhaps?'

'No, my hobby seems to be being a policeman. Actually, I do have a secret hobby that very few know about.'

'I promise not to tell anyone. But, wait, I want to guess. You too have a collection of antique guns.'

'No. Who has a collection of antique guns?'

'Guillaume,' she said.

'No. I like to read crime novels, when I have the time, and watch crime movies and television series and prove the detectives wrong.'

She didn't understand. No one understood.

'Prove to whom?'

'To myself. With every crime novel I read, I conduct my own investigation and prove that the detective in the book is mistaken, or else deliberately misleads the readers, and that the true solution is not the one he presents.'

He was willing to swear that this was the case with every crime novel he'd ever read.

'So give me an example,' she said.

'Which detective novels do you like?' he asked. 'Do you know Hercule Poirot, for example? Now that I think of it, he's Belgian. I read his first investigation a short while ago, Agatha Christie's first book, and discovered that he frames one of the characters who is completely innocent. It's called *The Mysterious Affair at Styles*.'

'What do you mean by "frames"?'

'Exactly that. Poirot is investigating the poisoning of a wealthy elderly woman. At the end of the book, he accuses her maidservant of the murder, but she is innocent. He's framed her, and I can prove it.'

'But why would he do that?' There was real astonishment in Marianka's eyes.

'He has any number of reasons to do that. But it's a very long story,' he replied.

He suddenly noticed a blue-white-and-red flag in the second-floor window of one of the beautiful buildings along the avenue. He approached the building and found it was the Slovenian Consulate.

'So your favorite avenue in Brussels is the one with the Slovenian Consulate, but, no, you don't miss it,' he said, and she smiled as she said, 'It has nothing to do with that. It's just a really beautiful avenue. You should see it in December, before Christmas, all lit up.'

I almost wish I could, he thought.


They waited outside the hotel for the taxi.

'We saw everything, didn't we?' he asked, and Marianka said, 'Not at all. We could have seen lots more. It's a shame you had only half a day.'

'I know,' he said. 'But thank you, anyway.'

Before he got into the taxi she gave him her card and asked him to e-mail her about how the search for Ofer turned out.

'If you find out that he's in Koper after all, I could be of help,' she said.

The taxi drove off.

Then Jean-Marc Karot called to say good-bye. 'The investigation's over,' he said.

'What investigation?'

'Johanna Getz. That's why I couldn't come to get you today. We arrested the murderer this morning.'

Were the police in Belgium so much better? How did they do it so fast?

'Who was it?' Avraham asked, and Jean-Marc said, 'A neighbor. A different neighbor – not the landlord. A psychopath who lives on the first floor.'

'Why did he do it?'

'That's still unclear. Everything's unclear. His interrogation is still going on, but it was him, we have no doubt. He didn't even resist when we knocked on his door.'

Jean-Marc again apologized for not having spent much time with him during his stay in Brussels, and on his last day in particular. 'You simply came during the wrong week,' he said.

## 10

He knew all along that Michal would find out sooner or later.

It happened on Thursday, when they were both home in the afternoon – exactly two weeks after the start of the investigation.

Ze'ev was working at his desk on the balcony. Just like on the day he had watched Avraham and his policemen through the half-open shutters. Michal was in the kitchen, feeding Elie, to the sounds of his favorite CD of children's songs, and then she laid him down in his bed for an afternoon nap.

The black notebook beckoned him, called him to open it. It was risky in the middle of the day. He reread the first three letters and the opening paragraph of the fourth he had written the night before. After her shower, Michal came over to the balcony and asked if he'd like to have some lunch with her; he said he'd make do with a sandwich at his desk because he didn't want to take a break from his work. Was he hinting at something? Was this the route he wanted their conversation to take?

He didn't feel quite ready to confess to her about joining the writing workshop, but he could not hide the birth of his writing for long. Not from Michal. She was there with him when all previous attempts had failed, when he was frustrated that he had no place and no time for writing, when he was scared that it would escape him, never to return. But what happened after he told her was inconceivable. One of the most terrible days of his life.

It was one of the very first things Ze'ev had told Michal when they first met. He was a graduate of the Hebrew University's Department of English Literature, and she had a degree in political science from Tel Aviv. Just like everyone else, they had met during their teaching diploma studies at the Kibbutzim College. Such a long time ago. They all used to ask one another if they really wanted to be schoolteachers, and everyone would say no. Except for her. She was twenty-seven at the time, and he was a year younger. Both were single, after being involved in more or less serious relationships. Ze'ev had told her that he wrote, or rather that he wanted to write, and Michal hadn't asked what, only said that it was wonderful, and that she hoped to read his stories one day. He was not sure then whether she was implying a long-term relationship or was simply expressing a general confidence in his ability to write and be published.

As Michal approached, he closed the notebook. She ran her fingers through his hair above his neck. He didn't turn around.

'Is there something you want to tell me?' she asked, and he said, 'No. Why?'

'I think there is. You've been working on something for a while now. Did you think I hadn't noticed?'

If he had responded to her question, his answer would have been a profoundly complex one. He thought she both noticed and didn't notice. He hoped she noticed, and hoped she didn't notice too. They once agreed that she would never ask if he was working on anything because it only rubbed salt in his wounds. Now, however, he could respond differently.

'It's very preliminary,' he said. 'I'm not sure if I can talk about it yet.'

He was excited; she could feel it, and she was affected by it. 'Just a moment,' she said. 'Let me make myself a cup of coffee before you tell me. Should I get you one too?'

While Michal was in the kitchen, he decided to tell her everything. His desire overpowered his fear.

'Now I'm ready,' she said in a celebratory tone as she returned to the balcony. She sat down on the brown armchair and placed her mug on the wicker coffee table.

He turned in his chair to face her.

'Okay,' he said. 'So, I've been going to this writing workshop for the past few weeks.'

She didn't appear shocked or uncomfortable.

'I hadn't planned on going, and I'm sorry I never told you about it. It all happened by chance. I was passing by the central library in Tel Aviv and saw this sign and went in to see what it was like. I hadn't planned on staying. The instructor is Michael Rosin, if you know the name. He's a young writer, quite well-known. And we've become friends. He was the main reason I stayed. I'm sorry I haven't told you until now.'

'Wait a minute – when did this all happen? How come I didn't know until now?' She really seemed happy.

'When I told you I was going to work at the library – on Sunday afternoons. That's where the workshop is. It wasn't really a lie.'

'Do you think I care? The main thing is that you are finally doing it. Is it helping? Do you feel something will come out of your being there?'

She could have reminded him of how he always put down writing workshops every time she had suggested he join one to get past his writer's block. She didn't.

'Yes. I know for sure something good is happening,' he said.

Michal was the only person who truly believed in him – even during the weeks or months when he stopped believing in himself, when out of sheer frustration and despair he ceased to dream of the moment he would read her a story he had written, a finished story, and watch her be swept up by its magic. Now he could do it, but he didn't know if this was a good place to start. The things he had written were hard to swallow, and Michal might struggle to read them.

The second letter contained Ofer's most piercing lines – in Ze'ev's eyes, at least. It was written after the long conversation with Avraham, in the office, and inspired by the insights born there. Ofer analyzed his parents' fear of him, of his otherness. He tried to explain the root of it, to himself and to them. The letter ended with the harsh sentence: '*For years, you tried to starve me, to deny me what I needed; you wanted to crush me so that my life would be no better than yours, so that the wretchedness of your lives would not be reflected, like by a distorted mirror, in mine.*' He had again signed the letter: '*No longer yours. Ofer.*' And underneath, he had written, '*To be continued?*'

In its style, the second letter was more sophisticated than the previous one. He repeated expressions that appeared in the first letter, along with grammatical constructions he had identified when rereading it, so as to maintain a credible and consistent voice for Ofer. He also included expressions he had picked up in the classroom or at recess and had copied down in his notebook at the end of each school day. He had learned, too, to use his elbows and arms so as not to touch the blank sheet of paper with his fingers when transcribing the final version. He had bought a different envelope, and hadn't discarded the surgical gloves in the building's trash bin, but rather had stuffed them into the pocket of his jeans and later dumped them in a bin near his school. The letter had remained in the mailbox for two days before disappearing.

Michal looked at him excitedly, expectantly.

'Well, what do you write there?'

'Just a moment, let me explain.'

She was impatient. 'Does the instructor give you assignments? How does it work?'

'In principle, yes. Michael gives the students a writing exercise on a particular subject, and they bring their work to class and discuss it. But that's not what I'm doing. I've simply come up with my own idea – from outside the workshop, though maybe inspired by it – and I am working on something longer and more serious.'

Michal smiled at him, as if it was clear to her that he wouldn't be wasting his time on routine writing exercises.

'So, can the author kindly tell me what it is that he is writing about?'

'I'm not sure,' Ze'ev replied.

His indecision was sincere; it wasn't a means to pique her curiosity. He hadn't been able to see the reactions of his previous readers – not of Ofer's parents, and not of the police – and could only imagine. But he'd be able to see Michal's face while she read.

'It's up to you,' she said. 'I'd really love to read it. And maybe we should celebrate in some way.'

'Celebrate? There's nothing to celebrate just yet. First you'd have to read it and tell me if you like it.'

Should he give it to her or not?

He placed the open notebook on the desk in front of her. Her excitement had won him over.

'I haven't typed it up on the computer yet,' he said. 'It's all in the notebook for the meantime. Right now there are three letters, or three chapters.'

'Ah, okay, it's a story in letters,' she said and began reading.


Elie was sleeping soundly, but Ze'ev could feel his son's slumber weighing heavily on him. More than anything else, he feared Elie would wake crying and that Michal would have to stop reading to go see to him, or that he'd have to get up for the boy and would not be there to see her reactions. He followed her eyes as they moved from one word on to another, not missing a single expression on her face. If Elie were to wake, they wouldn't be able to discuss the text right then and there, and would have to wait until the evening. By then, the excitement would have waned.

The third letter was the longest – and the most complex, he thought, because it was reflexive and referred to the process of reading the previous ones and to the possibility that whoever had received them might be questioning the identity and credibility of the author. Like the first two, the third letter opened with 'Father and Mother,' which Ofer then followed up with a series of direct questions relating to the previous correspondence.

*Where did you read the two letters I sent you? In my room? In the living room? And what thoughts went through your mind when you read them? Did you tell yourselves that it isn't me, that it can't be me, in order to protect yourselves from what was written in them? Did you try to convince yourselves that someone else wrote them in my name so that you wouldn't have to deal with the pain in what I was trying to say? And what did you do with them after you read them? Did you destroy them so that you would never again have to read those words that you don't want to hear? But I will never stop writing.*

Wearing a pair of thin leather gloves he bought at an automotive supply store, he had placed the third letter in the mailbox in the middle of the day, quite brazenly.

Ze'ev tried to guess Michal's thoughts as she read. She looked solemn. At one point, she was unable to make out the words *'when I was buried,'* and asked him to help her, and there was also a moment when she lifted her head from the page and gave him an odd look. 'What?' he asked, and her eyes returned to the black notebook.

After she had finished, she just said, 'What is this?' and Ze'ev asked, 'What do you mean?'

'Are these our Ofer's letters? Ofer our neighbor?'

He knew she'd be a perfect reader – precisely because Ofer's disappearance and the fruitless search for him had seeped deep into her thoughts and her dreams.

'Yes,' he said, 'they're letters he writes to his parents, explaining what's happened.'

She didn't respond. He waited a moment before asking, 'What do you think?'

She still didn't say a word about the letters themselves, neither their content nor their style. 'What do you mean by "explaining what's happened"? How do you know what has happened?'

'I don't know,' he said. 'I'm trying to imagine. That's the whole point – I'm trying to see things from his perspective and to understand what happened there.'

'But how can you write such things without knowing what really happened?'

'Of course I can. It isn't a true-crime novel or a newspaper article. I'm not interested in what truly happened. What interests me is the emotional processes he underwent – or, rather, that I imagine he underwent – and that led to his disappearance.'

She went silent. This was not the reaction he had expected. He wondered if their conversation could be heard on the floor above them. She flipped back through some of the pages in the notebook, and reread the first letter.

'So, what have you got to say?' he asked quietly.

'That it frightens me.' There was no enthusiasm in her voice.

He tried to smile. 'Frightening is good, right? That's what literature should be.'

'I don't know what literature should be.'

'The only question is how it affected you, from the point of view of the reading process. Were you focused? Did you want to read on, or did you get bored? Did you feel that there was an authentic voice of a teenager speaking to his parents?'

'I think so.'

'That's the important thing! I agree that I'm doing something a bit frightening here. Getting into the mind of a sixteen-year-old, and writing in the first person – which can be pretty dangerous for a writer. The question is whether I'm going in the right direction or not.'

She stubbornly refused to answer. 'Why did you choose Ofer, of all people?' she asked.

'Because I know Ofer, and because I consider him to be an intriguing character. His story fascinates me. But, you realize, of course, that it's not just about Ofer, right? That there are other characters, other people, maybe even me, combined there in him?'

'Aren't you afraid that someone will read it and think you're mixed up in what happened to Ofer?'

'Are you serious? Of course not. Besides, I think I really was involved somehow in what's happened to him, even though we don't know what it is yet. I did have an influence on him and his life, and that's also why I feel close to the character and his story.'

He didn't know quite how to interpret the strange look she gave him.

She suddenly asked, 'What did they say at the workshop?' and he said, 'They haven't said anything yet. I haven't presented it. And I'm not sure I will, either. I may give it to Michael Rosin to read. But the truth is, I'm afraid to reveal the idea – I mean the idea itself, and the structure of the book. Just think about it; it's going to be a novel comprised entirely of a missing boy's letters to his parents. I don't think anything like that has ever been written – not in Hebrew, anyway.'

'It frightens me,' she said again. She still held the black notebook, looking at the black handwriting, the correction lines and arrows on the page. She was not reading.

'Frightening is good,' he repeated, wondering if he should

read her the quote about the ax and the frozen sea from Kafka's letter that he had found on the Internet a few days earlier.

'If you decide to publish it, you have to change the names,' Michal said. 'Do you know how his parents would react?' and without thinking twice Ze'ev said, 'I may find out soon enough. I sent them the letters.'

Was it a mistake to tell her? Later, while waiting for her call, for a sign that she hadn't abandoned him, that he hadn't been left all on his own, he thought he should have continued to hide it all from her, that there was a lesson to be learned here. But things had never been like that between them.

Michal didn't believe him; he could still take back his words.

'You did what?' she asked.

'I sent them the letters,' he simply said again. 'In fact, I put them in their mailbox.'

She refused to believe it.

'Don't worry. They aren't signed or anything. And I had no choice; the letters are addressed to them. The person writing these letters has specific addressees in mind whom he wishes to terrify.'

'I don't believe that you put them in their mailbox,' Michal said, her eyes welling with tears.

Once again he had a chance to take his words back and say, 'Just kidding, of course I didn't put the letters in their mailbox' – but he didn't.

Michal stood up and walked away.

He found her in the kitchen, sitting with her elbows resting on the table and her hands covering her eyes. He was at a loss for words. He tried to hold her, but she shrugged him off.

'Ze'evi,' she said, 'you didn't really put the letters in their mailbox, right? You're just trying to mess with me, right?'

He didn't answer her.

'I can't believe you did this. How could you have done such a thing? Have you lost your mind?'

Her sadness startled him – and overcame him too.

'They don't know it was me,' he said.

'What does it matter if they don't know it's you? Do you realize what you have done?'

Of course he realized what he had done. That's precisely why he had sent the letters.

He tried to play with her hair. She continued to speak with her hands still covering her eyes and her head bent over the table. 'You have to go to the police and tell them it was you. They must be looking for the person who sent the letters. They may even think that Ofer sent them.'

'What do you mean, go to the police?' he asked, and Michal suddenly lifted her head and dropped her hands from her face, uncovering her brown eyes, which were now wide open and fixed on him. 'Ze'evi, did something happen between you and Ofer?' she asked.

Her question stunned him. It was the second time someone had implied something of the sort – and Michal, of all people.

The most difficult moment of that terrible afternoon was when they heard Elie had woken – probably because of the pitch of their raised voices. The fact that he hadn't woken to silence but to the sounds of his father and mother, however, meant no crying. They could hear him in his room, babbling to himself in words that only he understood, perhaps trying to imitate their conversation in his infant fashion. Michal wiped the tears from her cheeks before going to see to him, but on returning with the infant in her arms suddenly broke down sobbing, deposited the surprised baby in his father's arms, and went into the bathroom, shutting the door behind her. She hurried out moments later, snatched Elie from Ze'ev's hands, and went with him into the bedroom. Ze'ev followed and sat down on the bed. Elie was oblivious to the situation; he looked happy to be on his parents' bed, crawling back and forth between them.

'Do you really want me to go to the police?' he asked, and she said, 'Ze'evi, you have a child. How could you have even thought of doing such a thing? I just don't get it.'

He tried to move closer to her. Elie grabbed hold of his hands and pulled himself up onto his feet for a moment, before flopping forward onto his father. The literary discussion was over and they were not going to have one again. In an instant, once Michal realized that the letters she had read were intended for real recipients, they were transformed from true writing into something immoral, even criminal, a heavy rock that had been thrown at someone and injured him.

'That's the best thing to do,' she said. 'Do you think it's better to wait here for them to burst into the apartment, turn it upside down, and arrest you right here in front of Elie, in front of Ofer's parents?'

He couldn't understand why she was so sure the police would be able to arrest him. She was mixing up totally unrelated reasons and causes. He quietly tried to explain to her that there was no chance of anyone connecting him with the letters. He had taken care to write them on standard sheets of paper, and he used regular envelopes; he hadn't left any fingerprints, and no one had seen him slipping them in the mailbox.

A week-and-a-half had passed since he sent the first letter, and no one had found out. But now she infected him with her anxiety and roused his own fears.

'We can't hide it,' she repeated, and he kept saying, 'But why not? Why the hell not?'

'Because the police will find out in the end, and it would be best if they did from you. You go in and explain it all. And we can't hide it because it's a terrible thing. Ofer's parents may believe he's alive and well only because of these letters. We have to tell the police. And if you go to them and admit it, maybe they will agree not to tell Ofer's parents that we did it. What would we do here in the building? Do you think we'd be able to stay here after they find out that you were the one who wrote those letters?'

'And what do we do if they arrest me?' he asked.

'Well, first thing we do is talk to a lawyer. After all, you didn't do anything, you just wrote letters. And if you go and tell them the truth, and show remorse, then they won't suspect you of being involved in what happened to Ofer. Explain to them that you know nothing about his disappearance. That it was nothing more than a writing exercise.'

Despite her trying to sound calm and to protect him, her last sentence was meant to hurt him.

Ze'ev said, 'I don't need to consult with a lawyer. If need be, I'm willing to speak to Avi Avraham, I'm sure he'll under-stand,' and she said, 'So call him, then. Let's not wait. This needs to be done right away.'

It was so odd.

He eventually found Avraham's card tucked into the black

notebook, between the cover and the first page. He remembered placing it there only after looking first in his wallet and bag and then in the desk drawers.

Michal followed him to the balcony and was standing beside him with Elie in her arms when he heard Avraham's voice on the other end of the line. He told the inspector that he wished to speak to him about a certain matter, and Avraham replied that it couldn't be before Sunday or even Monday, as he was abroad, and asked if he had urgent information regarding the investigation. He said no, and that he was calling about a somewhat different matter. Avraham suggested that he call the police, but he explained that he was willing to speak only to him. The inspector sounded different, far away, as if caught up in some internal storm.

'I'll wait for your call on Sunday, then. You'll let me know when it would be convenient for me to come to the station,' Ze'ev said, ending the call.

Michal went to her parents' house to do some thinking, leaving Ze'ev alone in the apartment.

He dared not approach the balcony overlooking the street, from where passers-by who lifted their heads to look up at the windows would be able to see him. Only then did it dawn on him that it was all over. Everything that had opened up two weeks earlier had closed. Doors and windows, the other person inside him, the birth, Michael Rosin, the writing. The writing for which he had waited so long. Michal's emotional response and the conversation between them had turned the idea that had thrilled him into something sordid and frightening. He was done with the workshop. He was done with writing letters. The black notebook lay on the desk, closed, as repellent as a leprous hand. He didn't open it, and didn't read the opening paragraph of the fourth letter, which began with the sentence: *'Father and Mother, do you keep reading the words I'm sending you from where I am now?'*

Ze'ev felt like leaving the house and walking for hours in the dark to tire himself out, to exhaust his legs, and his fear – but it was impossible. His mind conjured up images of cold eyes staring at him from every corner, every balcony. Everyone knew by now. But knew what, for God's sake? The thought of having to go to school the next day as per usual and meet up with his students and the other teachers was unbearable, and he decided to again call in sick and ask the secretary to have a substitute teach his classes. He'd soon be losing his job, anyway. There was no reason for it, nothing in the world had changed, yet the slightest sound now startled him, as if a police siren was being set off in his head. He tried to calm himself. He drank a large mug of chamomile tea with no sugar. He felt nauseated and wanted to throw up. He kept telling himself that Avraham would understand. He'd have harsh words for him, no doubt, but he wouldn't arrest him. He was sure of that, despite not having much to back up his certainty other than the understanding that existed between them. And what was he doing abroad in the middle of an investigation? Was the trip related to the search for Ofer? Could Ofer have managed to leave Israel?

He thought again about Michael Rosin, about his bloodshot eyes and pungent odor. About his legs that barely managed to fit into the space in the small car. He was sorry they wouldn't meet again. He couldn't remember if he had left his telephone number and address with the secretary at the library, and thus didn't know if Michael would be able to contact him to find out why he had disappeared halfway through the workshop.

The thought that people he knew, particularly distant relatives and old acquaintances from his university days, would read about what had happened in the newspapers was paralyzing. Would Michael Rosin read it too? He wished he could stop thinking. If he were to lose his job, it would only be for the best.

He'd told Michal that he would leave the apartment and go to a hotel for the weekend, until he had a chance to speak to Avraham, until things got cleared up. 'Maybe you'll feel calmer without me here,' he had said to her – and meant it. Instead, however, she had left, and he wondered if she'd ever return. He fell asleep on the sofa in the living room, with the TV on, and unlike other nights, that night he dreamed of things that he vaguely remembered the next morning.

The door opened when he was still on the sofa, covered by a thin, multicolored blanket he had taken from his son's bed in the middle of the night. His bones felt stiff. The events of the day before came back to him slowly.

Michal entered – alone. She had left Elie with her parents. She sat down by his side.

'I'm sorry I left,' she said. 'Did you sleep okay?'

'Yes. Quite a lot, I think. What time is it? How was your night?'

'I want to talk to you, and I want you to explain to me why you did it, because I'm struggling to understand what happened.'

'I am too,' he said, beginning to cry for the first time since the day before.

She said, 'Don't cry, we'll get through this,' and he said, 'No, it's because I'm happy; I didn't think you'd come back.'

Michal touched his light hair.

She then went over to the balcony to open the shutters to air out the apartment, prepared two cups of coffee, and placed a pack of cigarettes on the living room table beside them.

'I guess we might as well start smoking again,' she said.

It felt like they had stepped into a time machine and gone back to the past. They didn't leave the apartment for the next forty-eight hours, barely moving from the living-room sofa – as if they were students once again, as if in a single weekend, with no sleep, they could relive all the years differently, and could wake up on Sunday morning to a world in which no letters had been written, in which they had never met Ofer, and in which there was no need to face the police.

They spoke about everything, not only Ofer's letters. About the difficult year they had had with Elie, about their careers, and the move to Holon. They drifted apart and got closer, and then moved away again. At times he thought Michal was ready to forgive him, and there were also moments, just like the very first moment, when the shock of the discovery and her inability to understand what he had done drove a wedge between them.

'When I first read the letters, I realized right away that they were more about you than about Ofer,' Michal said. 'And then I thought you should have sent them to me, that they were really addressed to me. You should have put anonymous letters in our mailbox.'

'To you? What are you talking about?' he replied. 'And I don't believe they are more about me than about Ofer. Perhaps they're about both of us. My parents are already dead, I can't send letters to them.'

'But you do realize, don't you, that you shouldn't have put

the letters in his parents' mailbox, even if you had decided that this is what you wanted to write? You're able to tell the difference between writing the letters and the terrible thing you did when you sent them, right?'

'Right now I don't know if I can tell the difference between. All I know is that what I've done frightens me, and your reaction does too. I don't care about the police. Only about you.'

He wasn't trying to make things easier for her by saying such things. He said them because at that moment he truly was seeking her absolution, even if the sin for which he sought it still remained unclear to him.

'Look at me, I'm fine,' she said. 'Forget about my reaction. They can't hurt me or Elie. I'm only afraid for you, and I'm trying to understand what you have been going through, Ze'evi.'

So he told her – almost everything, almost from the very beginning. He told her about his realization that this was the story he'd been waiting for, and about the moment when he knew the letters would be the way he'd achieve it. He didn't mention the call to the police.

On Friday night, during one of the disturbing moments in their long conversation, she again asked him, 'And you're sure that nothing happened between you and Ofer?' and he almost shouted, 'Enough! Stop asking me that! I can't take hearing you interrogate me that way. Is that why you left Elie with your parents?'

'Don't be crazy! I just don't want him to be here now.'

'Why?'

'Maybe because I'm afraid that the police will show up. And maybe because I can't be a mother right now. I just can't think about being one. I need to be with you alone.'

He thought these words from her were wonderful.

'Thank you for coming back,' he said quietly, and let his body soften to fold up in her arms.

'I couldn't bear to think of you here all alone. And I was afraid of what you might do.'

'I'll never again do anything without talking to you first, I promise,' he said, and smiled.

On Monday, at the appointed time, they went to the police station together.

## II

He returned to an entirely different investigation.

In fact, from then on, right through to its resolution, the case was no longer his – though officially he was still in charge of the team and in the end signed his name to the final summation before it was handed over to the state prosecutor. He even played an important role in the actions that led to the resolution, but he no longer managed the investigation, and he wasn't quite sure who did – if anyone at all.

He sat in Ilana's office at the precinct headquarters on Sunday morning, after three hours of sleep, trying to comprehend what she was implying. 'In fact, we've come to the conclusion that this investigation has been based on just a single working assumption thus far, and that we can't be sure it's correct,' Ilana said, and he listened to her, puzzled and exhausted.

The El Al flight from Brussels to Ben-Gurion International was delayed, and then Avraham had to wait close to forty minutes for his luggage, and didn't get back to Holon before 2:00 a.m. The apartment was cleaner than he remembered it, and in the refrigerator he found a carton of fresh milk and an unopened tub of cottage cheese; the sparkling vegetable drawer also contained a bag of ripe tomatoes and another with six cucumbers. There was a loaf of bread on the dining table. He turned on the TV just to hear its sound and unpacked his suitcase. In his absence, his mother had also organized his closet, and had placed his neatly folded blue police uniform shirts on a separate shelf. Only the green bed linen, which she hadn't changed, still smelled of him.

'I'm not sure I understand what you mean,' he said to Ilana as he took a pack of cigarettes out of his pocket.

Ilana stood up and opened the window overlooking Salame Street. It was a muggy morning and the open window did nothing to freshen the air in the room. She sat down facing him again. 'I mean that, contrary to the things that were said here at the first team meeting, we didn't allow for uncertainty. I'm sure you're aware of that. We were too quick to turn our theory of the case into a given fact, when it should only have been a hypothesis – namely, that Ofer went missing on Wednesday morning.'

'What do you mean? What should we have done?'

She had forgotten to put the ashtray on the desk.

'I'm saying it was a mistake because we don't know for sure that it's true. We have no physical evidence to back it up and no corroboration from any other source. To the contrary. For the past two-and-a-half weeks, we've been looking for someone, aside from his mother, who saw him on Wednesday morning – and we've come up with nothing. We don't have the faintest idea about what happened on Wednesday morning, and it doesn't make sense to any of us any longer. If you assume that something happened to him on the way to school on Wednesday, or that he decided to skip school and go elsewhere, or that someone persuaded him to do so, you should be able to find evidence or testimony to support this. Yet we haven't been able to locate anyone who saw him – not going down the stairs in the building, not leaving the building, not getting onto a bus, nothing. His picture has been distributed to all the bus and taxi drivers in the area, along with all the residents and shopkeepers, and no one has come forward to say they saw him on Wednesday. You made a television appearance, we ran ads, and still we got nothing from anyone who could swear to seeing him going in one direction or another on Wednesday morning. Do you see what I mean? We've been treading water since the investigation began, Avi. Time is running out. It may even be too late. And we've been forced to admit this to ourselves. We haven't been able to reconstruct the events of Wednesday from the moment he allegedly left the apartment. And so now we think we at least need to reevaluate this paradigm, to question it, or to add others and see where they take us. We have nothing to lose.'

He was silent, and lit up another cigarette – despite the stuffiness in the room and the absence of an ashtray. Ma'alul hadn't said a word to him about reevaluating the paradigm when they spoke after the bag was found, or the next afternoon, during his last conversation with him from Brussels. When exactly had the paradigm changed? And on whose initiative? The bottom line was that behind Ilana's professional speech lay a direct accusation: You failed to conduct the investigation as you should have, particularly the questioning of the parents.

He saw the mother sitting in front of him that first evening in his office at the police station. And he recalled the photographs of Ofer she had taken out of the small plastic bag and placed on his desk the following morning.

Ilana's barrage against him continued: 'Avi, all we know for certain is that he was at school on Tuesday. Eliyahu has reviewed the footage from the security cameras in the school-yard and by the gate. He's there. You can see him walking out of the gate. And we know, too, that he returned home on

Tuesday afternoon. We have statements from three people, aside from the mother – two students from the school who were behind him on the way home, and a neighbor who saw him entering the building before two p.m. And that's it. In fact, that's the last time we know his whereabouts based on testimony from a number of different people. Ofer went home, and that's where we need to start looking for him.'

It was the first time he had heard Ofer's name since Thursday, although it seemed to him that he hadn't heard it uttered for weeks.

'So where would you like us to look for him, Ilana?' he asked, unable to restrain himself. 'Do you think maybe he's hiding under the bed?'

He'd sensed uneasiness between them the moment he arrived at her office, at 9:30 a.m. She was waiting for him at the door, dressed in her uniform. There was no emotion in their embrace. She invited him to sit down as if he were a first-time guest, and he took his usual seat, the blue chair, the one on the right as you come in – but still couldn't feel comfortable there.

Ilana's first words seemed to travel across a wide expanse before reaching him. Different faces looked down at him from the old pictures on the walls. Though it wasn't the first time, it was different. An air of alienation that needed to be dispersed always existed between them whenever they would meet again after a long while. And it always did disperse. But on previous occasions, Avraham had always blamed only himself for this alienation, because it took time for him to feel at ease in her presence. Now the alienation came from Ilana. She too was responsible for the distance between them.

'Well, tell me about the trip,' she opened, and he countered, 'A waste of time. I shouldn't have gone.'

'Well, you definitely look good. You simply can't admit to having a good time.'

Perhaps that was true.

She asked him to tell her about Jean-Marc Karot and if he had run into a senior officer from the Brussels Police Division Centrale whom she had once met at a conference in Madrid. It was one of the two officers leading the Johanna Getz murder investigation, the one who had solved it, most likely. Avraham told her that his meeting with him had been canceled because of the murder. He wanted to tell her about the investigation that had interfered with his visit and had ended on the day of his departure.

'Wait, maybe you should tell Eliyahu and Eyal too, when they get here,' she said. 'You and I have other things to talk about.'

She then asked if he had met Jean-Marc's wife and if she was truly as beautiful as he had said. Surprised at the question, he answered that she was. He hadn't been present at the meeting between Jean-Marc and Ilana in Tel Aviv and didn't know what they had spoken about.

'And did you get a chance to see the city?' she asked, and he replied, 'Barely. Only on my last day.'

And all this while he felt that she was holding something back from him – and then learned that he was right. He, too, struggled to talk. His presence in the familiar office felt oddly foreign, despite an absence of just a few days. He asked Ilana to bring him up to speed on the progress in their investigation, and told her that he had maintained contact with Ma'alul during the course of the week. It was then that she dropped the bombshell regarding the change in the theory of the case.

At 10:00 a.m., Shrapstein and Ma'alul arrived, together.

Shrapstein settled naturally in the vacant chair, as if it were reserved for him, and Ilana left the room to look for a third chair for Ma'alul. Avraham stood up and Ma'alul shook his hand, saying, 'Our man in Belgium. You look much better.'

Despite the muggy morning, Ma'alul was wearing the gray Windbreaker again and Avraham thought for a moment that perhaps he was hiding his arms from them. Was there a teasing tone in Ma'alul's voice when he asked Avraham if he had had a good time in Brussels? Shrapstein completely ignored all reference to his trip, as if he hadn't gone and come back. They exchanged mute greetings, and then Shrapstein waited in silence for Ilana to return. He began speaking without waiting for her to open the meeting.

'First of all, the bag,' Shrapstein declared. 'We have the initial findings. There are no traces of blood or any other foreign substances on it or inside it. It's covered in fingerprints, some of which we can use and others not. It'll take at least two or three days to complete the lab tests on the contents.'

Shrapstein handed out a sheet of paper with a list of all the items that had been found in the bag, which Avraham, still stunned by the conversation about the altered theory of the case, had almost forgotten about. He asked Shrapstein if he had photographs of the bag and the dumpster in which it had been found and Shrapstein said, 'Not here with me.'

Avraham wanted to go to Jerusalem to hold the bag in his hands. Again he regretted not having been the first person to receive it and examine its contents, item by item. He was familiar with most of them from his phone call with Ma'alul – the ID, the pen, the two twenty-shekel notes. Shrapstein's records also included precise details of the school textbooks and folders that they had found inside the bag. Avraham read through the list. It included a civics textbook, *Being Citizens in Israel – A Democratic Jewish State*, one called *Sociology: Social Circles*, Sophocles' *Antigone*, in Hebrew translation, and a compilation of grammar exercises. The bag had also contained two A4-size spiral-bound notebooks, one lined and the other squared. Following the forensic testing at the lab in Jerusalem, all the items were to be returned to the investigation team. He read through the list of books twice – and something about it caught his attention.

Shrapstein continued. 'The bag doesn't appear to be offering us any leads at this stage. And the forensic examinations in and around the dumpster don't help much, either. There's nothing that looks like it belongs to Ofer. We're still looking for someone who may have seen the person who dumped the bag there. The problem is – and we may want to give this some thought – that we requested, and received, a gag order, following Avi's directions. That may have been a mistake, and perhaps we should go public with the information in the hope that it will lead us to someone who saw whoever threw the bag away. That aside, I spoke this morning with the legal department and there's no way a court will approve a wiretap at this stage because we don't have sufficient evidence. We'll have to come up with something more concrete. The question is, how do we get our hands on something more concrete without arousing their suspicions?'

Avraham lifted his head from the piece of paper, looking first at Shrapstein and then at Ilana. 'I don't get it,' he said. 'A wiretap on whom? Whom do we suspect?'

Ilana felt uncomfortable; there was something else she hadn't told him. 'A wiretap on the parents' telephones,' she said, and Shrapstein added, 'Their landlines and cell phones.'

'The parents? What for?'

The look on Shrapstein's face was one of pity. He didn't say a word; Ilana spoke for him. 'Earlier, I informed Avi of our decision over the weekend to reevaluate our working assumption regarding Wednesday morning,' she said. She turned back to Avraham. 'As I told you, we want to make sure it's correct – or, more precisely, to rule out the possibility that it may be wrong.'

'That I got already. But what do the parents have to do with it? Do you think they're lying and that they're going to say as much to someone over the phone?'

Sensing the anger that was rising in him again, Ilana tried to soften her tone.

'We don't think anything,' she said. 'We are reevaluating our initial theory of the case, that the parents revealed all in their interviews and that they don't know anything more than what they've said in their statements and aren't holding anything back from us. In order for us to work systematically, we have to rule out the possibility that they haven't informed us of everything they know – that's all.'

'But where does this come from all of a sudden?' Avraham raised his voice. 'If you want to rule out the possibility – whoever may have raised it – I'll call them in for questioning and we'll rule it out. Why do we need to tap their phones?'

'It came up because we've been stuck for two-and-a-half weeks now. And every second that goes by without any progress in the investigation scares me. And because I'm having to answer questions like: Why is it that after two-and-a-half weeks, we haven't the faintest idea of what happened to Ofer?

And also because after finding the bag, it is even more likely that we are dealing with a crime and not a runaway. Do you agree? But primarily because until now we have been working without examining other alternatives, despite stressing at the outset the need to refrain from restricting ourselves to a single working theory. I think it's time to put this into practice – before the case is handed over to a different team.'

Despite her definitive tone, Ilana sounded insecure to him. Shrapstein spoke up, as if to lend his support. She watched him as he spoke, like he was the divisional investigations officer and she his subordinate. He said, 'Another reason it came up is because I'm uncomfortable with the fact that Ofer's bag turned up in a dumpster in Tel Aviv only after his father returned from abroad.'

Avraham turned to look at him. The extent of the betrayal was only now beginning to dawn on him. Behind every new surprise lay another. 'The bag was found in the dumpster a week-and-a-half after the father's return, not the following day,' he quietly said.

They were silent for a while, all four of them. He had been party to long silences in that office in the past. Silences that had sparked thinking. Silences during which ideas had been tossed around from eye to eye. This was a different silence, the kind of silence that preceded a redeployment, a silence during which all the occupants of the room attempted to assess the new balance of power that was emerging and to consider where and how to position themselves. He tried to calm down, to take the insult on the chin.

'Okay, so tell me what you are really thinking,' he said, lighting another cigarette. 'Because what you seem to be saying is that I screwed up the interviews with the parents.'

'Not at all' – Ma'alul immediately tried to calm him down – 'we are simply suggesting that all angles should be examined.'

Shrapstein again broke in. 'Think about it. If we change the theory of the case and assume instead that Ofer Sharabi went missing on Tuesday afternoon – because that's the last time we know of his whereabouts for certain – the entire picture changes. It means he's been missing since before the father went away. And then the fact that the bag was found in the dumpster after the father's return is capable of taking on a different meaning. For the bag to turn up two weeks after his disappearance is odd. Don't you think it's worth looking into?'

Avraham could see Ma'alul nodding in his seat, and he tried to layer his words with a matter-of-fact tone.

'It seems so speculative to me,' he said. 'We could also assume that he disappeared on Monday and that the figure appearing in the footage from the school cameras is a double, couldn't we? If you believe the parents are withholding information concerning the investigation, then you're casting doubt on my inquiry. There's no other way of putting it. And I'm telling you they aren't withholding any information and are doing all they can to assist with the investigation. I'm the only one who has met and spoken with them at their apartment and has seen what they are going through. We'd be doing them a gross injustice by doubting their statements. I have no intention of doing so.'

'Do you have a different theory to explain why we've been unable to reconstruct the events of Wednesday?' Shrapstein asked carefully.

'I don't have a theory. I'm not looking for theories,' he said. 'I took statements from Ofer's parents and I know what they told me. You're the one spinning theories, aren't you? So does this mean you've finally dropped the theory of the neighborhood criminal? And now you've decided to go after the parents?'

Shrapstein didn't respond, and Ilana said, 'Enough of that, Avi. There's nothing personal going on here, and no one's being criticized. Let's just get back to thinking about the case in a mature and professional way.'

The room went silent again. He couldn't tell Ilana that he wanted to be dropped from the investigation team because without him there, they'd focus their inquiries on Rafael and Hannah Sharabi, and he wasn't willing to allow anyone else to interview them but himself.

Ilana's cell rang and she whispered, covering her mouth with her hand as she spoke. Ma'alul, meanwhile, used the interruption to change the subject, while Shrapstein pretended to be amused by a text message, though the look on his face said he would never forgive the affront. 'Go on, then, let's have it,' Ma'alul said. 'What did you do there?' and Avraham said, 'Really nothing.'

'What was the police division like?'

'They seemed skilled, but it's difficult to tell. The exchange program fell apart, because the entire division was working day and night on a high-profile murder investigation. They were under intense pressure, but they seem to have done a good job because by my last day there, they had a suspect in custody, the presumed murderer.'

Ilana excused herself from the room to continue her conversation. Ma'alul pushed for more about the Belgian case, and Avraham told him the little he knew. At the start of the week, following the discovery of Johanna Getz's body in a potato field on the outskirts of Brussels, her boyfriend was taken into custody and news of his arrest was published in the media. It was a deliberate ruse. The partner had a solid alibi; he had been at his family home in Antwerp the weekend of her disappearance. The police hoped that the arrest and its publication would cause the real murderer to be less careful. The partner was released two days later, and the police then arrested the owner of the victim's apartment – a retired school principal who lived in the same building, on the third floor, an eccentric-looking individual with piercing eyes and an Albert Einstein hairstyle. Without knowing much French and merely from browsing through the newspapers, Avraham had worked out that former students and colleagues of the man had come forward with sensational information about the principal's oddness and unusual habits. He didn't know if this arrest was also part of the investigation tactics. During his time in Brussels sitting in on meetings at police headquarters, he had seen dozens of construction plans from different times in the history of the building, which went up at the start of the twentieth century, and concluded the police were looking for side entrances, or maybe even doorways that had been blocked up over the course of the years. The assumption was that the assailant or assailants hadn't forcibly removed her from the apartment or the building through the main entrance. The former principal remained in custody until Saturday morning, when a second neighbor was arrested – a Dutch man, in his thirties, unemployed, who had arrived in Brussels a few years earlier. In all likelihood, he was the killer. Jean-Marc Karot had referred to him as a psychopath during their last conversation.

Ilana returned to the room at ease and smiling, and interrupted their conversation – 'What's happening? Have I missed the story?' she asked, and Ma'alul said, 'But how did they get on to him?'

'Truth is, I don't know,' Avraham admitted. 'Perhaps because of her sock.'

'What sock?'

'The body was found with one sock missing – a pink woolen sock. They were obsessed with the sock, and I couldn't work out why. They were sure it would lead them to the murderer. Who knows? Maybe it did. I'll call Jean-Marc this evening to thank him for hosting me and I'll ask him if they ever found it.'

The tension had begun to ease and they returned to their discussion of the case. Ilana led the meeting through to the end.

'First things first,' she said. 'I'd like everyone to settle down. As I said before, no one is being personally criticized here, and I don't want anything of that sort to hamper the investigation. Okay? We're not drawing any conclusions, and we aren't abandoning any lines of inquiry. We'll wait for the final results from the lab and see if there's anything there to work with. Aside from that, we'll continue to look for witnesses to the dumping of the bag. Eyal, I want you to continue working this line. Avi, you'll call in Ofer's parents for another interview and try to ascertain, with a degree of subtlety of course, if there are any contradictions in their stories, anything that gives off a whiff of concealment or obstruction of justice. For now, I don't want them sensing that we doubt their statements; be sensitive. It's important that you conduct the additional interviews with them. Okay? Does that work for you? If you like, stay behind for a few minutes and we can discuss the interrogation strategy. Are there any other lines of inquiry we'd like to follow?'

Just as they all stood to leave, Avraham suddenly said, 'Yes, I think we haven't exhausted our inquiries regarding the neighbor, the English teacher. Ze'ev Avni. He called me in Brussels on Thursday and asked for an urgent meeting. He sounded stressed. He said he had information unrelated to the investigation; still, he insisted on speaking only to me. He wants to talk, and I think has more to tell than he has until now.'

'This sounds like a direction worth pursuing,' Ma'alul said.

'I have a gut feeling that his involvement in this story is more significant than he has let on,' Avraham continued. 'And if we're considering wiretaps, I'd go for one on him.'

'So speak to him. I don't see a problem,' Ilana said. 'When's he coming in for questioning?'

'I need to call him. I'll ask him to come in today, or tomorrow morning perhaps.'

Ilana seemed calmer, and Avraham wondered whom she had been speaking to on the telephone and what they had spoken about. 'I don't see any clash between these two lines of inquiry,' she said. 'And we can put wiretaps on anyone we want.'

Avraham stopped off at the station on his way home and picked up the case file from his office. He then drove to Histadrut Street and parked his car a few buildings from the Sharabi family's apartment block, on the opposite side of the road.

He sat in the car and waited.

Despite Ilana's efforts to conclude the meeting on a concili-atory note, all he had wanted to do was to go home, to sleep an hour or two, to digest – or perhaps forget – what had happened, and to try to rethink how to move forward with the investigation. He had passed on her offer to join her for an early lunch and had remained in her office for just ten minutes after Ma'alul and Shrapstein left. 'You were way out of line just now,' Ilana had said, and he had chosen not to respond. 'You tried to humiliate him, and he didn't deserve it. He's working on the team with you, not against you. And I want you to know that the idea of reconsidering our theory of the case came from me, not him.' He couldn't see how that was supposed to make him feel better. And if she was indeed the one to propose the re-evaluation of their tactics, why hadn't she waited for his return? There was no point in asking, or perhaps he was simply unable to. At least the questioning of the parents was still his.

The shutters on the balcony of their apartment were open. No one stood in the window. He could have knocked on the door but was too tired and agitated, and anyway, he still wasn't sure how to go about 'subtly reassessing' their statements, as Ilana had requested.

The air conditioner had cooled the interior of the police car, but the steering wheel burned from sitting in the hot sun. Drivers who passed him by slowed down, assuming he was a cop looking to snag a speeder. A mailman with a red mailbag slung over his shoulder walked from building to building. He couldn't recall if the balcony of Ze'ev Avni's apartment faced the street or the rear courtyard.

A car pulled up alongside him. The driver signaled him to open his window and asked for directions to Jaffa – and just then, Avraham spotted Hannah Sharabi. She came out of the building, turned left, and walked slowly down the street. She was carrying a wallet and wearing gray sweatpants, a yellow shirt, and flip-flops. She went into the grocery store, the same one Ofer would visit every morning. A short while later, he saw her heading back home with two pink nylon bags. The wallet must have been in one of the bags, along with the purchases. Posters bearing pictures of Ofer still hung on the streetlight poles along the road, but she chose not to see them. He followed her with his eyes until she opened the entrance door of the building, where she disappeared into the hallway, and then he drove home.

He slept that entire afternoon and woke to sudden darkness. Later that evening, he called Rafael and Hannah Sharabi to tell them he was back from Brussels and would like them to join him the following afternoon at the police station so that he could update them on the investigation and they could all go through the list of items that had been found in Ofer's backpack. He then dialed the number of Ze'ev Avni's cell phone. His wife answered, and her voice seemed to tremble when she called her husband after he gave her his name. Ze'ev came on the line and Avraham invited him in for a meeting in his office at eight the next morning. He thought he might have to call the wife in for further questioning too.

His computer rested on a white wooden desk in a small room that served both as a study and a storeroom. He sat down and removed the transcripts of the interviews and his notes from the case file. Among the various pages, he found the record of Ma'alul's conversation with the girl Ofer was supposed to see a movie with on Friday, two days after his disappearance. He also came across a copy of the class schedule he had taken from Ofer's room that same Friday when he had spoken with his mother.

He wanted to write to Marianka, but didn't know what to say. His father called to ask how he was doing and about the trip to Brussels, and suggested that he drop by for dinner. Avraham declined the invitation, saying he was bogged down with work.

'You sound very tired,' his father said.

'I just woke up,' he replied. 'I barely slept last night, and I was at work all morning.'

'Okay, we're home if you decide to come. Mom's gone out for a walk but should be home soon. Did you see what she bought for you and put in the fridge?'

What could he say to Marianka? Thank her for the tour of the city, of course, but what else? He emptied out the ashtray in the trash can and poured himself a glass of cold water.

'*Dear Marianka,*' he began writing in English, '*I returned to Israel and to the case of the missing boy that I told you about (the boy who may be in Koper). I wanted to thank you again for the tour. Since this morning, everybody has asked me about the city and thanks to you I can tell them something about it. And how are you? Are you back in . . .*'

He deleted all he had written. She wasn't back at work yet; it was Sunday.

He called Jean-Marc but got no reply, and didn't leave a message.

Once again he began writing, once more in English: '*Marianka, I'm writing to thank you again for the tour. It was a good ending to a week that wasn't easy. I hope I didn't take up too much of your time and that you had a nice Sund –* ' And again he stopped and deleted the boring and trite lines.

There was no point in trying again.

## 12

That morning, the blue skies stretched out above them as they made their way to the police station, and the breeze, as light as a feather, that accompanied them on their way remained with him long after the case closed.

The weather broke during the night, and the heat had dissipated. They didn't follow the shortest route but walked along Hankin Street instead. Ze'ev took a seat at one of the steel-topped tables at Cup o' Joe outside the mall and Michal went into the café and returned with two mugs of coffee and a croissant for each of them – butter for her, almond for him. A woman in her forties was sitting at the table beside them, browsing through the job ads. They ate and drank in silence until Michal asked, 'Are you worried?' and Ze'ev said, smiling, 'Yes, but I'm ready.'

The evening before, similarly, they had spoken very little about what was about to happen the following day. There was nothing more to say. Elie was home again, and the small talk they had shared on various other matters reinforced the sense in both of them that nothing in their lives had changed – or at least kept at bay the fear that something had. Michal had been wonderful to him all weekend, as long as he didn't bring up that one question: Was writing the letters, and then sending them, really a crime?

He could sense the tension inside her, just beneath the calm facade she tried to maintain, for his sake, and sometimes he could see she was on the verge of tears, fighting back a breakdown with tremendous strength and determination. The crisis allowed him to see just how strong she was; it was a big gift, in this way, for both of them.

And there was another scene: a ray of morning sunshine casting flickers of light on the sheets, and his waking up in her arms, his head resting on her right shoulder, which was covered by an old white undershirt. He opened his eyes and immediately recalled what the day had in store for him – and felt a spark of anger. He looked over at Michal sleeping alongside him and knew he had no choice. They had both already informed their respective schools that they wouldn't be coming in, and Michal's mother arrived at 7:15 a.m. to look after Elie, though it was not her regular day. Elie stretched out his small arms toward his father when they left, struggling to get out of the grip of his grandmother. He took him from her and brought his lips up close to the boy's cheek, wanting to whisper something in his ear, but then allowing the moment to pass. It was the first time they had left the apartment together since Michal learned of the letters, and he was praying they wouldn't run into Ofer's parents on the stairs or in the parking lot, more for Michal's sake than his own.

'We haven't decided – should I wait for you here or somewhere else?' Michal said as they stood outside the police station.

'Don't wait,' Ze'ev replied. 'Who knows how long it'll take. I'll call when I get out, or as soon as I can.'

'Okay. I may go home, then. I'm not sure,' she said. 'Don't be afraid, Ze'evi. No matter what, I'm by your side.'

She waited at the entrance and watched him as he entered the station and closed the heavy glass door behind him.

Along with Michal's support, the thing that saved Ze'ev from folding under the terrible pressure brought to bear on him that day was the fact that he came prepared. Almost nothing during the course of the interrogation surprised him, aside from the end, which he couldn't have predicted. If a police interrogation is sometimes poetically compared to a game of chess, Ze'ev constantly remained two or three moves ahead of his opponent – until the board overturned on both of them and the pieces came crashing down.

He identified himself to the policeman behind the desk at the entrance. Avraham was waiting for him, and Ze'ev knew the way. He walked down the gray corridor and stopped outside the third door on the left. His fear left him the moment he pressed down on the door handle and the familiar room opened up before him, but seconds earlier, while waiting outside the closed door, he had felt so strange – as if he was about to meet his maker.

But it was only Avi Avraham.

The investigator, dressed in uniform, was squashed in between the desk and the wall. He asked Ze'ev to take a seat and watched the teacher's movements as he placed his bag at the leg of the desk, pulled back the chair, and sat down. Looking at the inspector, Ze'ev felt both excited and relieved. Avraham asked again for his ID card and used a blue pen to jot down a few words on a blank sheet of paper.

'How are you today?' Ze'ev asked, but got no response.

There was a recording device, which remained switched off for now, on the side of the desk next to the wall.

Ze'ev waited for Avraham to turn it on and formally begin their talk.

Avraham took his time. He continued writing, putting down the pen only a minute or two later and lifting his gaze from the page. 'I understand you'd like to speak to me about a different matter,' he then said. 'But I still need to ask you a number of questions regarding the investigation into the disappearance of Ofer Sharabi.'

'What I have to say is not an entirely different matter,' Ze'ev replied, and then went silent for a moment. 'Are you turning on the recording device or have we not started yet?' he asked.

He wouldn't be able to repeat what he had to say.

'Do you think I should turn it on?' Avraham asked, and Ze'ev thought he sounded sterner and less intimate than he had the last time they had met, as if he was playing some kind of childish interrogation game with him. There were no barriers or mask between them when they last spoke. For a while, at least, they had had a real conversation, not a question-and-answer session between an interrogator and a suspect, and he had hoped for the same this time too. That's why he had chosen Avraham. He knew he needed to tell him everything right away, without hesitation, just as he had planned. He said, 'I don't know if you should turn it on or not – I mean, from a legal standpoint.'

The device remained off.

'I'm listening,' Avraham said.

'Okay, so here it goes. Two weeks ago, the police received an anonymous call in which someone told them they should look for Ofer on the dunes around the H300 building project. I wanted to tell you that I made that call.'

That was the plan – to open with the telephone call, and move on to the letters afterward, precisely in keeping with the chronological order in which things had happened, so that Avraham would understand the chain of events. It was also easier to confess to the telephone call without betraying his soul.

Ze'ev was too tense to accurately read Avraham's expression, but he was able to discern a look of puzzlement in his eyes. He clearly had never considered that Ze'ev might have been the caller. Avraham moved his hand toward the recording device, but then retracted it. 'Go on,' he said, the blue pen in his hand once again.

'I surprised myself, too,' Ze'ev said. 'And I don't really have much more to say about it. That was just the way it all happened. I hadn't intended saying that the police should look for a body. I planned to say that I had seen Ofer there and that that's where the searches should be carried out. I must have added it because I was agitated. I would like to apologize for that.'

'When did you see him there?' Avraham asked. 'What day was it?'

Disappointed by the question, Ze'ev repeated what he thought he'd made clear in his previous statement. 'I didn't see him. That's what I'm trying to tell you. What I said on the telephone was fabricated. I made it up. That's what I want to apologize for.'

'Apologize. That's the most important thing,' Michal had repeatedly said to him.

Avraham still did not understand. 'If you didn't see him, why did you call?' he asked, and Ze'ev said, 'I don't know. I wish I had an explanation. I wanted to speak to you, to try to explain why I think I did what I did. But it's important that you know that I didn't see Ofer, and that the information was made up. And it was especially important for me to tell you all of this face-to-face, not just because you're in charge of the investigation, but also because I sat and spoke with you for two hours previously and concealed it, despite the trust that developed between us and the rapport we had. I should have just told you then. It may already be too late, and if so, I apologize again. That's why I am here. But I honestly had no intention of sabotaging the investigation. Finding Ofer is just as important to me as it is to you.'

He was left alone in the room, and not for the last time.

But in fact he wasn't entirely alone, thanks to Michal. During the difficult hours that followed, too, after he lost control over the discussion and the chess pieces came crashing down, she remained by his side. She didn't get mad about his failure to tell her about the phone call. She understood he only wanted to avoid upsetting her even more. She quietly absorbed his rage at being in that room, came up close to him, and whispered in his ear, 'You're doing it for me. For us.'

He planned on telling Avraham about the letters when he returned to the room, but when the police inspector entered once again, without explaining his reason for leaving, he immediately turned on the recording device and said, in an official tone, 'Interview with Ze'ev Avni. May twenty-second. Eight twenty-two a.m. Please repeat what you said to me just now.'

Ze'ev wasn't sure if he should direct his voice at the silver-colored metal box or the investigator who sat there in front of him. 'I said I want to apologize for the anonymous phone call to the police,' he said.

'The phone call regarding what matter?' Avraham asked.

'The matter of Ofer Sharabi.'

'In which you said what?'

'In which I said the police should look for Ofer on the dunes by the H300 building project.'

'That's not what was said in the call to the police.'

'In which I said the police should look for Ofer's body.'

'How did you come by this information about the location of Ofer's body?'

Despite being prepared for questions of the kind designed to trip him up, Ze'ev was both startled and disappointed to hear them from Avraham. For him, this wasn't the purpose of their conversation. 'I didn't have any information,' he said. 'I made it up. I meant to say something else.'

'What did you mean to say?' Avraham asked.

'That I saw Ofer. But that wouldn't have been true either. It was a mistake for which I take full responsibility and apologize.'

'When did you make the call?'

'On Friday, two-and-a-half weeks ago.'

'Do you recall the date?'

'No.'

'Friday, May sixth?'

'Probably.'

'At what time?'

'I don't remember exactly. In the evening, somewhere between nine and ten.'

'And where did you make the call from?'

'From a public telephone near the beach. I don't recall the name of the street.'

'And according to you, at the time you made the call, you knew you were providing the police with false information, right? So please explain to me why you called.'

Now, these were the important questions, as far as he was concerned, the kind of questions that could spark a real conversation. He hadn't only wanted to meet with Avi Avraham because Michal thought it was the right thing to do; he had tried to find his own justification for going to the police. And that's what he came up with: the justification for it all lay in the chance that, together with Avraham, with his help, he could truly work out what had happened to him. He wanted to go back with Avraham to the moment he saw the police cars parked outside the building and realized they were there for him. When he had spoken to Michal about that tremendous moment, it was as if the words were unfaithful to what he felt and what he truly wanted to say. He had hoped that with Avraham things would be different.

'As I told you, I really don't know what drove me to do it,' Ze'ev said. 'There were a few reasons, I think. I know that from the moment I learned that Ofer had disappeared, I felt a compelling need to be involved in the search and to help his family and the police – and Ofer, most of all. I also realized that I wanted to write about the subject. If you are looking for simple explanations, perhaps I was afraid that the police wouldn't take the matter seriously enough, and I wanted to make sure they carried out comprehensive searches. And maybe – and I know that what I'm about to say may sound terrible – maybe I wanted to see what searches look like and how they are carried out, so I'd be able to write about them. But all this explains nothing, and I'm sure there are other subconscious reasons that I'm not even aware of. Perhaps you'll understand better if you hear it all. I have more to tell you.'

'Just a moment,' Avraham said. 'Before you do, I'd like to understand what you mean by "other subconscious reasons."'

'The last time we spoke, I told you that Ofer and I had developed a very close relationship when I was tutoring him, and that I identified strongly with him and what he had been through. You and I met during the search on the dunes on Saturday, remember? And also before then, on Thursday evening, when you came to our apartment to take statements from me and my wife. I already felt then I wanted to be actively involved in the search. I had hoped to tell you about Ofer's personality and what I had recognized in him, but I wasn't able to then. You were also in a rush that day. Perhaps I also feared that if I didn't initiate the search, I wouldn't get the opportunity to speak with you again and tell you about Ofer.'

'You have a wife and child, don't you?' Avraham suddenly asked, breaking his train of thought.

'You met them. Why do you ask?'

'How old is the boy?'

'He'll be a year old soon. But why do you ask?'

Avraham ignored his question. The abrupt questions about Michal and Elie caused Ze'ev more discomfort than any others might have aroused.

'How long have you been living in Ofer's building?' Avraham continued, and Ze'ev replied, 'You know that, too. Just over a year now.'

'And do you have a private office at the school where you teach?'

'A private office? No, there's a staff room.'

'When you saw Ofer on the dunes, was he carrying his bag, the black bag?'

'I told you, I didn't see him there. Please, believe me.'

Avraham was silent for a moment, tapping his pen on the piece of paper in front of him and searching Ze'ev's eyes with his own. 'I think there's another reason for your calling the police and coming in here to speak to me,' he then said quietly.

Ze'ev looked directly at Avraham, with no fear, only curiosity. 'What reason?'

'In fact you've been pursuing me since the investigation began. The day it started, you invited me to your apartment, didn't you? The next day you called the police to say you had found Ofer's body, and then you joined the search and chased after me all day. That same week, you invited yourself for another interview with me, and here you are again, for the fourth time.'

The description of the police inspector being hounded by him was thought-provoking. Ze'ev hadn't seen it like that. He said, 'I'm sure you don't recall, but we ran into each other on the stairs of my building that same Friday on which I called the police. It was purely by chance; I wasn't following you, and you didn't even notice me. In any event, I wouldn't say I've been pursuing you. What are you implying, anyway?'

'I think *you're* trying to imply something,' Avraham said. 'You would like to tell me something about your relationship with Ofer, but it's difficult for you to do it. You want to and don't want to at the same time. Would you like me to help you?'

Even in retrospect Ze'ev was unable to assess how much time had passed from the start of their conversation until the moment the chessboard came crashing down to the floor without either of them overturning it.

He looked around. Before the crash, Avraham was taking the conversation in a direction that disgusted Ze'ev though probably was inevitable. Ze'ev answered all his questions while escaping them inwardly with the help of his writing. He wanted the crummy room at the police station to be etched in his memory, every tiny detail, so that he'd be able to describe it in a book one day, perhaps in a novel centered on a police detective – if he ever dared to write one. He tried to memorize the appearance of the walls of the room: close to one another, white and bare, but dark somehow, maybe because the paint was old. It was more a cell than a room. Fixed to the wall above the desk were three shelves, made from a yellowish wood, on which cardboard files and three books, the names of which he couldn't remember, were haphazardly piled. A gold-plated commendation plaque was also on display. There was no window. On one of the occasions on which Avraham left the room and Ze'ev was left alone for a while, he stood up to stretch his legs, leaned forward, and saw on the inspector's computer screen a photograph, in shades of blue, of a European city that he wasn't able to identify, either at dawn or sunset. At the bottom of the picture an orange light shone from behind a bedroom curtain.

The letters had not been mentioned yet, and he wasn't solely to blame for that. He had told Avraham that he had more to say, but the inspector insisted on asking him dark question after dark question about his 'relationship with Ofer' – though maybe he cooperated with that. He found it easier to respond to insinuations that were swallowed up by the questions he was being asked than to confess about the letters. 'If you like, I'll turn off the tape and you can just talk to me about what went on between you two,' Avraham said. 'If it has nothing to do with the disappearance, I promise it won't leave this room.'

It was almost humiliating.

'You don't have to turn it off. I came here to talk. And I already told you about our relationship. I was Ofer's private tutor for four months, and aside from teaching him English, I think we were close, that I was some kind of a mentor to him. I saw sides of him that no one else did, and I listened to him the way no one else could or wanted to.'

Avraham did surprise him with the next question, 'Do you think Ofer loved you?' and Ze'ev said, 'Loved me? What a strange question. Ofer felt that I was willing to give him something that others didn't. I don't know if he loved me.'

'And did you love him?'

'You're using that word again; I don't think it's the right word. I love my son; it's not the same thing. I think I identified with Ofer, that I saw parts of myself in him and that I had a lot of empathy for him. I wanted to help him.'

'And did you feel he wanted more, that he was asking you for more?'

'Not at all. But maybe I don't understand what you mean.'

'That he wanted you as a close friend, or to be his father – I have no idea. We understand from statements collected during the course of the investigation that Ofer was very attached to you. Loved you perhaps. Forgive me for using that word again, I know you don't like it.'

Ze'ev looked at him. For the first time he felt unsure of his ability to read Avraham's intentions. He didn't know if Avraham was telling the truth, if that's what the police had been told during their inquiries. It certainly could have been the truth. He wondered who the police had spoken to – Ofer's parents, without doubt – but would Ofer have told his friends about their relationship?

'No, I like the word,' Ze'ev said. 'I simply think you are not using it correctly.'

'And what do you have to say about what I have just told you?'

'I don't know what to say. I'm sure Ofer appreciated the way I listened to him and perceived him. I don't think that means he loved me.'

'Mr Avni, tell me, why in fact did Ofer stop coming to the lessons?'

He could have called him Ze'ev.

'He didn't stop. I told you the last time; his parents informed me that he no longer needed private English lessons, and I don't think it was only due to financial reasons, because I was willing to continue for free. Perhaps they weren't pleased with the relationship that developed between us.'

'Yes, that's what you said last time. I remember. But it's not entirely true, you know. I spoke to his parents and they told me explicitly that the lessons were stopped at Ofer's request. He didn't want you to come to their home any longer.'

Ze'ev recalled their last lesson: nothing out of the ordinary, in Ofer's room, preparation for a grammar test on the use of the present perfect tense. Ofer didn't say it would be their last one. At the start of the lesson, Ofer gave him back the Hitchcock box set, and Ze'ev tried to find out if he had watched any of the movies and what he had thought of them, but couldn't get Ofer to respond. Hannah Sharabi served him a cup of tea and date biscuits. It was raining by the time the lesson ended, and long drops of water were trickling down the windowpane. Hannah Sharabi offered him a jelly doughnut on the way out – it was the third or fourth night of Hanukkah. He remembered thinking that evening how wonderful it was to discover the rain from angles one wasn't accustomed to, through the windows of others. Two days later, Hannah knocked on their door and informed him, apologetically, that Ofer would be taking extra lessons in math, rather than English, from then on.

And Ze'ev didn't even know how Ofer did on the test. 'Perhaps it's easier for them to present it like that,' he said. 'This is the first I hear of Ofer wanting to stop the lessons.'

'Perhaps he wanted to stop them because he felt he loved you too much.'

'What is it with you and that word? I'm telling you, they are not telling the truth. Ofer wasn't the one who chose to end our lessons.'

'I'm sorry to disappoint you, but that's what they said in their interviews.'

'So they're either mistaken or lying,' Ze'ev replied.

Avraham went silent again. Perhaps he was waiting for Ze'ev to continue. 'You know what?' he finally said. 'I think you're right. I don't believe them either. And I'm sure that after they stopped the lessons, Ofer tried to meet with you, right?'

'What do you mean?'

'I mean that based on the statements we have collected during the course of the investigation, I am sure he tried to meet up with you after his parents stopped the lessons – maybe even without their knowledge.'

'I don't understand. Is your investigation centered on the lessons I gave to Ofer?'

'Among other things. The investigation is focusing on Ofer's life in general, and the lessons were an important part of it, don't you agree?'

'Yes. Of course. But I don't understand what you're asking me, then.'

'The question is, did Ofer initiate meetings between the two of you after the lessons were stopped? Because I know he wanted to. Perhaps he tried and you refused?'

Had Ofer really wanted to get together with him? During their chance meetings on the stairs, he had appeared so shy and embarrassed. He had avoided looking at Ze'ev, as if he wished to ignore him. They bumped into each other a few weeks before his disappearance, in the morning, outside the building. Ze'ev was unchaining his bike when Ofer came outside wearing a gray T-shirt. Ze'ev called out to him, and asked him how school was going, and Ofer said okay, and that he was late for classes, and took off. Ze'ev thought for a moment about offering him a ride on the back of the bike – Michal's helmet was in the trunk – but then decided against it, sensing Ofer's reluctance and feeling hurt by it.

'Ofer didn't initiate any meeting,' he said. 'To the contrary. As I told you before, I had the sense that he was avoiding me, perhaps because he felt guilty about the lessons being stopped. If he had approached me, I wouldn't have refused. I told you, I offered his parents to continue the private lessons free of charge.'

'So you want me to believe that you haven't spoken since December?' Avraham asked, and Ze'ev said, 'Certainly we spoke. A word or two when we ran into each other in the building. But can I say something for a moment?'

Avraham leaned back in his chair, and Ze'ev got the impression that the inspector was finally ready to listen.

'I understand from your questions that you believe my relationship with Ofer continued after the lessons were stopped, and I'm telling you that's not true. Your questions on the subject are a waste of time. I knew before coming here that you'd take this line of questioning, so I was prepared, but still, I think it's a shame. I didn't hide the fact that Ofer and I had a close relationship. If I had wanted to hide it, I don't think I'd be here, of my own accord, telling you about Ofer – "pursuing you," as you put it. Don't you think?'

Avraham didn't answer.

'You clearly suspect me of being involved in Ofer's disappearance, especially in light of what you now know about the phone call. Or at least you're pressing me, trying to find out if I am involved. That's your job. I get it. But it isn't true. Let me ask you again: If I was involved in Ofer's disappearance, do you think that I'd call the police or come here on my own initiative to speak about it? Or that I'd tell you the truth about the phone call? Anyway, I have something more to say, and then you can carry on asking me whatever you like.'

'I'm listening,' Avraham said.

'Okay. Let me first say that I know that what I'm about to tell you will only increase your suspicions. But, again, I ask you to think logically and understand that if I was in any way linked to Ofer's disappearance, I would never have chosen to come here and tell you what I am about to say.'

Was there a way to speak about the letters without being forced to express a sense of remorse that he didn't truly feel? He imagined himself praying in a synagogue, draped in a prayer shawl, tefillin wrapped around his arm and his forehead, but no God in his heart.

Avraham glanced briefly at the recording device to ensure that it was still on.

'I was also the one who wrote the letters in Ofer's name,'

Ze'ev said, and Avraham looked at him as if he had no idea what he was talking about.

The noise of the chessboard crashing to the floor came only later.

At first there was only silence.

'What letters are you talking about?' Avraham asked, and Ze'ev said, 'These,' and bent over to reach into his bag to retrieve the black notebook with the folded sheets of paper on which he had copied the near-final versions of the three letters he had sent. He handed them to Avraham.

A few days later, after Ze'ev understood what had happened with the letters, he realized that Avraham was not only their fourth reader but also the last. It was unlikely that anyone would ever want to read them – Michal wouldn't want to see them again, and neither would Ze'ev, most likely. Nonetheless, the three letters were the start of what he had hoped would be his first novel. But as it turned out, Avraham would forever be their final reader.

Avraham read through the letters quickly. Was he able to make out Ze'ev's handwriting? He placed the first one on the desk, facedown, and went on to the second. When he got to the third, he focused his attention on the lines that Ze'ev liked best, the series of poetic questions focusing on what Rafael and Hannah Sharabi had done after reading the letters: *'Where did you read the two letters I sent you? In my room? In the living room? And what thoughts went through your mind when you read them? Did you tell yourselves that it isn't me, that it can't be me, in order to protect yourselves from what was written in them? Did you try to convince yourselves that someone else wrote them in my name so that you wouldn't have to deal with the pain in what I was trying to say? And*

*what did you do with them after you read them? Did you destroy them
so that you would never again have to read those words that you don't
want to hear? But I will never stop writing.'*

He waited patiently for Avraham to finish reading and said,
'I made a few changes here and there, but these are the letters
that were sent.'

Avraham looked at him, and again Ze'ev could not identify what it was that stared out from his eyes. He thought it was
terror, but maybe that was only what he wanted to see.

'You wrote these in Ofer's name?' Avraham quietly asked.

'Yes,' Ze'ev replied.

'Why did you do that?' Avraham declared, more than
asked. For the first time Ze'ev felt that the police inspector was
truly interested in knowing what was going on inside him.

'It's a long story,' Ze'ev said. 'And I came here to tell it
to you.'

'You can tell it to me in a moment, but first tell me who
you sent them to. To the police, too?'

Did he really not know? Or was he again trying to test
Ze'ev's honesty? Surely this wasn't the first time he had seen the
letters. And suddenly he was terrified by the thought that his
letters hadn't reached their destination. Had someone removed
them from the mailbox ahead of Rafael and Hannah Sharabi?
He stifled a scream that was meant only for Michal's ears. If the
letters did not reach their destination and Avraham was seeing
them for the first time, it was rash of him to turn up and confess. It didn't make sense. Ofer's parents must have handed them
over to someone else on the investigation team who hadn't
informed Avraham and had hastily filed them away.

'I sent them to Ofer's parents – I mean, I slipped them into
their mailbox,' Ze'ev said.

'When was this?'

'The first one, about two weeks ago; the second, that same week; and the third, last week.'

Avraham took the letters and left the room. This time he didn't come back for an hour or more.

On his return, Avraham asked Ze'ev to accompany him to a different room, which looked even more like an interrogation cell, and again left him there alone, asking beforehand for his cell phone.

Ze'ev waited a long time.

Policemen he didn't know entered and left without saying a word. Were they checking to see if he was still there? That he wasn't doing anything he shouldn't be doing? Perhaps they were coming in simply to get a look at him, as if he were a rare species of animal that had been trapped and confined. His plan had gone wrong, and he no longer understood Avraham's actions. The questioning had ended precisely where it should have begun.

A young policewoman brought in a tray with lunch – roast meat, mashed potatoes, and boiled peas, along with a bottle of mineral water. He drank all the water in a single gulp but didn't touch the food. Avraham returned, accompanied by a policewoman who introduced herself as an officer from the Investigations and Intelligence Division. She asked if they could interrupt his meal. He pointed toward the full tray. He wasn't eating. They showed him a calendar and asked him to recall the precise dates on which he had placed the letters in the Sharabi mailbox. He wondered if this senior officer had also read them. She had long brown hair, a little too full for his liking, and blue eyes.

'The letters you wrote are a serious criminal offense – I'm sure you realize that,' she said in a tone that angered him, that one uses to address a child. 'But right now, all we want to know is what has happened to Ofer. That's all we are concerned with at this point. I'm going to ask you only once if you know what has happened to him, and I want an honest response. You know that all you say could be verified by means of a polygraph test, so it would be foolish for you to lie. Tell me now if you know what has happened to Ofer and where he is.'

He felt too tired and too hurt to have a conversation with an investigator he didn't know, and stuck to the story he had told Avraham.

'I've already said I don't know what has happened to him and that I'm not involved in his disappearance. I wish I knew where he was. If I had had anything to do with his disappearance, I wouldn't have chosen, on my own accord, to tell you about the letters and the phone call. I came here to apologize and to prevent any damage to your investigation, although I may already be too late for that.'

'So why did you write that you know what has happened to him?' she asked, and Ze'ev tried to control his tone of voice as he said, 'That's not what I wrote. I suspect you haven't read them. If you had, you'd see they are written by Ofer, from his perspective, through his character. And if you'd read them properly, you'd see they say nothing about what has happened to him, because I don't know.'

'So why did you write them?' Avraham burst in.

'I was trying to tell you but didn't get a chance because you ended our conversation,' he answered quietly. 'I realize it was a mistake to send the letters, but for me they were part of a novel I was working on. That's how I saw them, though I'm realizing now that probably seems disturbing to you. I wanted to write a book made up of letters from a missing boy to his parents. But I don't have any information about what happened to Ofer. And I'm willing to take a polygraph test whenever you like.'

This was not how he had wanted to share his story with Avraham. To tell him how he wrote the letters, how important they were. The senior investigations officer looked at him with contempt, maybe hatred. What she said about him writing the letters, that it was a serious criminal offense, was just ridiculous.

They left the room.

Ze'ev tasted the mashed potatoes and ate most of the peas using a white plastic spoon. Later that afternoon he knocked several times on the door of the interrogation room. Avraham eventually came in and Ze'ev asked how long he was still expected to wait and if he could speak to Michal.

'Your wife has already called,' was Avraham's reply, which frightened Ze'ev.

'Who spoke to her?' he asked. 'What did you tell her?'

'She was told that you're being questioned and that we'd keep her informed of any developments.'

'When am I getting out of here?'

'That's hard to say.'

'Can you at least tell me if I need a lawyer?'

'I don't know when we'll continue with the questioning, or in what manner,' Avraham replied. 'For now, we'd like to ask you to remain here. And you're okay with that, aren't you?'

'What do you mean, "you'd like to ask me"? Do I have a choice?'

'Yes. But if you say you want to leave, we will immediately arrest you. We have more than enough cause. In the meantime, though, we haven't decided what to do with you, and we'd appreciate it if you'd be patient.'

Ze'ev imagined he was waiting in line at the doctor's or at the Tax Authority and felt less intimidated. He then looked around the interrogation room to make a mental note of its appearance. Avraham had been shocked by the letters, as if he were seeing them for the first time, and Ze'ev recalled what Michael Rosin had said at the workshop about the one reader whom every text should terrify. Perhaps it wasn't Ofer's parents but Avraham who was his real addressee? When he thought that it was already evening, he asked Avraham if he could please phone his wife.

He knew right away that she was crying. In the background, he could hear the sound of Elie and his mother-in-law, who had stayed over. Had Michal told her where he was, and why?

'I can't talk now, but everything will be okay, Michali,' he said. 'I just wanted to tell you that I haven't been arrested. They aren't arresting me, do you understand? They just want to continue the questioning. Please don't cry.'

'But you're coming home today, right? How did they react?'

He looked over at Avraham, who could hear her. 'I don't know. I hope so.'

'Do you want me to call a lawyer?'

'I don't know what to tell you. I don't really understand what's happening. I hope I'll be home in a few hours. What did you say to your mother?'

Her crying pained him, but he couldn't suppress the anger he felt at knowing he was there because of her.

She didn't answer his question.

'Okay, Michali, I need to hang up now. Kisses for Elie,' he said. She asked him not to go, but he said he had no choice and hung up.

# 13

'Hello?'

Avraham recognized Hannah Sharabi's voice, though he had not heard it for a long time.

There was no tension in her voice. She had not been waiting for a call, but was not surprised when the phone rang so early in the morning.

'Is this the Sharabi residence?'

Ze'ev Avni sounded hesitant, rushed, and very tired. The hesitancy slowed his speech, almost to a standstill; the urgency fastened the syllables together. He sounded uncertain of his ability to say his piece. At that point in the conversation he could still end the call. He had come through a long night at the station, with no sleep and very little food. In the morning, when they brought him a cup of coffee in the interrogation room, he had taken one sip of the scalding-hot drink and drank no more, as if he had forgotten about it.

'Yes. Who is this?' Hannah Sharabi replied.

The conversation between Ze'ev Avni and Hannah Sharabi took place at 7:15 a.m., but Avraham heard it after 8:00 a.m., on the recording device in Shrapstein's office. He couldn't recall the location of the telephone in the Sharabi apartment. He imagined Hannah picking up the receiver in the kitchen while clearing the remains of breakfast from the table, or rushing to answer the phone from one of the children's rooms.

'I'm calling about Ofer,' came Avni's voice. There was silence at the other end of the line. 'Can you hear me?' he asked.

A moment later, Rafael Sharabi's voice could be heard from the recording device. He must have been nearby when the phone rang and Hannah had called him to her with a gesture of a hand or her pale face. 'Who is this? What do you want?' the father asked.

'I put Ofer's letters in the mailbox. I know where he is.'

Silence again. Rafael Sharabi could have hung up, just as Hannah could have, but he kept holding the receiver.

So he did it. Avraham wasn't sure that Avni would go through with it. He'd had a hunch — or maybe it was hope — that Avni would reject their offer at the very last minute.

'Can you hear me?' Avni asked Rafael Sharabi. 'I know where Ofer is, and I can tell you.'

Avni wasn't distorting his voice, yet it wasn't easy to make out the words. Was he covering the mouthpiece with his T-shirt?

'Who are you? Why are you calling us?' Rafael Sharabi asked, and Avni repeated his previous words. 'I know where Ofer is and what he's been doing since he went missing,' he said. 'I'll call in the evening to tell you.'

The call ended.

Shrapstein turned off the recorder and triumphantly smiled at Ilana and Avraham. Avraham was holding a white polystyrene cup filled with Turkish coffee; he must have had seven or eight of these since coming to the station some twenty-four hours earlier. Ilana drank her coffee. It had been a sleepless night for all of them.

'That's it. That was an hour ago,' Shrapstein said. 'He did it – that lunatic. Now it's just a waiting game.'

And they waited.

It all started the day before – the moment that lunatic, to use Shrapstein's words, knocked on his door.

Ze'ev Avni was wearing black trousers and a light-blue collared shirt, as if he had dressed up for an important work meeting. Only later did it occur to Avraham that his attire resembled a police uniform. He was sure the teacher was there to speak about a different matter, as he had indicated when they'd spoken during his trip to Brussels. It fitted the man's character, or at least what Avraham could make out of it. He'd probably want to speak about himself. Perhaps he suspected one of his students was using drugs.

And then Avni told him about the call to the police.

He confessed in a flowery tone, as if he were reciting an item on a news broadcast. Avraham left the office to inform Ilana and to check when exactly the call had come through and what had been said – although he hadn't forgotten. It was on his birthday, while he was at his parents' house, the last time he had visited them.

'What do you think it all means?' Ilana asked.

'That I was right,' Avraham replied with an air of confidence. 'That my gut feeling was right. He's involved far more than he has let on until now.'

He felt scared by the thought of where it all might lead, but he also felt a sense of exhilaration. He had been right all along. Now the investigation was his again and a safe distance away from Ofer's parents.

'What are you going to do with him?' Ilana asked, and he

said, 'I don't know yet. I'll continue with the questioning, and then I think we should book him – for obstructing a police investigation, to begin with – and get a search warrant for his apartment and computer. He may also have an office at the school. I'll check.'

'Keep me posted on your progress and let me know if you need anything,' Ilana said.

Avraham returned to his office to find Avni standing in front of the shelves on the wall and staring at the cardboard files. The teacher turned to face him, surprised. Ofer's case file wasn't on the shelves. Avraham had taken it home the day before, and had placed it in his desk drawer that morning.

He switched on the recorder and asked Avni to repeat his confession.

What exactly was he thinking at this stage of the investigation? He tried not to let his hopes get ahead of the information he now had, but it was impossible not to after two-and-a-half weeks of barren inquiries and countless small failures, coupled with the sense that the case was slipping away and with his ever-increasing concern for Ofer's fate. He needed to continue questioning Avni without jumping to conclusions; the investigation had to remain open to every possibility, but he believed he now had the end of the thread that would lead to Ofer, that it was in his grasp, between his fingers – and it was stronger than him. Had Avni helped Ofer to hide somewhere? That was the first possibility. The second was more disturbing. He looked at the teacher sitting in front of him, examining his posture, his eyes, but could not yet see anything definitive in them.

Avni's interrogation unfolded in various directions, taking sharp twists and turns that were designed to rattle the teacher and undermine his self-confidence. Avraham tried to surprise him with a question about Ofer's backpack, and scared him with short, direct questions about his family. But he got the impression that frightening Avni wasn't the way to go; it would be better to make him feel appreciated and understood. Without planning to, he asked if Avni thought Ofer loved him, and the teacher appeared taken aback. He kept pounding into him that Ofer had insisted the private lessons stop, and felt that Avni was losing his confidence, that he was about to say something he had not planned on confessing. He was on the threshold of victory, on the verge of confirming his intuition, just about to prove that Shrapstein and Ilana were wrong, that he was right – when Avni told him about the letters.

It took a while to sink in.

He left the room again and called Ma'alul, to ask if he had heard anything about anonymous letters sent to Ofer's parents while he was in Brussels. Ma'alul knew nothing about them. 'Why do you ask? What letters?' he asked, but Avraham had already hung up and walked into Shrapstein's office without knocking. It was panic rather than understanding that he was feeling. 'Did Ofer's parents try to contact you while I was in Brussels?' Shrapstein said no. He had never heard of any letters. Avraham stood outside the station and smoked a cigarette. After two hot days, the morning was fresh, almost cool. He spotted a young woman at a distance, near the entrance to the Technology Institute, who turned around when she saw him and walked off. Was it Avni's wife?

He thought about what he should tell Ilana over the phone.

'What do you make of it?' she asked, as if she wanted the words to come from his mouth and not hers, and he said, 'That apparently Ofer's parents have concealed the letters, God knows why. But they've kept information from us.'

'And you believe that he put the letters in their mailbox?'

He hesitated before replying. 'I think so. Why would he confess to something like that if it wasn't true?'

Ilana was at the station within half an hour. She took the letters from him.

Because Avni was waiting in his office, they crowded into Shrapstein's cool room. Ilana insisted on including him in the decision.

At Ilana's request, Avraham gave them a brief rundown on Avni – thirty-five years old, married with a baby, and living in the building on Histadrut Street for just over a year; before then in Tel Aviv, where he taught English at a high school. Tutored Ofer for four months in the winter and claims to have developed a close relationship with the boy. May have a some-what distorted view of reality. The investigation revealed that Ofer asked to end the lessons. He claims to have felt an uncontrollable urge to intervene in the investigation from day one. He therefore called the station two days into the inquiries and passed on false – or so he says – information about the location of Ofer's body. He began writing the letters for the same reason. He also participated in some of the searches. All the above made it obvious why Avraham became suspicious. Avni came across as not completely stable, so his statement required verification, but it did not seem he was lying. He had con-fessed to both the phone call and the letters voluntarily.

They then spoke about the parents.

Shrapstein opposed Ilana's suggestion – that they get a search warrant for the Sharabi apartment in order to find the letters and other evidence of their efforts to impede an investigation. 'If they've destroyed the letters, we'll have a problem,' he said, 'because they'll know we doubt their stories and will become even more cautious. Perhaps we should just detain them and bring them in for questioning for forty-eight hours?'

Avraham wanted to voice a protest but felt he had lost that right. Ilana was of two minds. She said, 'It's too soon. I can't detain the parents of a missing youth so easily – even if they did receive the letters. We have no proof other than what we've been told by that teacher, and he's fed false information to the police once before. I can't imagine why they didn't report the letters either. Maybe just stupidity and nothing more.'

Ilana's words gave him hope. 'Perhaps they didn't receive them?' he suggested. 'Someone may have taken the letters out of their mailbox, right?'

The other two didn't respond. Standing on Shrapstein's desk was a framed photograph of his wife and two small children. Ze'ev Avni's letters, written in black ink, lay next to it.

'I suggest we go back to the idea of the wiretap,' Shrapstein said. 'We have enough evidence now to get an okay from the court.'

'What will that give us?' Ilana asked, and Shrapstein said, 'You never know. If they failed to report the letters, there's a chance they may be concealing more information.'

Ilana looked over at Avraham. Was she expecting him to say something? She then excused herself and left the room, leaving them alone. Shrapstein kept silent at first, although he clearly wanted to say something. 'Do you think he's completely crazy?' he finally asked, and Avraham said, 'I can't figure him out – I don't understand why he wrote the letters, and particularly in Ofer's name, and even more so why he's now come to tell me about them.'

Shrapstein couldn't hold back. 'Perhaps he's fallen in love with you, too,' he quipped.

Avraham went out to smoke another cigarette.

Ilana returned to the office after him, and she sounded decisive again. 'Okay, Eyal, there's been a decision. You and I are going to the district court because I need to be there in order to file a request for a wiretap. We'll set it up immediately. We'll also request an arrest warrant for the parents, but we won't use it just yet. We'll wait to see what else comes out of the interrogation of the teacher. You'll continue with that, Avi. Get the exact dates on which he put the letters in the mailbox, and find out if he saw either the father or the mother take them out. And send Ma'alul over to have a look at the mailbox.'

He suddenly remembered that Rafael and Hannah Sharabi had arranged to come to the station that afternoon. 'Cancel it,' Ilana ordered. 'I don't want them here right now. We need to prepare for that interview. For now, continue with the teacher.'

'But what do I do with him? Should I arrest him?'

Ilana looked at Shrapstein again.

'I think not – not just yet,' Shrapstein said. 'He came in of his own accord, and as long as he isn't asking to leave, it's best not to arrest him. An arrest means a lawyer, and the entire building would soon know, including Ofer's parents. It wouldn't be in our best interest for them to know he's been arrested, right?'

No. Not now.

Ze'ev Avni was still waiting in his office.

★

Avraham's conversation with Rafael and Hannah Sharabi was the most difficult part of that day. There was no reply from their home line and he got hold of the father on his cell phone. He told him something about a meeting that was running late and asked that they not come down to the station, and he promised to be in touch to schedule their talk for another time. 'We haven't heard anything new,' the father replied in a steady voice to his question, adding, 'Have you received the results of the tests on the bag yet?'

He stopped himself from saying anything and ruining the investigation. How could you have concealed the letters? Why the hell did you do that? What are you afraid of? Why are you complicating things for yourselves for no reason? How could you not have told me about letters written in Ofer's name and placed in your mailbox, even if you thought he didn't write them? He said, 'The results haven't come back yet. I'll let you know the moment they do, but it won't be before tomorrow.'

To have his office back, Avraham moved Ze'ev Avni to an empty interrogation room and then ordered a tray of lunch for the teacher. He ate alone while waiting for Shrapstein and Ilana, as if he were afraid to continue the questioning without them. At one point, he went into the interrogation room and sat silently facing Avni for a minute or two. 'I'd really like to tell you why I wrote those letters in Ofer's name – how the idea was born and why I didn't think it was such a terrible thing to do,' the teacher began. 'Can you listen to me now?' Avraham left the room because he could not bear to hear Avni's voice, and maybe also to put more pressure on him. He still believed Avni would break down and confess that he never sent the letters.

Shrapstein and Ilana returned from the district court in the early afternoon with an easily attained green light for a wiretap and an arrest warrant. They must have come up with the idea on their way to court, or on their way back, and the next day, too, when they each sat in their offices at the station and waited, Avraham still didn't know whose it really was. Ilana was sufficiently shrewd to let Shrapstein present it to him.

'The idea is to wear Avni down without arresting him, to have him stay here as late as possible, the whole night if need be. To scare him. He doesn't look like a hard nut to crack. If you like, we can do it in shifts; you stay with him now, and I'll keep him company through the night. We'll let him stew awhile alone in the interrogation room, too. Occasionally, we'll stand outside the door and I'll say something like, "I'm sure it's him; let's just arrest him now." We want him panicking. And when he's ready, we'll hint that he can help himself by cooperating with us.'

Avraham wasn't sure he understood. 'Cooperate with us how?' he asked.

'We'll subtly imply that we're willing to forget his confession and will return the letters and ignore all he's done, because of lack of public interest, if he makes a call to Ofer's parents and tells them that he wrote the letters and knows where Ofer is,' Shrapstein replied.

Avraham was stunned. His eyes rested on Ilana. 'What will that give us?'

'The call will be recorded. And if, within a few hours, they don't report an anonymous call from someone who says he knows where Ofer is, we won't need to think twice about arresting them.'

'The only question is, how are you going to imply something like that subtly to him?' Ilana said, and Shrapstein smiled. 'We'll find a way. Mark my words, after a night at the station, without his family, convinced that he is going to be arrested and won't see his wife and child for who knows how long, and then given a chance to go home, he'll do whatever we want. He said he wanted to help with the investigation, didn't he? Okay, we'll give him the chance to do that.'

Avraham recalled the panic he had seen in Avni's eyes at the mention of his wife and son during the interrogation. Would he do whatever they wanted? Most people would behave exactly as Shrapstein had said. 'Is that even legal?' he asked, and Shrapstein said, 'Why not? Besides, do you think he's going to tell anyone?'

Ilana looked at a tall man passing through the parking lot outside the window of Shrapstein's office.

A policewoman entered. 'The guy you put in the interrogation room won't stop banging on the door and calling for Avi,' she said. 'What should we do with him?'

Avraham sat in his office and turned on the recording device to listen once again to the conversation between Avni and the parents. Avni was speaking directly to him alone now. 'I put Ofer's letters in the mailbox. I know where Ofer is,' he said.

Where was Avni right now? Avraham assumed the teacher had locked himself up at home. When they sent him out on his mission from the station early that morning, they told him he was free to do anything he pleased, but that wasn't entirely true. Ilana had requisitioned a team of detectives to keep an eye on him until the case was solved. 'The fact that the parents have held back information doesn't mean we know what has happened to Ofer,' she had said. 'And until we do, I want to keep the teacher in our sights.'

Meanwhile, they just waited.

And each of them waited differently.

Shrapstein was likely hoping that the parents wouldn't phone in to report the anonymous call and that his suppositions would be proved right. Avraham heard each second crash down, and with each thud it was more difficult to keep his eyes open. And Ilana? He didn't know what she was waiting for.

He needed to prepare for the questioning of the parents in the event that they failed to call and were brought into the station the following day to be confronted. He made a note of the dates on which the letters had been sent, and read through them again to select the fragments he would read out during the questioning. There were lines that made his blood run cold. *'No longer yours, Ofer.'* They had decided that if the parents failed to report the call, they'd be brought in together and questioned separately. They'd do it the following morning, after the children were dropped off at kindergarten and school. Shrapstein would take the father and he the mother. But they might have had countless reasons not to call right away! Perhaps they weren't sure who to contact first? Or maybe they were waiting for the next call because the anonymous caller had promised to contact them again? Avraham repeatedly checked to ensure his cell phone was on and the reception was good. He listened for the sound of any ring coming from the front desk or one of the other offices. The door could open at any minute. Everything could still change.

He removed various documents from the case file and spread them out over his desk. His attention was drawn to the list of items found in Ofer's backpack, just as it had been the first time he saw it, two days earlier, in Ilana's office. He also came across the copy of Ofer's class schedule. He stared at both documents. His eyes almost closed. And suddenly they opened.

He went out to smoke another cigarette.

A few minutes after returning to his office, he checked his e-mail, which he hadn't done since the morning of the day before. He had more than twenty new messages, most of which were junk mail.

But there was a message from Marianka.

The phone in his office rang just as he started reading her message, making him jump to his feet. Someone from the state attorney's office asking about the evidentiary material in the Igor Kintiev case. He had completely forgotten about him.

Marianka had written to him in English:

*Avi, you promised to update me about your investigation, but you probably haven't had time since you got back. Did you find him? I've been thinking a lot about what you told me about the missing boy, and about you too. I'm sure you will find him and pray together with you that nothing has happened to him. My thoughts are with you. Write to me when you have a chance. Marianka.*

The line '*My thoughts are with you*' might have meant she was thinking only of him, or of both him and Ofer, he couldn't tell.

He promised himself he would reply.

Ilana called to ask if there had been any developments and to see how he was feeling.

But there were no developments, and how did she think he was feeling?

'You're taking a vacation when this case is over,' she said.

'It was really hard for me to see you like that yesterday and today,' and he said only, 'Yes.'

'And you must go home to get some sleep. You've been at the station since yesterday morning. Do you know what the time is?'

It was 5:30 p.m.

'Nothing's going to happen now, Avi. They aren't going to call. And that means tomorrow's going to be a long and exhausting day. The interrogation of Ofer's mother won't be easy for you. You'll need all your strength for it.'

He took her advice, because he was used to doing so, and too tired to think. And again he stopped on the way home outside that damned building on Histadrut Street, which he was drawn to as if it were an old childhood haunt one returns to without really understanding why. The apartment in which Ofer had lived up until just a few weeks ago was shrouded in darkness. He'd be entering it the following day accompanied by three or four other policemen, and asking Rafael and Hannah Sharabi to come with him to the station for questioning. If they refused, he'd pull out the arrest warrant.

It was unbelievable – Ze'ev Avni was walking down the street.

At first Avraham thought that his eyes were playing tricks on him, that his exhaustion was messing with his mind. But it was indeed Avni, walking back to the building, pushing a stroller. His wife was by his side.

When, in the early hours of that morning, Avni understood their offer and was persuaded that he was not being framed for a crime he hadn't committed and that nothing he said on the telephone would be used against him, he asked to be left alone for a few minutes in the interrogation room to think about it.

They waited for him in the corridor and entered when he knocked on the door.

'I'll do it,' he said, 'although I'm not exactly sure what you're after.' He looked Avraham directly in the eyes when he added: 'I want you to know that I am doing it for you, because I trust you, and because you are asking me to do it. Until now I have hampered your investigation, and if you are asking me to, I am willing to help. And also because of my family. I think it's what my wife would want me to do. Nevertheless, I get the feeling that of all the allegedly improper things I have done until now, this is the worst.'

Now he could see Avni at the entrance to the building, undoing the straps of the stroller, lifting up his son in his one arm and folding the stroller with the other. He hadn't spotted any detectives in the area but assumed someone was watching them.

No one could hear him whisper in the car, 'I'll be seeing you again, Ze'ev.'


His cell rang at 11:00 p.m. He woke up startled, with his clothes on, in the armchair in front of the TV.

It was Ilana again. She wanted to make sure everything was ready.

'I'll be at the station tomorrow morning at six thirty,' he said. 'We'll be in front of their building at seven and will wait for the children to leave.'

'Do whatever you can to get them to come in without using the warrants,' Ilana instructed.

He turned out the lights.

The following day, a little after 7:00 a.m., exactly three weeks since that Wednesday morning when the mother had entered his office, two white police cars pulled up a short distance from the building. Farther down the street, outside the convenience store, a dairy truck was unloading.

Hannah Sharabi came out to the street at 7:25. A girl walked beside her, clumsily, hesitantly, heavily. It was Danit, and he was seeing her for the first time. She was taller and broader than her mother, and her eyes were fixed on the sidewalk. They waited together in front of the building, their hands constantly clasped. Then a yellow minibus pulled up and the driver stepped out to help Danit get on. Hannah waited for her daughter to take her seat and waved good-bye to her.

At 7:45 a.m., Rafael Sharabi drove their younger son to kindergarten. Shrapstein's car followed him. The father returned home some twenty minutes later, and shortly thereafter came the knock on the door.

There was no need for the arrest warrants.

Rafael Sharabi asked, 'But why like this? We were waiting for your call – we would have come in whenever you liked.' Though disconcerted, neither refused to accompany the police to the station for questioning.

Did they realize that the interviews would be different from the previous talks to which they had been summoned? Even if they did, they didn't show it – not then, and not when the policemen asked them to get into separate cars.

Avraham sat in the front seat, the mother behind him. Not a word was spoken between them during the short drive, and he refrained from studying her face in the rearview mirror.

They were brought into the station via the back entrance, through the parking lot, and taken to separate interrogation rooms.

## 14

Across the desk from him sat a mother. But this time she was no longer just another mother.

Three weeks earlier, Avraham had tried to get rid of her. He had asked if she knew why no one wrote detective novels in Hebrew, and she had not understood. He had sworn since never to repeat that question. He had sent her out to look for her son by herself, despite the fact that she had been alone. Her husband was on a ship bound for Trieste. And he had regretted what he had done that very same evening. The following day, he had seen her entering the station and had frozen in his tracks. She hadn't spoken much. She had placed the photographs of her son, in a nylon bag, on his desk. That same day, he had gone to her home. He had tried to have a quiet conversation with her, to no avail. The following day, his birthday, he had sat beside her on a bed in the room of her missing son. They had opened his drawers together. But then this was also the mother who had received three letters written in her son's name and had said nothing about them. The mother who was told in an anonymous telephone call that someone knew where Ofer was, and she did not report it to the police.

Did he now know a lot more about her than he had at the start of the investigation?

She served in the navy and married Rafael Sharabi at the age of twenty-one, and sometimes she would not see him for a month or two when he was at sea. She worked at a kinder-garten. A few years later she had her first son, and soon after a daughter, who was severely handicapped. Had they discovered it immediately or did it take them a few months to notice? Earlier that morning, Avraham had seen them standing together on the sidewalk, holding hands, the daughter a head taller than the mother but frozen and helpless. Hannah Sharabi raised the two children alone. Her husband was at sea. And having no choice, she accepted it. She quit her job to protect her daughter from the violence or indifference that surrounded her, and refused to send her away to an institution even when she grew up and her husband wanted her to do it. During the investigation he had perceived her to be submissive and meek. She never raised her voice; she hadn't demanded anything of him or criticized him. Her refusal to send Danit away was the only evidence of her ability to stand her ground. Not to break. When her daughter had grown up, Hannah had another child, perhaps thanks to advances in medical technology.

'Do you know why you are here?' he asked her. 'Do you know why we brought you both in for questioning?'

The conversation was being videotaped by a camera mounted on the ceiling of the interrogation room. He rested his elbows on the desk, clasped his hands together, and cov-ered his mouth when he wasn't speaking. Her chair was a foot or so away from the desk. Most of the time, she didn't look directly at the investigator sitting opposite her. Her gaze went through him and focused on the door, as if she were waiting for someone to open it and put an end to the interrogation, or perhaps as if planning an escape.

'No,' she said, and because no response came from him, she asked, 'Have you discovered something about Ofer?'

Avraham said, 'Yes,' and nothing more.

This was the first interrogation since the start of the investigation that he had planned down to the last detail, just as he liked to do. His strategy had unfolded clearly the moment he started working on it the previous afternoon, and he had meticulously thought through every word. Also the silences.

Realizing he wasn't going to add anything, she asked, 'Why aren't you telling me what you've found?' and he said, 'I want to give you the chance to tell me first.'

A look of confusion appeared on her face. 'Tell you what first?'

'If you know anything new about what happened to Ofer.'

It was her last chance. But she said, 'No, other than the bag you found.'

He tried to catch her eyes and then gave her yet another chance.

'Hannah, I want you to think hard before you answer me. I'm asking you if, since the search for Ofer began, you have informed me, or the police, of everything you know. Take your time. Think about my question.'

He was glad that no one was watching, or would ever watch, the video of Hannah Sharabi's interrogation. The film would go into the archives along with the rest of the case evidence and eventually would probably be destroyed or erased; he wasn't an expert on police storage procedures.

Interrogators are supposed to extract incriminating information from their suspects, but anyone watching the interrogation video would know that this was not what Avraham tried to do. When he watched it a few days later, he realized that some of the things she had said were unintelligible – one of the drawbacks of videotaped documentation. But that particular conversation he would always be able to reconstruct.

She told him she had informed the police of all she knew, and on film he looks like he is mulling over her answer, pondering. He opens the closed cardboard case file lying on the corner of the desk and removes sheets of paper wrapped in plastic.

'You didn't tell me that you received these letters,' Avraham said, though he hadn't yet handed them to her.

'What's that?' she asked.

'Letters that were put in your mailbox. Actually, these are not the original letters; those you removed. These are copies. Would you like me to tell you the exact dates on which they were in your mailbox?'

She didn't respond. Fixed her gaze on the door more fiercely. 'Would you like me to tell you how the letters are related to Ofer or do you already know?' he asked, and she said, 'I don't know. How did you find them?'

Disregarding her question, he began reading the first letter. '"*Father and Mother, I know you've been looking for me for a few days now, but I suggest you stop looking because you won't find me, and neither will the police, not even with tracker dogs. The notices you posted in the streets say I disappeared on Wednesday morning, but all three of us know that isn't true. We all know that I disappeared long before then, without you even noticing, because you didn't pay attention, and that I didn't disappear in a single day either, but it was a gradual process of disappearing, at the end of which you thought I was still at home only because you never even tried to look.*"' He stopped reading. The remainder of the letter horrified him. He tried to read the look on her face, and, even later, upon review, he didn't see any sign of astonishment. The thought that crossed his mind shook him.

He was right. Avni, the lunatic, was right.

With every passing moment, it became more possible that Ofer hadn't disappeared on Wednesday morning.

'What is that?' Hannah Sharabi asked again, and Avraham composed himself. 'You know whose name is on the letter. Here, read it: "*No longer yours, Ofer.*"' He put the letter in front of her.

'That's not Ofer's handwriting,' she said, and he responded immediately with a question that he had not planned: 'Why would Ofer write such a thing – that you all know he didn't disappear on Wednesday morning but before?'

'That's not his handwriting,' she repeated. 'He didn't write it. Where did you get that letter from?'

'We didn't get it, Hannah. You got it,' he said quietly. 'We only received a copy. Come now, explain to me why you didn't inform us.'

She was silent for a few moments and then said, 'I never saw that letter. And Ofer didn't write it.'

Was it possible that she hadn't seen the letter? He had never run into such a situation during an interrogation. He tried to make her slip, break down and confess, say she had seen the letter, but inside he also hoped she would continue to deny it. While watching the videotape of the interview later, he thought that had he continued to ask her about the content of the letters, as if he didn't know that Ofer hadn't written them, had he thrown the accusations of the teenager at her, she would have broken. But instead he said, 'I know Ofer didn't write them. And I know that they were in your mailbox, and that they are not there now. Could your husband have found them and not told you?' That possibility had only just then crossed his mind. Not that Rafael Sharabi had kept them from his wife – he had thought of that already – but that the father was not familiar with his son's handwriting and might have thought that Ofer had really written the letters. He couldn't picture Rafael Sharabi checking his son's homework or reading through his tests. And if that was what he had thought, then perhaps he kept them from his wife to protect her.

'No, he would give them to me,' Hannah said.

'Perhaps the children?'

'The children don't open the mail. Even Ofer didn't.'

Avraham looked at his watch and left the room.

Shrapstein was waiting for him in the old interrogation room at the far end of the corridor. 'Well?' he asked as Avraham entered.

He shook his head. 'She hadn't seen the letters, she hadn't heard about them, she knew it wasn't Ofer who wrote them,' he said.

'Same with him,' Shrapstein replied.

'And do you believe him? How does he look to you?'

'He's frightened. And I don't believe a word he says. I'm telling you, the moment I drop the phone call on him, he'll crack.'

Avraham hesitated for a moment before he said, 'I have almost no doubt now that they got the letters,' and Shrapstein asked, 'Why? Did she let something slip?'

'No. Because of you. I mean, because of the father. I don't believe the father would know Ofer's handwriting. If he knew that Ofer didn't write them, it's only because she told him before.'

Shrapstein looked at him in surprise. 'You're forgetting there could be another reason,' he said.

'What other reason?'

'That he knows that Ofer couldn't have written them.'

There were things he preferred not to think about.

They decided that Shrapstein would update Ilana, and Shrapstein told him, 'Avi, I'm moving on to the phone call the moment I go back in.'

Cars passed by slowly as he went out to have a cigarette. Drivers always slowed down on Fichman Street, near the station. There wasn't a street in Holon with fewer accidents. He lit his cigarette. The skies above were a spotless blue. That first evening, he had described to Hannah Sharabi what might have happened to Ofer. Perhaps he forgot to prepare for an exam and decided not to go to school, he had said. By the following day already, it was clear that this wasn't the case. He recalled that on his way home that evening, he had imagined Ofer all alone in a dark public park somewhere, putting his black backpack down on a bench and preparing for sleep. Was he still allowed to have some hope? Or perhaps he should pray, as Marianka had written?

Avraham, too, moved on to the phone call as soon as he returned to the interrogation room. And Hannah Sharabi's eyes again avoided his when he said, 'Look, Hannah, let me explain to you why it's so difficult for me to believe that you haven't seen those letters before, and why I find it difficult to believe that you aren't concealing any information from me. It's because of the phone call, which you didn't report to us, either.'

'What phone call?' she immediately answered – and something in her voice changed. Now she did look at him, and he saw alarm in her eyes. She placed her left hand on the desk.

'The call you received yesterday morning. Do you recall?'

She pretended to be trying to remember. 'Yes,' she finally said.

'And can you explain why you didn't report it?'

She didn't respond, and he asked, 'Can you tell me what was said in the call?'

'Someone said he knew Ofer. And that he would call later to tell us where he is.'

He chose to remain silent for a long minute, to give her a chance to understand for herself the significance of her statement. His next words were spoken in a voice that became louder, ending in a scream of true rage, no pretenses. 'We've been looking for your son for three weeks with I don't even know how many policemen, turning over every rock. I myself go to sleep with Ofer Sharabi in my head and I wake up with him in the morning – and you get a phone call from someone who tells you that he knows where Ofer is and you don't report it. And then you come here and continue to hide things from me and tell me that you've given me all the information you have. Have you completely lost your minds? Over and above the fact that you're putting your son at risk, do you realize that what you are doing is a serious criminal offense? Have you ever heard of obstructing a police investigation? Do you know that I could arrest you both?'

He expected she would not respond.

He stood up and began pacing back and forth in the narrow room, from one side to the other, over and over. He lowered his voice again, almost to a whisper, and wasn't sure she heard him when he said, 'Nothing you say could explain it. Nothing at all. But I want you to try anyway. Why didn't you tell us?'

His pacing was effective. Hannah Sharabi tried to track his movements, making it simple for him to catch her eyes. And for the first time he saw fear. He almost felt sorry and thought about leaving the room again, precisely at that moment, to allow her to compose herself. She, too, looked like she hadn't slept for three weeks. Rafael Sharabi had told him during his interview that she was plagued by nightmares. The small purse she was carrying with her that first evening, and the following day, was nowhere to be seen – as if from the moment her husband returned, she no longer needed a wallet or keys or a cell phone.

'We didn't think he really knew Ofer. We thought someone was harassing us – a lunatic,' she said quietly, echoing Shrapstein's words, as if she had been listening in on the conversations of the team of investigators, not just the other way around.

'I don't believe you.' He continued to pace through the room – now in ever tighter circles, around the desk, and around her, such that some of his words were spoken behind her back. 'I don't believe that a mother whose son has been missing for three weeks gets a call from someone who says he knows where this child is and she doesn't take it seriously. That would never happen. There's no such mother in the world. All you had to do was call me and say, "Some lunatic just called us to say he knows where Ofer is. Make of it what you will." He said he'd call in the evening to tell you where Ofer is, didn't he? And what if he really does know something? We'd be able to trace the call and locate him. Do you know a mother out there who would give up on a chance like that?'

'He didn't call,' she said, and he burst out: 'But you didn't know that then! No one could have known that. What am I supposed to think about what you've done? You're either stupid – but really stupid – to think there was no need to report the call, or you don't care what happened to Ofer, or you know what happened to him and that's why the call didn't seem important. Which do you choose? Which of those three options seems right to you?'

He waited for Shrapstein in the old interrogation room at the far end of the corridor for five minutes – but Shrapstein didn't come.

They had agreed to meet up every half-hour unless their interrogation reached a critical point. It was 10:04 a.m. Had Rafael Sharabi already crumbled, as Shrapstein had foreseen? And if so, what was exposed among the ruins?

He was tenser than he had ever been during an interrogation. His exhaustion was a factor, of course. Perhaps he should have taken up Ilana's offer to let her do the questioning of Hannah Sharabi in his stead.

He asked one of the duty officers to tell Shrapstein he was outside if she saw him in the corridor, then lit a cigarette and sat down on the stairs leading up to the station. He still wasn't sure how to tell Hannah Sharabi about what had been frightening him since the afternoon of the day before. He was about to reach the moment in the interrogation when, according to the plan, he would ask about something no one knew. Neither Shrapstein nor Ilana. And he had to ask – not to make her crumble, no, on the contrary – so that she would give him an answer that relieved him.

He regretted his outburst. As he left the room, slamming the door behind him, Hannah Sharabi had stared at him, humiliated, overcome with hatred.

Watching the videotape, he noticed a degree of hesitancy and anxiety in his stride as he returned to the room and slowly dragged his chair from its original position – across the desk from Hannah Sharabi's seat – to its new one, at the corner of the desk, alongside her, just a whisper away. They were now sitting close to each other, just as they had on Ofer's bed.

'What do you want from me?' she asked, and he said, 'One more thing, and then you can leave.'

How he wanted to believe that.

'I'd like to share with you one more problem that has been bothering me about Ofer's disappearance, okay? From the first time you came into the station, you have been saying that Ofer left home that Wednesday at seven forty-five a.m. and was on his way to school, right?'

'Yes.'

'And are you sure he was on his way to school? Did you know then or do you know now if he had other plans?'

'I've already told you – no.'

Did he see a glimmer of hope in the corner of her eye? Relief perhaps? He was back to inquiring about Ofer, about the morning of his disappearance, after all the questions about the letters and the phone call they had concealed. Her cheeks still shook.

He reached over for the cardboard case file and withdrew a sheet of paper. 'This is Ofer's class schedule. I took it out of the drawer in his room, if you recall. In fact, we found it together. And yesterday evening I verified it with his home-room teacher. According to the schedule for Wednesday, Ofer should have started the day with two hours of algebra, followed by an hour of English, an hour of PE, an hour of sociology, and an hour of literature.'

He looked at her, expecting a response. She had no idea where he was going.

He withdrew another sheet of paper from the case file. 'Don't be afraid,' he said. 'I'm not trying to trip you up. I want to help you.'

She remained silent.

'This is a list of the books that were found in Ofer's bag. A civics book, a sociology book, a copy of *Antigone* – that must be for the literature class – and a grammar book. No algebra book, and no English book, despite the fact that his first three hours on a Wednesday were in algebra and English. That doesn't sound like Ofer, does it? What do you make of it?'

She didn't reach for the page with the list of the items found in the bag. Her hands rested on her knees, just as they had almost throughout the interrogation.

'To me,' he went on, 'it means that if Ofer prepared the bag himself, he had no intention of going to school that Wednesday morning. Does that sound reasonable to you?'

Again she put her left hand on the desk, just as she had done earlier, when he surprised her with the question about the phone call. He was very close to her now, his face almost brushing against her left cheek and ear, where the ends of her black hair rested. Because of their proximity, she didn't know where to look when she replied, in a broken voice, 'So maybe he knew he wasn't . . .'

He cut in to her words. 'That's what I thought. But something confused me. You told me that Ofer was very organized. I saw it for myself when I was in his room, remember?'

She nodded.

'And that's what confused me. Let's assume he had no intention of going to school that Wednesday. If that's the case, he would probably have left the books he returned home with from school on Tuesday in the bag, right?'

He waited for her to say something but she didn't speak and he continued. Again he looked over the class schedule. 'From eight to nine, Bible studies; from nine to ten, geometry; then two hours of English, an hour of geography, and an hour of history. You see? The same problem. Yesterday, your husband asked me on the phone if we had come across anything in the bag. So here's the problem: the only conclusion we could possibly draw from Ofer's bag is that he had no intention of going to school. Otherwise, he would have taken the right books with him. On the other hand, if he planned to run away from home, why take any schoolbooks? Assuming he went to school on Tuesday with the right books, we're left with the following absurd scenario: on Tuesday, when Ofer prepared to run away or disappear, he removed the books he had taken to school that day and replaced them with others. Just any books. Does that make sense to you? Does it sound like something Ofer would do?'

He pulled his face away from her, and his voice cracked when, for the first time, he spoke the sentence he hadn't formulated in his mind ahead of their conversation. And he thought he could see tears in her eyes.

'There's one more possibility. That Ofer returned home on Tuesday, removed his schoolbooks from the bag, maybe did his homework, maybe placed his books on the shelf. And that someone else put the books we found into the bag – I'm not sure exactly when. But it wasn't Ofer. It was someone who didn't know Ofer's schedule, or didn't think about it, but simply stuffed some books in the bag before throwing it into the dumpster.'

He moved his face close to her cheek again, and waited.

'Hannah,' he said, 'there was a grammar book in the bag,

and Ofer doesn't do grammar anymore. You know that he took his final grammar exam last year.'

She stared fiercely at the closed door once again. The muscles of her face clenched tight as if in an effort to prevent it from disintegrating. If she could, he thought, she'd let her face fall into her hands.

Neither of them spoke. There was nothing more to say. His interrogation was finished.

She suddenly said, 'Get away from me,' and he asked, 'What?'

'Leave me alone. Don't come close to me.'

He pulled his face back and stood up.

And then he paced again – this time not to trap her gaze, but to calm himself.

He looked at her from time to time, and she seemed to have regained her composure. Her cheeks tightened. The intensity with which she fixed her eyes on the door handle frightened him.

He couldn't keep her in the interrogation room forever.

And suddenly he was filled with hatred. He wanted to hit her, to grab her hair and smash her head into the wall, over and over again.

The interrogation was being videotaped.

The door opened and Shrapstein appeared. 'Come here a moment, Avi,' he said, and Avraham replied, 'Not now, I'm in the middle of something.'

Shrapstein screamed at him. 'Avi, I'm telling you to get the fuck out here already.'

He stepped out – because of the scream.

Shrapstein looked stunned. His eyes were void of even the slightest joy when he said, 'That's it. He confessed.'

# 15

Ilana was immediately summoned from Tel Aviv, and they shut themselves off in the conference room to carefully analyze each aspect of the father's confession and its bearings on the remainder of the investigation. They had doubts about some of the details he had given them because he had taken all the blame and cleared his wife of any responsibility. Shrapstein thought they should break the mother too, root out the truth from both of them. Ilana wasn't sure, but leaned toward making do with the father's confession for the time being. They had enough to bring the parents up before a court and have them remanded to custody.

Avraham stayed out of their conversation. Shrapstein's words still echoed loud in his ears: 'Get the fuck out here already.' And he was still seeing how the mother's eyes locked in on him with terror as he left the room.

She understood.

Rafael Sharabi cracked after Shrapstein told him that the police were in possession of further incriminating evidence in addition to the information about the letters and the anonymous phone call. Perhaps even a body. Shrapstein's interrogation tactics were entirely different from Avraham's. He threatened, sent up smoke screens, referred frequently to the interrogation that was taking place in the adjacent room, and took the interview down the thin, blurred boundary of what the law permitted. And he never lost his nerve.

Could Avraham also have broken the father?

Just like his wife, Rafael Sharabi had lied to him in their interview. And he had believed him. He had continued to believe even after the team meeting where questions were raised about the parents' statements. And he still believed during his interrogation of the mother, even when he lashed out at her, even when he was filled with the urge to smash her silence against the wall.

He needed a cigarette but couldn't leave the room. Shrapstein and Ilana sat glued to the small television screen. Ilana was stone-faced. She instructed him to call Ma'alul, who was on his way to the station, and ask him to inform the welfare authorities.

Shrapstein too had been in possession of a trump card he hadn't revealed, or hadn't said anything about playing – the father's fingerprints on the bag. The finding was insignificant; the father's prints on the bag were expected. Even a novice lawyer, had there been one in the room at the time, would have crushed Shrapstein's vague insinuations as easily as stamping out a cigarette butt. But that was the advantage of the strategy he had woven: the parents weren't taken into custody for questioning – they were there willingly, alone, without legal representation.

Shrapstein presented the father with the letters, and then slammed him with the phone call, finally telling him repeatedly that his prints would prove that he had been the last person to touch the bag, not Ofer. And Rafael Sharabi was indeed terrified. From the start, far more than his wife. Avraham studied the father's face, the sunken cheeks covered by a silvery beard. He was dressed in jeans, a white polo shirt, and white sneakers. His features were deepened with pain. He looked like a man who was starving himself. Gone was the softness Avraham had seen in him when they first met. He was afraid of Shrapstein, perhaps because he had not met him before, and perhaps because until the moment of confession Shrapstein was scorchingly firm. It was clear from the moment the father sat down in front of him that the interrogation would culminate in the revelation of what he was hiding.

'Don't you understand why you have to talk to me?' Shrapstein said. 'Your wife is being questioned in the adjacent room, and you know she won't be able to take it. I've just come from there and have seen what she's going through. It's ugly. You don't know Inspector Avi Avraham; he'll get whatever he wants out of her, no matter how. Tell me the truth and you'll spare your wife and yourself a lot of suffering, believe me. Do you realize he wanted us to arrest you both yesterday and send you off to the Abu Kabir detention center? Is that where you want to end up? Is that where you want her to end up?'

At this point Rafael Sharabi still tried to defend himself. He said, 'Arrest us for what? For letters we didn't get? We'll get a lawyer,' and Shrapstein replied, 'Go ahead, with pleasure. You know what that tells us, but no problem. What I can promise you is that it's going to take some time for us to get you to a phone, and then some more for a lawyer to arrive; meanwhile, your wife in the other room will be screaming out whatever it is you're hiding – not speaking it, screaming it. But whatever you want.'

'I hope you didn't at any time advise him not to speak to a lawyer,' Ilana said, looking over at Shrapstein.

'Never,' Shrapstein quietly responded.

The videotape showed Rafael Sharabi on the verge of making the hardest decision of his life. He clenched his fingers into a fist and rested the fist on the desk, almost exactly as his wife had done.

The door to the conference room opened and Ma'alul entered. 'I spoke to welfare. They're sending someone,' he said to Ilana, and then touched Avraham's shoulder, without saying a word, without explaining if the gesture was an expression of greeting or consolation.

The digital clock at the bottom of the monitor raced forward. Rafael Sharabi sat in his chair, his back hunched, his head between his hands. Shrapstein towered over him. 'Don't you realize you're finished?' he said. 'Do you really not get it? The only way to help yourself and your wife, and Ofer too, is to tell the truth.'

A whimper came from between the father's hands.

Shrapstein fired his final shot. He whispered in his ear, 'Tell me, do you really not understand why you are here? Do you think we would have brought you only because of the phone call? I'll be straight with you. We have the letters; we have the phone call; we have your prints to prove that no one touched the bag after you. And we have Ofer, too.'

Rafael Sharabi withdrew his hands from his face and looked up at Shrapstein, who had gone silent. 'Have you found him?' the father asked, and Shrapstein didn't blink as he said, 'Why do you think you are here?'

And that was it.

The wail burst forth from within him and Avraham couldn't understand how he hadn't heard it from next door.

Ilana stood up. 'Stop the tape for a moment,' she said. 'I can't bear to see it.'

Ma'alul left the room.

A full two hours went by before Avraham returned to the interrogation room in which he had left the mother. She followed his return with her eyes. He dragged his chair back to its original position and sat down opposite her. The chair games were unnecessary now.

'That's it, it's all over,' he said, to which she didn't respond.

Her left hand rested on the desk. Before he returned to the room, Ilana had asked if he'd like her to stand in for him, or join him, for the remainder of the interrogation. He had said no. Now, faced with the frozen mother, he thought he might have made a mistake. He couldn't bring himself to look at her – either out of hatred or pity, he couldn't tell which.

'I know what happened to Ofer – you don't need to hide it anymore. And I don't understand why you lied. You made a terrible mistake.'

'Have you found Ofer?' she asked, and he responded without raising his voice: 'Enough already. Hannah, your husband provided us with a detailed confession, and you and I are going to go through it now. I want you to consider every detail in his statement, and for the good of both you and your children, I want you to tell me the truth this time.'

A sheet of paper with a summary of the father's statement, arranged as a bulleted list, lay on the desk in front of him. 'On Tuesday evening, May third, you and your husband went out to meet with friends. Can you recall the time?'

'We've already told you – at around nine.' Her voice trembled.

Avraham remembered the description of that day well. Ofer returned home from school at 2:00 p.m. His parents weren't sure what he did, and didn't ask. He ate lunch alone, played on the computer, watched TV, and did his homework in his room. Rafael Sharabi slept for a few hours in the bedroom and packed a suitcase for his trip when he woke. Hannah waited for her younger son and daughter to return from kindergarten and school. They sat down to have supper at 7:00 p.m. The father then bathed the small boy and put him to bed in the room he shared with Ofer. His wife bathed Danit and helped her with her nightdress and into bed. Ofer returned to his room after his younger brother had fallen asleep. He sat down in front of the computer without turning on the light.

'Can you give me the names of your friends and tell me where you met up?'

She was still hesitant. Was she unsure of exactly what her husband had said? Or perhaps she wanted to believe that the investigator's dramatic exit from the room and his return two hours later was just an interrogation ploy.

'Remember what I asked of you, Hannah?' he said. 'We know everything now, and if there is something we aren't yet aware of, we'll find out easily enough. I want the names of the friends you met with and the café where you spent the evening.'

'Somewhere in the center of town,' she blurted out. 'I don't remember the name.'

'Okay. According to your husband's confession, he returned home alone at ten thirty because he felt unwell, and you stayed behind with your friends. We don't believe this.'

The entire investigation team was of the same opinion – the parents had coordinated their stories. But he noticed a hint of surprise in her eyes, and she seemed to be struggling to decipher his intentions. What had surprised her? Was it possible that they weren't in sync and that Rafael Sharabi had made a statement that exonerated his wife without her knowledge? Avraham was never able to clarify that particular detail.

'It's true,' she whispered. 'That's what happened.'

'That's not what you told us in your previous statements,' Avraham said. 'You both told us you returned home together. And we can easily verify it. You realize that, don't you? We'll bring your friends in for questioning and find out.'

'Rafael wasn't feeling well and needed to go to bed early because of work. I wanted to stay longer.'

Without either of them saying it, this was the first moment when they both acknowledged that Ofer wasn't missing. That he never went missing. Ofer hadn't run away from home, he wasn't in Rio de Janeiro, he wasn't in Koper, and he wasn't in Tel Aviv. The story she had told him, and which he had told himself over the past three weeks, lost its steam. And Avraham didn't want to hear the story he was forcing her to tell him now.

'Can I see my husband?' she asked, and he said, 'Not yet. You may be able to see each other later.'

The thing he failed to understand at that point in the interrogation was that Hannah Sharabi hadn't cracked. To the contrary. She might have changed her story and stuck to almost every detail of her husband's confession, yet she still refused to divulge anything he didn't already know. He could press her and try to 'root out the truth,' as Shrapstein had demanded, or he could allow her to tell her story – at least for now, as Ilana had said.

'So tell me,' he continued. 'How long after your husband did you get home?'

'How long?'

'How much time passed between the moment your husband went home and you came back to the apartment?'

'I don't know exactly how long. Maybe an hour.'

'And how did you get there? Do you recall?'

'Get where?'

'How did you get home? On foot? By taxi? Did your friends drive you home?'

'I walked,' she replied, and he said, 'And as I understand it, when you came home Ofer was already dead.'

They were both startled by how suddenly and how directly he said it. He was even more surprised than her. He had heard it two hours earlier but only at that moment did the full impact of the truth hit him.

Ofer was already dead.

Was he trying to take it back, say something that would take the certainty of that question away, when he quickly repeated it using different words, ones that could imply that Ofer was still alive? He asked, 'Where was Ofer when you got home?' and she said, 'In his room.' He saw her face tightening again.

That was not what Rafael Sharabi said in his confession. Avraham felt a surge of rage, and tried to contain it. He wanted her to tell the truth. And at the same time he didn't. Ilana had instructed him not to press her too hard, not at this stage. 'It's enough that she corroborates his story, even if it is not an exact match,' she had said.

'Your husband said something different,' he said, and Hannah Sharabi replied, 'That's how I remember it.'

'So try to reconstruct it. Do you remember opening the door to the building? Did you open it, or did you use the intercom to call your husband, who then let you in?'

'I came in by myself,' she lied, and he thought back to that Friday, two days after she had reported Ofer missing, and about how he had waited outside the entrance to the building. He had tried the intercom and got no reply. A neighbor let him in, and he caught her just after her shower. They drank coffee at the counter that separated the kitchen from the dining room. She asked if there was anything new in the investigation. All that time she knew what had happened to Ofer.

'How did you open your apartment door? Did you also open that door yourself?' he asked, and she said, 'Yes.' The apartment opened up for him too – in his memory. The living room on the left. The dining room and the kitchen on the right. Across from the entrance – a narrow doorway to the passage that led to the bedrooms. Ofer's room was at the far end.

'You entered the apartment and then what did you see?' he asked, and she said, 'Nothing.'

'Was the apartment lit? Was it dark? What did you see?'

'A light was on. There was no one there. It was quiet.' The television was not on and no one sat on the sofas in the living room. The kitchen cupboards and the dining table and the walls were silent too. The light was weak. But that's not how it happened.

'Where was your husband?'

'In the bathroom.' She saw a light through the small glass pane in the bathroom door. Some noise came from there, maybe the water flowing. But that's not how it happened.

'So what did you do inside the apartment? Describe it to me. What was the first thing that you did? Where did you go?'

'I knocked on the bathroom door and asked Rafael how he was feeling.'

'And then? Did he stay in the bathroom? Did you find Ofer by yourself?'

'No, Rafael came out. He had vomited.' The bathroom door opened and she saw her husband. Could she tell right away from the look on his face that something was wrong? But that's not how it happened. She had been in the apartment with him, the whole time. Avraham had no doubt at all.

They both went silent.

He could still stop the interrogation, leave the room, and ask Ilana to take over.

'How did you discover Ofer?' he asked.

'Rafael told me something happened to Ofer. He took me to his room,' she said.

'You're sure that Ofer was in his room?'

'Yes. He was lying on the floor.'

'Was he bleeding?'

'No. There was no blood. He was lying on the floor, and there was no blood at all.'

He could have stopped there. Ilana had authorized him to do so. The fact that there was a disparity between the two versions of events with regard to the room in which Ofer had been found was of no significance at this stage in the investigation. But he could no longer suppress the rage building up inside him over the lies she had told for the past three weeks. Only later that night, when writing up the summary report of the investigation, did he understand what it was that he wanted her to tell him, and why she had refused to tell him that, even with all the facts laid out before them.

'According to your husband's confession, Ofer was not in his room,' he insisted, and she said again, 'That's how I remember it.'

'Your husband said he was in Danit's room.'

It was the only room in the apartment he hadn't gone into, hadn't even considered entering, and it had always remained shut when he was there. That's why he could not open its door in his imagination, either.

'When I arrived, he was in his room.' There was no hesitation in her voice. Only hatred.

'Hannah, do you know what Ofer was doing in Danit's room?' he asked, and she answered quietly, 'He wasn't there, I told you.'

'That's not what your husband said.'

She didn't answer. Her eyes were shielded from him.

'Was that the first time you found Ofer in Danit's room?'

She wouldn't have answered, even if he had asked a thousand times. He should have stopped asking.

'Hannah, I'm asking you if that was the first time you found Ofer there.'

She didn't hear his questions anymore.

At the tips of his fingers he felt that he was about to pounce on her, like before. 'Don't you realize I'm going to ask you the same question over and over and over again until you answer me?' he yelled. 'Tell me how long it had been going on for. How many times did Ofer hurt Danit? When did he start abusing her?'

He didn't want to know, so why did he not relent?

'Don't you understand that you have to talk to me if you want to help your children? You have a daughter that needs looking after.'

Now she heard him and she turned her face toward him. With contempt. She said, 'Don't tell me how to look after my children. I would never hurt my children – no matter who asks me to do it,' and he said, 'Your husband told us that he returned home and found Ofer in Danit's room. Ofer didn't hear him come in. You know what he was doing in her room, don't you?'

Also later, that night, when he watched the recording of the interrogation in his office and prepared to write up the report, he was unable to read his own face for a sign of what he had wanted her to say.

'Don't tell me how to look after my children. I won't let anyone hurt them,' she repeated.

The recording was coming to an end. And the investigation too. Perhaps by the following day he wouldn't recall a thing from the past three weeks. Their exchanges became rapid and urgent.

'What did your husband tell you?'

'He didn't say anything. There was a fight between him and Ofer.'

'And what was the fight about?'

'He didn't say.'

'And you expect me to believe that you didn't ask?'

'I don't expect anything. Would it help Ofer if I asked?'

'And then what happened?'

'When?'

'When your husband and Ofer fought. What happened during the fight?'

'Rafael pushed him against the wall and Ofer hit his head and fell. It was an accident. It was in Ofer's room.'

'And how did you react to what he told you?'

'How do you think I reacted to it?'

The video showed him about to lose his nerve.

'I don't know how you reacted. I'm looking at you sitting here now, lying to me, and I don't know. You haven't stopped lying to me. For three weeks now, you haven't said a single truthful word about your son. I'm struggling to understand just what kind of a mother you are. I'm asking you to tell me how your son died, and you aren't able to. I'm asking you to look at him, to look at your son – and you aren't capable of doing that, even now that he is dead.'

She didn't respond.

And he finally relented.

'So what did you do?' he asked, drained of all strength, and she muttered, 'What could I do?'

'What did you do with Ofer when you found him dead in Danit's room? Or in his, whichever you like.'

'What did I do? I hugged him. That's it. What else was there to do?'

Shrapstein wanted 'five minutes with the mother' to root out of her whatever needed to be rooted out. 'There's no way she wasn't home at the time. I don't buy that story about her returning home after him,' he said. They all knew he was right.

Ilana was hesitant and asked Avraham for his thoughts on the matter. He said, 'Do whatever you think is right, Ilana. It makes no difference to me.'

She decided to suspend the interrogations. 'Let's give them a few hours, or days, to digest it all,' she said. 'They haven't been lying only to us all this time; they've been lying to themselves too. It'll be easier for them to talk in a few days. And even if we are right and the mother was there, I'm not sure what to do with that. I'm not certain it would add anything to our case if we recommend pressing charges against her.'

Shrapstein objected. 'She's no less guilty than her husband, and she played a more active role in concealing it,' he said, but Ilana was adamant. 'The final decision will come from the state prosecutor,' she said, summing up the discussion.

At 4:00 p.m. a representative from welfare services showed up. Just as Avraham was beginning to update her on the case, Ilana entered his office without knocking. The two women knew each other and Ilana addressed her as Etti. She was in her fifties and her hair was graying, just like Ilana's.

'Both parents will remain in custody, so something has to be done about the children,' he said. 'It appears that the sister, who has a handicap, was assaulted.'

'By whom?' Etti asked.

He was slow to answer and Ilana spoke in his stead. 'By her brother, the boy who was killed,' she said. 'It appears the father caught him in the act and a violent struggle broke out between them.'

Avraham hadn't had a cigarette in hours.

Etti asked if the children had any other family, and Ilana replied, 'A grandfather and grandmother,' and he interjected, 'The daughter and mother are very close. I don't think the mother will willingly let anyone but herself look after the girl.' That morning, through the window of the same police car he was about to use to bring the mother in for questioning, he had seen them waiting together on the sidewalk for Danit's ride to school. Hannah Sharabi hadn't let go of her daughter's hand for even a moment.

'And will the mother be remaining in custody too?' the social worker asked.

'Yes, at least overnight,' Ilana replied.

'Was she involved in what happened to her son?'

'We don't know yet to what extent,' Ilana said. 'She was certainly involved in concealing the matter. They've given statements that exonerate her, hoping, probably, that she'll be able to stay with the children.'

The door opened and Ma'alul informed them that Danit had arrived at the station.

Ilana and Etti hurried out of the office. Avraham didn't know if he should go with them. He stopped at the doorway. A young woman, presumably a staff member from the school Danit attended, was escorting the tall teenager. Danit allowed the young woman to lead her through the reception area, among the policemen, who froze in their tracks. Her steps were small and cautious.

Ilana asked for the conference room to be vacated and Avraham then watched as she entered the interrogation room in which Hannah Sharabi was waiting, emerged with the mother, and escorted her to the room into which her daughter had been taken. Ilana remained outside, closing the door behind the mother. Through the closed door and the walls, he heard Hannah Sharabi break down into bitter tears for the first time.

Thirty minutes later, Etti and the young woman escorted Danit out of the station. He didn't know where they were going.

It was around 11:00 p.m. when Avraham finally found the time to sit down and write the summary report for the remand hearing. He took hold of the blue pen, and within seconds his fingers were stained with ink – just like always. Aside from himself and Shrapstein, there was almost no one at the station. Ilana had gone home earlier in the evening. Ma'alul too.

The first words were easy to write. He summarized the circumstances of opening the case. But he soon reached the point at which he needed to describe the interrogation that had started that morning and found he was stuck. He went into Shrapstein's room and said, 'I think it's going to take me a while,' and Shrapstein asked, 'Then maybe I'll go home and take a look at it in the morning?'

There was no reason for him not to.

The nights were still pleasant, not too humid. The lights from the mall, the municipal library, and the museum instilled life in the dark. Avraham smoked one last cigarette. The building on Histadrut Street wasn't visible from the station, although it was close by. It lay hidden behind the sandy lots, between other apartment buildings where all the windows and shutters were already closed. They would open again in the morning.

Avraham returned to his office.

He was supposed to describe in dry, simple sentences how Rafael Sharabi arrived home early and found Ofer in his sister's room. He had to describe how the father lost his self-control, pulled the boy off his sister, hit him, and slammed him against the wall; how Ofer's head smashed against the wall and how he fell, lifeless, to the floor. He was supposed to write that, a few hours later, the father folded his son's body into a large suitcase, and that in the early hours of the morning, he dragged the suitcase down the dark stairs of the building and put it into the trunk of his car. According to his confession, his wife wanted to inform the police right away, but he warned her not to do so. He forced her to go to the station the following day and report their son missing. She didn't want to do it, but she feared her husband. The father covered up what he had done out of fear of his expected punishment, and also because he feared for the fate of his family without him. He was supposed to describe how, the following night, more than twelve hours after the cargo ship he was on left Ashdod Port, Rafael Sharabi threw the suitcase containing the body of his son overboard far out at sea. Far away from any shore. And that when he returned to Israel, his wife again pleaded with him to tell the police what happened, but he insisted they say nothing about it. They realized later that Ofer's bag had been forgotten in his room, and the father stuffed a few books inside and threw it into the dumpster. He was supposed to write that the search for Ofer out at sea would continue in keeping with financial considerations, unless the suitcase with his body washed up onshore beforehand.

But he could not write a word. His pen dropped.

The file lay open in front of him, and Ze'ev Avni's handwriting in black ink caught his eye from among the pile of documents. Suddenly, he picked up the pen and began writing:

*Dear Dad and Mom,*

*I'm writing to you so you don't worry about me. I want you to know I've arrived safely.*

*Despite everything that happened, I'm well. I'm now in Koper, a small and pretty provincial city. I think you'd like it here, Dad, because of the beautiful port. I've decided to stay here for now, but who knows, perhaps I'll be back one day.*

*I'm sorry about everything.*

*Yours,*

*Ofer*

Avraham had no one to send the letter to.

He crumpled the page and slipped it into his pocket so that no one would find it.

## 16

He replied to Marianka's e-mail early Saturday morning, from home. He told her the investigation had ended and that Ofer was dead. If and how a search for his body would continue remained unclear. The Cypriot, Turkish, and Greek authorities had been asked to notify the police in Israel in the event that a suitcase containing the body of a dead boy washed ashore or was found out at sea by local fishermen. He added no details because he had decided not to discuss anything that happened with anyone.

Her reply came after thirty minutes. Marianka expressed her condolences and asked how he was. She ended her short message with the words '*Sometimes prayers don't help.*' He responded immediately, writing to her that he was not well and that he was planning to take a vacation to get over it all. How was she doing? he asked. This time she answered several hours later, at night, and he read her message at 6:30 the following morning, Sunday, shortly after he woke up. She told him that she and Guillaume had broken up and that she too was going through a rough time. Their shifts together in the traffic police were not making the split any easier. She was also planning a vacation. Not sure if he was writing it just out of politeness, he invited her to spend her holiday in Israel and promised to pay her back for the tour of Brussels. It was 5:30 a.m. in Belgium but she wrote back immediately, one sentence, '*Are you serious?*' and he answered with one word.

*Yes.*

Reports about the case and its resolution appeared in the newspapers on Sunday, the same day that Rafael Sharabi appeared in court for a remand hearing ahead of his indictment. Ofer's death came under the headline FAMILY TRAGEDY IN HOLON. No details were given of the circumstances leading up to the violent confrontation and the teenager's ensuing death, as the court had imposed a gag order covering most of the details of the investigation owing to the involvement of minors; meanwhile, anyone familiar with the case knew why the press was treading relatively lightly with regard to a father who had killed his own son. Rafael Sharabi's lawyers claimed he was a devoted father, that the tragedy had destroyed him, and one report said that the state prosecutor was considering dropping the charges for obstruction of justice and likely would not oppose a light sentence. Very little was written about Ofer, as if he had been forgotten or had gone missing again.

Avraham rejected offers from the press office to give TV and radio interviews, and for the two days during which the media followed the story, Shrapstein appeared on three television news shows and several morning radio programs. He was asked about 'the complicated investigation, the details of which remain under a gag order,' and smiled knowingly at the mention of 'sophisticated investigative tactics that led to solving the case.' He too expressed compassion for the father's plight, and in response to a question from one of the interviewers said that Rafael Sharabi had expressed heartfelt remorse for concealing the tragedy. When asked to describe his feelings about the resolution of the case, Shrapstein repeated the same line in all the interviews: 'It was undoubtedly one of my most difficult moments as an Israel Police investigator . . . but that's our job.'

On Sunday evening, just after Channel 10 aired a short report on the 'Holon tragedy,' Avraham's phone rang. He knew who was on the line before lifting the receiver.

His mother was agitated. 'Are you watching the news?' she asked, and he said, 'No. Why?' lowering the sound coming from the television set.

'You took part in the case of the teenager who was murdered by his father, didn't you? I just saw the report on TV, but they didn't mention you. I'm sure I've seen that father before. I think he uses the same jogging path I do.'

Avraham confirmed that he had been involved in the investigation. He couldn't deny it because his parents had heard about his brief television appearance when Ofer was still a missing-persons case.

'I'm telling you, I felt right from the beginning that the father must have done something to him. I don't know why, I just had a feeling. Did you interrogate the father yourself?'

He said he hadn't.

'And do you know that officer, Shrapstein? He was interviewed for the report. Do you work with him? He's a very impressive young man.'

'He is impressive,' Avraham responded, and she asked, 'Do you know how old he is? Is he married?'

His meeting with Ilana was scheduled for Monday morning. He arrived late and she welcomed him warmly.

'I was waiting for you,' she said. She was wearing a purple dress that didn't suit her and that he hadn't seen before.

They always met for a postmortem after a big case, generally in her office, but sometimes at a restaurant, for lunch or dinner. They would drink a toast, analyze the investigation process, and look for errors to avoid in future cases. They both knew that was not going to happen this time. There had been too many errors, and there was no cause to celebrate.

Why did it seem to him that their relationship would never go back to the way it was before the case? Ilana had stood by him, and might even have prevented him from making graver mistakes than the ones he had. She had also supported his decision not to participate in the reconstruction. He couldn't go back to the apartment. Something deep inside him simply refused to open the door to Danit's room, from which the mother had shut him out. Shrapstein had taken Rafael Sharabi to the building on Histadrut Street – late Thursday night so as to avoid prying eyes, as much as possible – and had watched as the father shoved Ma'alul, in the role of Ofer, against the wall. Because a long time had passed, they didn't find any signs of the struggle or remains of the violent confrontation that happened there. Rafael Sharabi pushed Ma'alul against a pink wall partly covered by a dresser with toys, and afterward he pushed him against a second wall, a white one. When Ilana described the reconstruction, Avraham suddenly recalled the statement made by Ze'ev Avni's wife on the first day of the investigation. They were sitting in the kitchen of the Avni apartment and she was holding their son in her arms. She remembered hearing an argument or fight from the apartment above and was almost sure it had been on Tuesday evening. He hadn't ignored her statement; he had tried to confirm it with other neighbors, but without success. And yet it had all been there in front of him.

'When does your vacation begin?' Ilana asked, and he said, 'Maybe on Monday. I haven't given a definite date yet.'

'And when do you get back?'

'I haven't decided how much time to take off.' There were thoughts he was not ready to share with her.

He liked her office, the photograph of Lions Gate Bridge and the familiar faces in the other pictures, the window that was opened only for him and that had often breathed life into him. But he didn't want it to be his home anymore.

Ilana suggested that he refrain from taking on any other cases before beginning his vacation and he nodded.

'Why do you think this case was so difficult for you?' she suddenly asked.

'It was difficult for everyone, wasn't it?' he replied, trying to avoid the question, but she said, 'Yes, it was, but for you in particular.'

The question troubled him too, and he had no answer. Perhaps it was the geographic proximity, or maybe the feeling of having lost control.

'I think it's a sense of guilt,' she said. 'You felt guilty toward Ofer and his parents from the start, and it prevented you from seeing what was really happening there. And in the end – well, you know how it ended.'

But he didn't feel that he knew. And he believed Ilana was wrong in thinking that guilt was the problem. He didn't want to continue speaking about himself and asked if the state prosecutor had made a decision regarding Hannah Sharabi. It turned out that she had been released. A decision regarding an indictment against her, if there was to be one at all, had yet to be made. The children had been returned to their mother for now. Ilana told him that Ma'alul's inquiries with the friends

Ofer's parents had met the evening of the tragedy indicated that Hannah Sharabi had indeed returned home after her husband and not with him, just as she had said. Nevertheless, there was still no proof that she was not in the apartment at the time Ofer was killed.

None of that interested him anymore.

He didn't have any words, and a part of their meeting passed in silence.

'Are you going away?' Ilana asked, and he said, 'Where would I go? I'll stay at home. Maybe I'll finally clean the place up.'

Avraham was unable to get hold of the IT Division when he returned to the station. Someone there needed to take down Ofer's photograph from the police website's missing-persons page. The thin boy with the hint of a black mustache looked at him from the computer screen. The other missing people stared at him from their small images too. Some had been there for a long time. There were teenagers, boys and girls, who were last seen in 2008, 1996, 1994. He clicked on one of the thumbnails. Full name: Michael Lutenko. Gender: Male. Born: 1980. Native language: Russian. Other languages: Hebrew. Height: 5'8". Nose shape: Medium. Build: Slight. Skin: Light. Glasses: None. Residence: Ramat Gan. Last seen in: Ramat Gan. Date of disappearance: 23 June 1997.

There was a soft knock on the door. Lital Levy, the policewoman who had called on his birthday to tell him about the anonymous call regarding Ofer, walked in, saying, 'Someone left this for you.' She handed him a brown envelope with black letters addressed *To Inspector Avi Avraham*.

'Is he still here?' he asked, quickly getting up from his chair, and she said no. She still managed to ask if he wanted to have lunch with her, but Avraham had already rushed out of the station. Ze'ev Avni was gone.

He read the letter while sitting on the stairs outside, smoking a cigarette.

*Dear Inspector Avraham,*

 *A letter from me must surely come as a surprise to you. To be honest, I never imagined writing to you until I saw the newspaper reports about Ofer and realized that I, too, need closure. This period in my life will undoubtedly remain with me forever, but I would like to move on, just as you will move on. More than anything, I'd like to meet and speak with you – not at the police station, but somewhere more pleasant and friendly – and to continue, or rather to begin, the conversation I had hoped to have with you and wasn't able to, but because that isn't very practical (is it?), I have resorted instead to writing you a letter, a symbolic (or ironic, some would say) act, of course, in light of the circumstances surrounding our acquaintanceship.*

 *First, it's important that you know that I have yet to come to terms with what I did, even after finding out (more or less – I admit that not everything is clear to me) just how central a role I played in exposing Ofer's parents – and perhaps particularly for that very reason. Obviously, Rafael Sharabi must pay for his crime; I wouldn't want it any other way, but I do have a problem with the fact that I played a part in the trap you laid for him (am I correct in my assumptions?). In retrospect, I would have liked to have refused your 'generous offer,' or, more precisely, to have been the kind of person who could do that. Regrettably, I am not that man yet. When I agonize over the cowardice that led me to accept*

294

your 'offer,' I try to convince myself that I had no choice – because of both my wife and my son – and I also tell myself that I am now in possession of compromising information about the police. We are almost in equal positions now, don't you think? You know things about me that I wouldn't want others to know, and I know something about you that you wouldn't want revealed (this is not a threat).

The second thing I wanted to say is that I was deeply disappointed with our meeting. (I hope you are capable of appreciating my frankness.) When we first met, I felt that we could share a true dialogue; apparently I misjudged you. From the first moment you misunderstood me and my intentions, you were quick to judge me, and you turned all I told you about my close relationship with Ofer into suspicions against me – so much so that it is difficult even now to think about my intimate friendship with Ofer without doubting my intentions. And for that, I cannot easily forgive you. In the end, you exploited my faith in you and my appreciation for you to achieve your own objectives. (By the way, have you already been promoted or received a commendation following your 'success'?)

There's one more thing I need to write – more to myself than to you – and it has to do with the act of writing. What I had begun I shall not continue, do not worry about that, although today I understand the true power of the letters I wrote. In fact, without my knowing anything (do you believe me now?), those letters contained the truth – the literary truth and the factual truth – long before all of you found out. Maybe that's what people mean when they speak about inspiration. I feel a certain sense of satisfaction (also a shiver) when I think about Ofer's parents reading his letters, with

*the accusations he dared to make at them, while concealing
their guilt from everyone. This encourages me not to stop
writing, despite all the attempts to intimidate me (others' too,
not only yours). I don't yet know what I will write, but I
know it will happen — and not too far down the line, either.
Who knows, maybe a book about police investigators? My
son, Elie, has reached the age at which he enjoys listening to
the stories I make up for him — even if he doesn't understand
everything — and maybe children's literature is the right
direction for me.*

    *Shall we part as friends?*

*Ze'ev Avni*

*P.S. If, by chance, you come looking for me, you probably
won't find me at the same address in a few weeks. We plan
to move, although no one in our building knows of my
involvement (and I'd like it to stay that way). It's not the
kind of place in which we want to raise Elie, and I wanted to
move, anyway.*

Should he file the letter in the case file? Throw it in the
trash? Keep it for the next case in which Ze'ev Avni turns out
to be involved? In all his years on the police force he had never
come across anyone like Avni, who had made every effort to
become the subject of a police investigation. Apparently Avni
had an urge to confess something, but Avraham had been
unable to discover exactly what it was. And perhaps Avni
couldn't, either.

★

Marianka arrived the following week, on Monday, at 4:00 p.m.

She was dressed in blue jeans, a pink T-shirt, flowery and short-sleeved, and sneakers. Her brown hair was cut short. They kissed each other on the cheek, twice, and he took her silver suitcase and wheeled it behind him to the parking lot – all the while hounded by thoughts of the suitcase into which Ofer's dead body was stuffed. He had the feeling she saw the shadow darkening over his face.

He'd spent the week ahead of her visit getting his apartment in order. Several months had gone by since a woman last visited his place, and it had been almost two years since someone had spent the night there with him. On Thursday, his last day at work before his vacation, he left the station early to go to the Holon industrial area to buy a fold-out bed. He then cleared out the small room that served both as his office and a storage room, moving cartons of old documents – some related to his police work, and others to his personal life – to a storeroom downstairs, and taking the two dusty fans and old stereo system down to the trash room; the small desk and computer he moved to the living room. As evening fell, he polished the windows by the gloomy light that cleaved through from the dirty glass of the lamp hanging from the ceiling, and hoped he hadn't missed anything. The following morning he scrubbed the remaining rooms in the apartment, especially the kitchen, and then drove into Tel Aviv to shop for fruit and vegetables, spices and salted snacks at the Carmel market, where he also bought new linens for the fold-out bed, which was delivered on Sunday morning.

He didn't know if they'd be eating in. He didn't even know if they'd be spending all of Marianka's time in Israel together. To be on the safe side, he spent hours browsing through the

Internet on Saturday in search of Tel Aviv's finest restaurants. He also decided that if Marianka wanted to eat lunch or dinner at home, he would tell her that he usually ate out and suggest they do the shopping together in a local supermarket. He didn't know whether to make plans for the evenings too.

Marianka liked the apartment. She stepped carefully through the living room, as if she was walking around the house of a total stranger, looked at the picture on the wall – a framed black-and-white photograph of a father and son riding a bike along a country road – read the names on the CDs arranged on a tall metal stand, and then stopped by the bookcase. 'These are the detective novels you told me about, aren't they?' Almost all of them were translations into Hebrew.

'Yes, they are. Let me show you the guest room,' he replied and led her to the small room, which – without the carton boxes and computer desk and with the fold-out bed, as well as the blue cushions and small lampshade he had managed to buy that morning – looked spacious and bright.

He suggested they go to Tel Aviv or Jaffa for dinner, to discuss her vacation plans, but Marianka was tired from all the traveling and the hours spent sitting down on the airplane, and wanted to stretch her legs. She asked if they could walk to Tel Aviv, and he laughed.

'Then we'll walk around here. I want to walk,' she insisted, and he said, 'But there is nothing to see here, and nowhere to eat.'

'You live here, don't you?' she said. 'So there must be something to see. I'm in a city I've never been to before. How could that be boring? By the way, what did you say its name was?'

They walked through the streets of Holon.

She studied the apartment buildings, the faces of the passers-by and the clothes they were wearing, as if she had just arrived in New York or was on an undercover detective assignment. And she walked slowly in Holon. There was only one street they could not visit, and he led her far away from there. On the way back to his apartment, they passed by his parents' home.

'So when do I finally meet them?' she asked, and he said, 'They'll come to our wedding, you'll see them there.'

It was all so strange and different, as if they had just kept on walking through the streets of Brussels. They spoke in English, and Avraham thought to himself that this was the first time he was speaking a foreign language in the city where he had been born and had lived almost his entire life.

'What happened with Guillaume?' he asked, and she said, 'Nothing special. I knew I wasn't in love with him after two weeks, but I couldn't end it. It's the second time I've made the mistake of going out with someone from work.'

'And how did he take it?'

She smiled. 'He wasn't in love with me, either. I think he's secretly in love with Elise, Jean-Marc's wife.'

That made sense.

It was while he was rummaging in his pocket for the keys at the entrance to his building that Marianka suddenly said, 'I haven't asked you about the case, not because I don't want to but because I felt you don't want me to. If you're able to speak about what happened and what you are going through, I want to listen.'

They ate tomatoes, yellow peppers, mangoes, grapes, water-melon, and thick slices of bread – because that's all there was. And they watched a little TV because Marianka wanted to hear some Hebrew. Then they made plans for the rest of the week. Shortly after 10:00 p.m. Marianka took a shower and emerged from the bathroom in pajamas. She kissed his cheek, said goodnight, and went to her room. He washed the dishes in the kitchen. When he sat in the living room and started reading a book, something he hadn't done in weeks, she came back and sat beside him, folding her legs and putting her bare feet on the sofa. She asked him, 'Can I sit closer?' and his heart felt heavy with excitement when he told her, 'Yes.'

After that the wonderful struggle between them began.

He didn't always understand what she was asking of him. From time to time, she would withdraw, place a finger on his lips, and ask him to stop; there were moments when he felt her body drawing him in. He suggested they move to the bedroom, but she wanted to stay where they were, and asked him to turn out the light, searching for his eyes in the darkness even when he shut them. He wanted to keep them open so as not to stop seeing the hands that were touching him and the fragile body wrapped in his arms – but wasn't always able to. He could not believe that such a miracle was happening inside him.

They listened to David Bowie's 'Absolute Beginners' in the dark living room, naked.

'Just so it's clear, I'm sleeping in my own room,' said Marianka, and Avraham didn't fully comprehend that she really meant it.

'Not that I'm complaining, but why did you do that?' he asked, and she said, 'Because I wanted to, and also because I didn't want to. And because it's forbidden. And because now everything between us will be much easier than before. Though it was very easy already.'

He slept in his bed, and when he woke the following morning and stepped out of his room, he saw her through the open bathroom door, brushing her teeth.

Had it not still been so close to the conclusion of the investigation, it would probably have been the most beautiful week of his life. On Tuesday, they drove to Masada and the Dead Sea, and Avraham watched from the beach as Marianka hesitantly entered the dense water and rubbed mud on her cheeks and forehead. He hated the Dead Sea, from childhood. Early Wednesday morning, he drove her to East Jerusalem, from where she continued alone by taxi to Bethlehem. He regretted rejecting her pleas to come along, particularly when he found her so quiet and pensive when she returned. She touched his face and hands in a fuller way. She told him she had sat for over an hour in the Church of the Nativity and thought about her life. 'What did you ask for?' he inquired, and she said, 'I didn't ask for anything. It's not a wishing well, you know, it's a church. I felt that I want to live differently and that I don't know how.'

Later that evening, she turned down his offer to take a walk along the beach in Tel Aviv, choosing instead to read in her room, and he fell asleep stricken with anxiety and despair. When he opened his eyes in the morning, she was sleeping beside him.

Marianka wasn't joking when she said she'd like to meet his parents, so he called his mother on Thursday and told her he had a guest from Belgium. 'Would you like to come for dinner tomorrow?' his mother immediately suggested – and to her amazement, he didn't refuse. She called twice that same day to ask what Belgians like to eat and if meatballs in a sauce would be sufficiently respectable. 'What's the problem?' came his father's voice in the background. 'Just prepare for her some rice and beans; I'm sure she isn't familiar with that.' Marianka insisted that they could not arrive without a bottle of wine.

Much to his surprise, the meal didn't end in disaster. His parents had dressed up for the occasion, and his father even wore shoes. They had set the table in the living room and his mother had placed a green vase with a nice bouquet of white lilies in the center. Marianka wore a black dress, and he saw her putting makeup on for the first time. His parents didn't ask about the nature of their relationship, and he and Marianka didn't offer any explanations. His mother grilled Marianka about the origin of her name, and she told them she was born in Slovenia and had immigrated to Brussels with her family.

'Oh, so you're not really from Belgium,' his mother said, clearly disappointed.

'So what?' his father said. 'And we're from here? My parents were born in Iraq. And where do you think she was born? In Hungary!' And his mother hissed at him in Hebrew, 'What are you talking nonsense for? You think she cares where I come from?'

He felt Marianka's fingers climbing up his thigh under the table. His mother cleared the dishes from the first course and he followed her into the kitchen to help.

'She's charming,' his mother whispered, 'and very pretty. Where did you meet her?' and he said, 'We met in Belgium,' adding nothing more. Marianka stayed at the table. He saw from the kitchen that she fixed her serious eyes on his father. She really was so beautiful, and he wondered whether in Belgian or Slovenian terms he, for his part, could be considered a handsome man.

The conversation in English proved difficult for his father, who made an effort at first but then switched to Hebrew and waited for someone to translate what he said, until he grew weary of that and went silent. He buried his gaze in his plate and still drew the food to his mouth with careful movements after everyone had finished eating. Avraham had told Marianka of his condition before dinner, and she listened to his father patiently, even when he mumbled unintelligible words in Hebrew. Toward the end of the meal, his father suddenly whispered, as if to himself, 'It's good that you're leaving the country. There's nothing for you here,' and then addressed Marianka in slow Hebrew, saying, 'I will miss him very much. Do you know how much I love him?'

The next day they went to Jerusalem. It was Saturday, the last day.

They began their tour in the western part of the city and he took her first to the old Nahlaot neighborhood. They walked among the alleyways where his grandfather had once lived and where he himself had rented an apartment for a year during his studies, a long time ago. The city was empty and still. The air was stifling and hard to breathe, laden with the sorrow of their parting.

Ever since she arrived, Marianka had been asking him to take her to the Mount of Olives. Her father, who had visited Israel many years earlier, had told her of the sacredness of the mountain and the spectacular view of Jerusalem from its peak. Avraham struggled at first to find his way along the new roads leading to the eastern part of the city. It was animated and noisy there, and the higher they climbed, the more the commotion of the tourists grew. They sat on a wooden bench and looked out over the city that lay spread out before them, flat and stony. Cameras clicked around them and the golden Dome of the Rock blazed. Avraham spoke less and less and Marianka tried to comfort him. A distance had opened up between them even before her plane left the ground.

'Do you know that that's the gate through which the Messiah will one day enter Jerusalem?' she asked, pointing toward the Old City.

'No doubt,' he said.

'You don't believe that? The Jews also believe that the resurrection of the dead will begin from the Mount of Olives. I think the prophet Elijah is supposed to blow a shofar from here,' she said seriously, and he replied, 'I don't think it will be heard in Holon. And where do you know all of that from?'

'My father,' she said. 'He didn't just teach me karate.'

They both went silent for a long time before Avraham could no longer hold back the sadness within him and said, 'The worst thing is that sometimes I think he's better off dead. I am so angry at him without even knowing him.'

'Who?' Marianka asked.

'Ofer. The teenager who went missing. The boy we were looking for.'

And for the first time since leaving the station that night, he spoke about what had happened. He told her about his interrogation of Hannah Sharabi and her refusal to speak, her blind refusal to admit to what had happened in Danit's room, the room whose door was shut to him. That was why they had hidden the daughter from him to begin with. 'I am really so angry that I thought a few times that it was good that he died the way he did. And I am frightened by the thought.' Marianka let go of his hand.

'I don't understand how you can be so sure that he assaulted her,' she said as he lit a cigarette. 'I don't believe that's what happened.'

That wasn't a question of belief.

'Are you listening to me, Avi? I don't understand why you choose to believe the father and not the mother. Did you not consider the possibility that she had been telling the truth? That she found him in his own room, as she said? That Ofer didn't hurt his sister?'

He suspended his dimmed gaze on her. 'What do you mean?'

'That Ofer's father lied. After all, he clearly has a motive to do so. The story he told you about Ofer and his sister will surely influence the sentence he receives, right?'

'Yes – and rightly so, don't you think?'

'So you agree, then, that if the fight between them broke out over something else, you'd be treating him differently? What if he came up with the story to give himself a justifiable motive and extenuating circumstances and all of you were drawn into it and failed to listen to what the mother was trying to tell you?'

Shrapstein had been absolutely sure that Rafael Sharabi had cracked to pieces and had told the truth, and that Hannah Sharabi had kept on lying. And everyone had accepted his position.

'I'm telling you, I don't believe that the mother lied,' Marianka insisted. 'Ofer's mother told you the truth. You've already confirmed that she didn't lie when she told you she returned home after the father, right? And didn't you wonder about the fact that the father returned home early? This is mere conjecture, but perhaps he was the one who assaulted the daughter? Perhaps he thought that Ofer was sleeping and went into her room, and maybe Ofer was awake or was waked by noise coming from the girl's room and found his father there? That would explain not only why the father killed him but also why it was so important for him to conceal what really happened, to come up with the story of Ofer's disappearance. Did it never occur to any of you that Ofer might have been trying to protect his sister?'

Marianka's words shocked him. 'I would never hurt my children – no matter who asks me to do that,' Hannah Sharabi had said to him during the interrogation. And he recalled Ilana's description of the reconstruction in which the father had pushed Ma'alul first against one wall and then against another.

'But why would she not have told us explicitly that her husband was lying?' he asked.

'She said she was afraid of him, didn't she? And she did tell you explicitly. You told me she kept insisting that she found Ofer in his own room and that he hadn't harmed his sister. You simply decided to believe the father's version of events and not what the mother told you.'

Ilana didn't answer his call.

He left her a message, asking her to call him, insisting that it was urgent. His whole world was spinning around him. He wanted to get back into the car and go to the station right then and there; he wanted to open the file and watch the video recordings again; he wanted to get Rafael Sharabi back into an interrogation room and question him himself. And he wasn't willing to let go of Marianka. He stood facing her, his back to the old city.

'You can't go,' he whispered, and she said, 'I have to be back at work on Monday.'

'So quit your job.'

'And then what?'

Or he could quit. He didn't really want to go back anyway. Leaving the station that night, he had told himself that it had probably been his final case.

'You can't quit,' Marianka said. 'Don't you remember saying that even when you aren't a policeman you're a policeman?'

But maybe now he could? He sat beside her on the bench again.

'Don't let a single case break you,' she said. 'And I understand how difficult it was. Besides, the investigation isn't over. Didn't you tell me how you can always prove the detective wrong? Didn't you say that the true solution is always different from the one that's given? See? It's happened to you too.'

'It doesn't happen in real life – only in detective novels,' he said, but he hoped that he was wrong.

He saw Ofer again, putting his backpack on the park bench and resting his head on it.

He closed his eyes.

The skies darkened.

They stopped by his apartment to collect Marianka's suitcase, then drove to the airport.

Avraham promised to try to extend his vacation and to come to her, perhaps even in two or three days.

They held each other as if they would never meet again, but that was not true.

They met.

*To be continued . . .*

# ACKNOWLEDGEMENTS

The setting of *The Missing File* is Holon, my home town, but I wrote it far away from Israel, in a peaceful Cambridgeshire village called Impington.

I would like to thank Claire Wachtel, my editor at HarperCollins US, for preparing the English edition of the novel, and Jon Riley at Quercus for bringing it back to the UK. I could not have imagined Avraham Avraham in better hands.

To Ronit Zafran, Marianne Fritch, Marc Koralnik and Eva Koralnik at the Liepman literary agency I owe the fact that Avraham speaks English now, along with many other languages that I do not.

Special thanks to my editor and friend, Shira Hadad, the most sensitive and encouraging reader a writer can hope for.

D. A. Mishani

# Why are there so few detective novels
# written in Hebrew?

Israeli literature, when it emerged in the mid-19th century, started very much within the Jewish national project of reviving the Hebrew language. So the literature was really connected to national issues. It had to deal with Jewish identity, Jewish past, Jewish future. The detective genre deals with violence, with urban existence – which didn't have anything to do with those national themes. In the 1930s, when the first translations of the Sherlock Holmes stories were published, they were denounced. Because Hebrew is a sacred language and even when we're secularizing it, it should still be used for national purposes.

There's also another, sociological reason. In the States, when you think of a protagonist, you can think of Dirty Harry. Or the sheriff in Westerns. But in Israel, the protagonists have always been 'the soldier' or 'the spy.' Traditionally members of the police in Israel were Sephardic Jews. They often came from lower classes. It was – I think maybe it's changing now – but it was very difficult to conceive of a police officer as a hero.

Avi Avraham is from a family of Sephardic Jews. He comes from a suburb of Tel Aviv. It's not a poor suburb, but lower middle class. He's not glamorous. I wanted to write the detective that I like in Hebrew, and to try to see if it's possible to bring this genre that I admire to Israel.

The detective novel emerged in the middle of the 19th century in London, New York, Paris. One of the main reasons is that people were living in urban communities. The detective is the guy that goes around in the city where nobody knows each other. When there's a serious crime going on and nobody knows who did it. In Israel, you have less ways to disappear. It's supposed to be a community where everybody knows each other.

The fact that there are more and more crime novels in Israel now – original and in translation – is one of the symptoms of a society that is changing from communal to more urban. I don't know if it's a question of moving from a bad system to a good system or the other way around. It's two different social control systems. Israel is moving from a more communal social control system to a more, I would say, modern, Western system. And – for sure, it's good for a crime writer.

D. A. Mishani

*Taken from an interview with Lidia Jean Kott of NPR Books*

COMING SOON

# THE POSSIBILITY OF VIOLENCE

## D. A. Mishani

Translated from the Hebrew by Todd Hasak-Lowy

**An explosive device is found in a suitcase near
a nursery. A few hours later there comes a threat:
'the suitcase was only the beginning'.**

**And it is.**

Inspector Avraham Avraham must act fast. He has a few suspects,
but one of them, a father of two, has disappeared. Avraham may
guess that the man is trying to escape his guilty conscience. But he
cannot guess the deepest, darkest reasons that will make a father
run. Nor the extent to which this case – even more than his last –
will deceive and devastate him.

'Mishani, with an almost frightening skill, succeeded to shatter
the very intimate parts of my soul . . . This is such a difficult task
to achieve for a detective story in general and for an Israeli one in
particular, that I find it difficult to restrain the superlatives'
*Time Out Tel Aviv*

# Quercus